The Big Empty

The Evolved Book 1

Richard Quarry

ALSO BY RICHARD QUARRY

THE EVOLVED SERIES:
The Big Empty
Point of No Return
The Outcasts
The Evolved
Holobrain
Grinder
The God Machine

The Further Tales of Odysseus:
Man of Many Turnings
Odysseus and the Eye of Odin

The Dance of Light and Dark
Dance of Sword and Heron
Dance of Deer and Shadow
Dance of Cat and Amber
Dance of Wolf and Moon
Dance of Ring and Dragon

Stand-alones
Absent From Felicity
Geneslide

Blue Dread
Trade All My Tomorrows
What Rough Beast
Midnight Choir

Collections:
Soldier of Discontent and other stories
Lord Under London and other cases of Nat Frayne
The Dread Men and other cases of Nat Frayne
Questing Song and other stories
Devolution Day and other f&sf stories

Chapter 1

BECK EGAN INADVERTENTLY TWISTED the bosun's chair to the right with his body English as he tried to mentally urge the lattice back into alignment. Glancing down between his white-booted feet, he saw the tiny blue marble of Earth far, far away. Funny, but after fourteen years at L5, every time he went EVA he still always thought of the planet as "down."

"Yukio," he spoke into his helmet, "slow to one kph relative." A crawl, but he didn't dare allow her to bring the structure into the ring any faster. "And watch your alignment."

"Yes ... sir," came the reply. Clearly she wasn't happy with his interference.

The thrusters on the sled flared briefly, slowing the vehicle, though not quite to the speed he'd specified. The lattice gripped in the sled's pincer arms, an open four-sided pyramid eight meters high, wobbled to either side before she managed to line her aiming beam up on the target.

Which was a forest of similar lattices welded base-to-point within one floor of a ring eighty meters from edge to edge. Five floors had already been filled, and this, the sixth, was a little over half done. When filled in, the ring, close to three hundred meters in diameter, would form the skin for a second torus at the far end of the *Banneker's* manufacturing spindle.

To the dismay of Beck Egan, and most others who lived aboard.

The original torus rotated six hundred meters up the manufacturing spindle. The donut-shaped torus itself was hidden by its radiation shield, a massive, stationary ring of mine tailings and asteroidal rock, glinting ochre, buff, and marble beneath the light of a brilliant yellow moon. Through a slit in the shield the five spokes circled, pulling the white-painted Hub, whose upper and lower surfaces bristled with landing docks, slowly around. The motion was barely perceptible from down here, yet fast enough to provide three-quarters gravity to those standing with their feet on the outer floor of the *Banneker*.

The colony had not been built with a lower torus in mind. Beck Egan knew this better than most. He'd been among that first generation who built it.

No problem, the Earth-bound engineers of Space Command assured the inhabitants. We've worked it all out so that the counter-rotation will keep the whole system in balance.

Meaning, no chance at all the momentum of the lower torus won't swing the upper, inhabited torus past its safeguards right into the stationary radiation shield, smashing both to pieces.

Earth representatives had blanketed L5 for months, staging promotions and poring over the figures with torus engineers. Not just the *Banneker*, but the other habitats as well.

Beck had no doubt the numbers worked out.

On Earth.

But on Earth, any glitches in construction could be worked out as they came up. "Back to the drawing board" didn't work so well when that drawing board might be rubble drifting in vacuum and surrounded by a corona of freeze-dried bodies. Already the magnetic buffers that kept the torus hull and shield from grinding together when gyroscopic stability came past its margins were showing readings higher than any in the history of the *Banneker*. No, they hadn't yet approached critical.

Nor was the lower torus yet more than an empty frame.

But Beck Egan was a Rigger, no less and most definitely no more. So if he wanted to refuse to participate in the project, he could voice his objections from Earth. Where there weren't a whole lot of openings in EVA construction.

And now, of all times, he had been detailed to oversee a crew of Earth trainees.

Yukio slowly eased the sled toward the frame. The damn lattice still wobbled.

"Engage magnets," Beck ordered the crew working among the lattices already in place. Four of them, all Earthers in their bulky white suits lacking all sensor inputs and power enhancements. "Yukio, begin reverse."

"But I'm still thirty meters out."

"Begin reverse now."

If he let her go any further she was bound to ram the lattice into something. Probably so slowly that it would bend to absorb the impact. The lattices were, after all, designed as shock absorbers. That's why they also filled the skin of the upper torus. But a hard enough impact might bend it past its breaking point, causing it to shatter in a storm of lightweight titanium balls that could injure or kill the crew inside the existing structure.

Who, Beck noticed, instead of standing behind cover like any Rigger would, floated free, loosely holding to the pyramid arms to get a better view.

"Magnets on maximum strength," he ordered, rather harshly. During his fourteen years as a Rigger he'd seen too many people, too many friends, die in space to indulge the Earther's neophyte enthusiasm.

"Yukio, release."

"But—"

"Just obey the goddamn order!"

As the sled hit neutral speed relative to the crawling rotation of the ring, the pincer arms opened and the lattice floated free. Further out than regulation, but the electromagnets, carefully placed under his supervision on both the this and the lattices among which the newcomer would mesh like teeth, should pull it into place.

Just in case, Beck powered his chair closer in. The floating seat's thrusters weren't intended to change the momentum of large drifting objects. For that matter, neither was this unpowered Earther suit. Fortunately the titanium balls making up the pyramid were mostly empty space. The whole structure massed well short of two hundred kilograms. If he had to, he could apply a mild shove to help the magnets steady its approach.

Entering the ring frame, Beck approached the fused lattices cautiously, uneasy at having to rely solely on visual. For this sort of work his normal Rigger's suit, with its pigtail attachments transmitting a multiplicity of inputs from its sensors to implanted neural nets in his brain, would provide a far wider spectrum of data.

But such were the orders from Space Command: you train Earth recruits, you wear Earth suits to give you a better grasp of their experience.

Okay, their experience was pathetic. Cheap and nasty. Much quicker than having the neural nets implanted, then spending the endless hours drilling to make them useful, but the resulting ninety-day wonders would be dying in droves if Space Command actually tried to use them for anything more than maintaining solar satellites in high Earth orbit.

Beck eased in closer to the tip of the pyramid as it glided to within ten meters of its bedding point. Despite the electromagnets' pull, a slight instability still remained.

The point of the pyramid swung toward him. Tipping his sled he extended one of the control arms to make contact — barely. With a very light hand on the controls, or as light as these over-padded sausage fingers would permit, he directed the point toward where he wanted it to end up. Ferrying around objects in space with a lot of inertia and no particular reason to stop was like petting a strange cat. Best give it plenty of warning, and be ready to pull back quick.

By now the gap in the wall of lattices lay barely eight meters away. Confident of the trajectory, Beck eased the sled away from the pyramid. Proud of his touch; disengagement was so smooth it wouldn't have loosed a tennis ball set on the point of the lattice.

The structure glided the last few meters in.

Three of the Earth crew, positioned in the lattices above and to either side, extended telescoping arms bolted to the existing flanges. Another stood by with the bonding gun.

Allll-most there. Just don't anyone make any fast moves.

The servo hands clamped onto the arms of the pyramid.

"All servos on automatic," Beck transmitted. The extensor arms, like the Riggers' suit he didn't have, applied power amplified on a logarithmic scale. Too dangerous for what he regarded as half-trained workers to play with.

The lattice shuddered slightly as the servo arms abruptly slowed its momentum for the last few centimeters of travel.

Done.

Beck let out the breath he'd been unconsciously holding. Despite his worries, the situation was well under control.

Until suddenly, unbelievably, it all went wrong.

Chapter 2

One second Beck was watching the pyramid eased into place by the extensor arms.

Then ... what?

Later Beck wasn't quite sure of the exact sequence. Trying to reconstruct it he thought he could picture one of the servo arms clamped to the lattices failing to contract. Thus the two exerted their force against the maverick on both ends.

But did he actually have his attention fixed on that exact point at that exact moment?

Because it just shouldn't happen like that. Any excessive resistance from the third arm should have triggered the other two to switch off. And if that failed, then the third arm itself should be programmed to fold at any pressure that might cause structural damage to the pyramids.

And even if every failsafe built into the extensor arms went snafu at the same moment, the lattices should still hold their integrity. After all, when completed they would form the bulwark of the skin that stood between the torus inhabitants and open space. All three arms together shouldn't force one to shatter.

Only it hadn't shattered, had it?

It exploded. Not just at the bending point; all over. The titanium balls burst forth in a storm of inch-thick projectiles lighter than steel, but much harder.

Impossible.

That was what Beck Egan would insist throughout multiple questionings, depositions, and findings. Mostly undertaken to prove his own malfeasance.

But that came later. At the time he found himself staring in utter disbelief as what had a moment before been empty space suddenly filled with one-inch balls of shrapnel tearing outward, ricocheting off whatever they hit.

Beck Egan was was not known for slow reflexes. But he was still trying to understand what he was seeing when within a second or two of the lattice breaking apart the first fatality occurred.

Emina Cortez. Beck couldn't tell who it was at the time. Might not even have remembered her name in truth, but it came to haunt him later. Every time he tried to erase from his memory the picture of the violently whirling extension arm, torn from its mounts, smashing one end right through her faceplate. The resultant spray of blood immediately froze into thin sheets of ice glittering red-gold in the light of the construction torches, then broke into glowing needles as the titanium balls spread like a swarm of angry bees.

An instant later the first shrapnel reached him. He'd already spun the sled so that its back was to the storm. He extended his legs to expose the minimum amount of suit. His boots rattled at the onslaught but were not breached. Impacts against the back of the chair shoved it stuttering away from the explosion. He couldn't hear them through the vacuum but they jarred his neck and spine. Klaxons sounded in his earpieces as he stabbed down on the sled's red emergency button.

Adrenalin emptied Beck's mind of all but a panicked sense of urgency. No fear, no horror, no plan, just an acute awareness that he had people back in there and he had to get them out *now*.

A white suit floated past, faceplate shattered and shards of ice still spitting out from the cavity.

The titanium balls ricocheting inside the lattice would shed some energy with each impact. Otherwise with no atmosphere to resist them they would go flying forever. Would his suit, this Earth suit, stand up to the barrage?

If not, there was no point going back to the lattice because the people in there were already dead.

Screams told him otherwise.

If you asked Beck in that moment what his name was he might not have been able to answer. Adrenalin was was strobing his mind; his heart pulsed like a neutron star. Had this been a Rigger's suit he could have given a voice command that would trigger an injection to ease the thundering pain in his chest.

Now he had only his fear.

The storm of shrapnel, though still thick, diminished as the pellets not ricocheting inside the lattices flew off into space. Approaching the lattices he unbuckled from the sled. The chair was too unwieldy to maneuver around in there. Sliding loose, he slid his belt around to bring the aux thrusters to his back. Engaging the jetpacs with his left hand because the voice command on this idiot suit was hopelessly imprecise, he flew into the hard spatter of balls.

Cracks formed as his faceplate took hits. Three people remained in the shrapnel zone, and at least two were screaming about being blind. He could see through myriad bugs'-eye images their white suits gyrate amid the storm of balls streaking under the lights. One of the extensor arms, still clanging away from one pyramid arm to another, bashed him on the back of the head. Going into a slow spin he saw the blue ball of Earth flickering by through the lattices like an old-time movie projector.

Within a couple of seconds he'd recovered his bearings. Swinging from pillar to pillar Beck soon discovered why the Earth workers were hollering about being blind. The succession of isolated cracks against his faceplate swelled into one continuous *splat!* of impacts that shook his head so violently it felt like jaws clamping down on the back of his neck. They also produced such a dense spiderweb of cracks he couldn't see a thing.

Soon one of the balls would crack through.

"Hug the beams!" he shouted. "Press your face into them to protect your faceplate!"

Before the cracks obliterated his vision entirely he got one very deliberate fix on the nearest of the writhing white suits. He swung over and grabbed them from behind. Reaching down to engage the pitiful thrusters, he navigated his way out like a paramecium, going till he bumped into something then backing off, angling to the side, and trying again.

Finally he emerged. Outside the lattices the shrapnel had thinned down. But he was also virtually blind; his vision just a blurry field of light and darkness. One good tap should serve to shatter what remained of his faceplate.

"Yukio!" he shouted. "Take this person to the aid station. Everyone, stop screaming!"

Surprisingly they quieted, though one kept moaning "*Ohgod ohgod ohgod ohgod*" into her helmet.

Where were the frigging emergency crews?

Non-existent. This had been listed as a training exercise, not a construction procedure, avoiding a host of regulations.

But other crews were on their way. He could hear them. The nearest would arrive within four minutes.

And if one of the faceplates got breached in that time?

"Yukio! Hold for a moment. I'm going back in. My vision is poor. I need you to guide me to the nearest survivor."

He could see just enough to sail back into the lattices, one arm held across his face. A Rigger's suit would not only have been stronger, he'd have had infrared and radar to guide him. This was the last time he ever went EVA in an Earth suit. Screw the directives and screw Earth.

Gliding forward, his hands touched a beam. He pulled himself in.

"To the left," came a voice.

"*Oh my God oh my God oh my God.*"

He groped his way past one beam, then two.

Ahead of him he saw several glints of white spread across his faceplate. Reaching out, he touched something moving.

Beck gripped down, pulled in. Two hands grabbed his arms.

"*Help me! I can't see!*"

"Be still!"

Too late. In her panic she lunged at him, knocking them both free of any perch. Now she grabbed on tight with all her strength, tying up his arms. The titanium balls beat against the two suits savagely. Soon they'd open a breach in one or both of their faceplates.

For the first time he was grateful these *weren't* Riggers' powered suits. For then their strength would have been equal.

But Beck was a powerful man. Swinging his right forearm over her clutching left arm, he levered her across his body, breaking her grip. He grabbed her shoulder to swing her around, lifting at the same time to drive himself downward. Catching her around her waist with his right arm, he engaged thrusters with his left.

Unfortunately he now had two problems. One was that he couldn't see where to go. Yukio shouted directions to him, but they didn't always agree, and "not so far!" lacked the necessary precision.

The other problem was the woman, who in her blind, literally, panic, flailed about trying to grab anything at all. And consistently beat what Beck would have sworn were the odds.

The thrusters weren't strong enough to break the woman's grip. Or to anchor Beck in space while he tried to twist her loose.

Finally he had to pull himself up her body, wrench her arms loose and bunch them behind her back so tightly she screeched, and hold her elbows together with his right arm while he used his left to ward off oncoming beams Yukio could not compensate for the fact that to a man flying blind in zero grav *up* and *down* were of most circumscribed utility, and even *left* and *right* changed too fast to do much good.

God, if there'd only been another Rigger here! Even in the sled!

Beck was thus bemoaning his fate and banging his head against the lattice arms when he heard the worst sound that can ever come to you in space. A hiss.

Or rather, a *hiss-s-s-ss!* more virulent than any serpent.

His suit had been breached.

Shit!

His right thigh. He knew from that cutting-torch burn.

Immediately his suit went on max support, pumping warm air to keep his body from being flash-frozen. It could keep that up for two minutes. Then the tourniquet point below his groin would squeeze down and he'd survive, probably, but the leg would be a write-off.

Beck knew a whole bunch of Riggers with prosthetic legs or arms. A whole bunch of dead ones, too.

Still holding the woman's arms with his right, he jerked loose the seal kit from his belt modules. Though he couldn't see the breach through his cracked helmet, that sensation of having a corkscrew drilling into his leg guided him well enough. He slapped down against the suit below the pain and drew the kit upward. Hopefully that would seal the breach for now.

The process only took seconds, but all the time he and the the woman he held, now screaming, bounced blindly among the girders as she kicked and twisted. Beck was frantic that he'd smash either of their faceplates into a beam.

And he was lost. Lost as you can only be in space, without even up or down to give you at least some bearings.

Worst of all, his mind was suffocating.

That's what it felt like. Every part of his brain that had been implanted with the neural nets was screaming out for information. And this stupid suit had none to give. His brain was sucking itself inside out trying to answer that most basic existential question: not who am I, but *where?*

Cries from the sled filled his ears. More freaking directions he had no way to follow.

I'm going to die in this stupid Earth suit, clutching this stupid Earther.

His life didn't exactly flash in front of his eyes, but Beck did experience a sudden appraisal of his place in the universe. His life in space. If it ended here, too bad, but fitting. No complaints.

Then Maeda.

At once regret flooded him for what they'd had, and for what they'd lost.

Oh, Maeda.

While love might remain, the precious spirit that animated it had dribbled away over the past several years.

Which left him alone, and sad, and somehow frightened.

Maeda, he called. Less to the woman he lived with than the one he'd loved years ago. For what they'd once had together.

Maeda.

But even as he thought this, Beck was reaching down to the thruster control module on his waist belt.

He had to go *somewhere*. The Earth woman he held was still shrieking, indicating her faceplate had not yet been shattered. But one of them would be soon.

A peculiar sensation came to him. Deep, deep in his head. So deep he wasn't at first sure whether he felt it or not. Yet....

A sense of direction began to assemble within his mind.

Couldn't be.

But he sure as hell had no place else to go.

Beck dialed up max power from his thrusters, and headed toward where the tiny voice beckoned.

Chapter 3

The dolphin swam lazily in the glass tank bolted in the center of the lab. A Maui's dolphin, only four feet long, it lay lightly anaesthetized while tubes did its breathing for it. A pump at the front of the tank set up currents to keep the dolphin swimming forward.

It had so many hookups clustered around its head that Maeda Rao imagined it as a space mermaid, with the fishlike body in full view but the traditional beautiful face with flowing blue-green hair now covered over by a bulbous open-face helmet with numerous modules for all sorts of bizarre alien functions. The mermaid-dolphin would be only partially aware of the signals it was sending to and receiving from the array of machines spread around the tank.

Maeda sat belted into a padded chair facing the tank. Though the three-quarters g of the lab was sufficient to hold her in place, she chose to belt in anyway because sometimes during the experiments she got lost in the signals going to her own head. Unknowingly she might gyrate strongly enough to come out of the fugue in a looping trajectory into a soft but embarrassing landing on the floor.

Alongside her stood a silver-plated machine with slightly concave aides and a semi-circular top, that for some reason brought to her mind a Victorian breakfast warmer. Wires in plastic harnesses ran in and out of the machine, reinforced by a broad-spectrum battery of wireless emissions.

Some of the wires ran into a connector plugged into Maeda Rao's pigtail — not hair, but the short black strip emerging from the base of her skull. For though trained as a neuroscientist, Maeda had first come into space back in the wild old days, a dozen years gone, when all who intended to live long-term in the habitats had first to qualify as a space-walker in the event of a sector breach, and were not infrequently called into support roles while the Riggers went and patched up whatever imperiled life support.

As the science conducted aboard the toruses turned increasingly toward the enhanced sensory apparatus that enabled the Riggers to work in an environment where danger came from too many angles in too many forms to rely on visual and auditory warnings alone, the pigtail became more and more vital to their work, and hers.

Or at least, Maeda thought with a twinge of shame, it had, back when she was still a true scientist. Back before the "tube neurosis" that afflicted so many of the torus' long-term residents sapped her mind of its sharpness, turning it toward vague inspirations that struck her as enormously immediate and profound, but like any dream or drug vision, faded away when you tried to translate it into coherent form.

Now she thought of herself as the fish anesthesiologist-in-chief. As well as dogs, bats, snakes, toads, electric eels, small sharks; anything at all with some sensory apparatus that might conceivably be useful for living in space. You produce it, she'd zap it.

Maeda had other functions, of course. Since it was too expensive to put people into space and maintain them there as menial laborers, she cleaned cages and tanks, assisted the two veterinarians, set up wired and wireless connections ... and sometimes, when her mind wasn't wandering beyond its own gravitational well, even helped map out the "transferences" done in the lab.

In these the circuitry of the host animal's brain was transcribed into neural nets. These could then be replicated, adjusted, and implanted into the Riggers. Thus enabling inputs from their suit sensors to be "felt" inside their own brain instead of read on screens. Which in the early days of habitat construction at LaGrange 5 had led to many a Rigger dying of task saturation while trying to sort all that data presented in two dimensions into the three-dimensional world about to kill him.

Such a transference was taking place now. Inside the silver-plated machine a neural net received data from the dolphin's brain, something in the manner of an old-style electromagnetic recording, or even earlier, a needle scoring grooves into a wax cylinder.

The transcription happened in more dimensions of course, and carried infinitely more data. Nor did the neural net emerge wholly ready to furnish the user's brain with miraculous new perceptions once implanted. The nerve tissue provided the raw material, a basic diagram for constructing a permanent circuitry. But before the host brain could make use of it the connections had to be laid down through thousands of repetitions of stimulus and response.

The sense impression Maeda worked on now was one vital to the Riggers: echo-location. It had been long known that humans, in particular the blind, could learn to orient themselves through subtle gradients of sound. That was a long way from receiving some form of reflected signal from the suit's sensors and having a complete, instant, and instinctive image of your surroundings, especially where lack of gravity made disorientation a constant hazard. Working in space, where danger could come at you from any angle, at any speed, without a sound, you did not have time to differentiate up from down before taking action.

Unfortunately, the basic neural net, once optimized through a process of reduction toward echo-location or any other sensory mode, could not simply be duplicated. The technology to fine-tune brain tissue to such exactitude did not yet exist.

The process was expensive and time-consuming. Maeda's own husband, for example, Beck Egan, had spent fourteen years as a Rigger, working in space. But over that time a total of three of those years had been spent training his brain to work with the new inputs.

His success rate, remarkably, had been above ninety percent. The average for Riggers as a whole was closer to sixty. The degree of mental concentration one needed to maintain for weeks at a time in order to join the circuits from the net to the brain in workable fashion was just too exhausting. Thus most Riggers might spend half their service time in training, and still not fully master the sensory enhancements.

A fully-enhanced Rigger like Beck Egan could interpret infrared, echo-location, magnetic fields, and motion detection. He could even perceive full three-dimensional visual input directly to his visual centers, bypassing the two-dimensional input even the most sophisticated Virtual Reality could not overcome.

That was what made senior Riggers like Beck such valuable commodity.

So here sat Maeda, in her box of a laboratory with glass-smooth walls fashioned from ore tailings whose underlying sickly mauve was so pervasive it leached the life out of even the brightest colors painted over it. Her task: conduct yet another transcription session. Necessary work, yes. But rote. Not exactly fulfilling her early dreams of stunningly original scientific breakthroughs.

Still, she was a more or less functioning member of the torus culture. She had a reason for being here.

And needed it. For if she could not meet minimum job performance standards, she would have to apply for a visa on the grounds of being Beck Egan's wife. Which might or not be granted, and maybe later rather than sooner. The economics of life in space were harsh. Food, air, and even space to live in could not be squandered on the non-productive.

Beck had long promised he'd follow her back to Earth if Maeda was forced to leave, either at her own choice or Space Command's. And for a long time she believed him.

Not any more. He might love her. Might even love her almost as much as he thought he did.

But he didn't need her. Not Beck. He only *needed* space. The Big Empty. Which seemed to fill him even as it hollowed her out.

And so she smothered her discontents and tried to keep her attention fixed on the dolphin's sensory perceptions. Right now the semi-conscious mammal was tracking an assortment of darting images like fleeing mackerel. In its normal state it would perceive it was not swimming at pursuit speed, and knowing the images unreal, would soon abandon the chase. A current strong enough to keep the dolphin swimming at more than a quarter of its top speed would be too dangerous.

Now, rendered much more susceptible by sedation, the dolphin pursued the images by emitting signals that had the fish been real, would bounce off them back to the fatty sheath across its forehead, which would amplify the vibrations so that the dolphin could decipher them into direction, size, and speed. Though the fish were in fact no more than signals transmitted to the optic nerves, reflective disks mirrored their apparent movement, so that the dolphin continued to get feedback, and accordingly continued its emissions.

Maeda's most important task was to monitor the state of sedation. Not through chemical readings; the time lag rendered them useless. And not through any recording of brain waves, which just got you into a game of catch-up that quickly devolved into a negative feedback loop.

Instead, she more or less *melded*, as they said in the lab, into the mind of the dolphin. Shared its perceptions as far as possible, and increased or impeded the strength of the sedating agent.

How, no one was really sure. The most convenient explanation was that Maeda's hookups stimulated enough centers in her own brain that she could instinctively sense the degree of activation in the host animal. The key element as far as the lab was concerned was that the transference session not be too short, too weak, too strong, or too uneven. Any of these could scramble the forming neural net into incoherence. Which meant not only that the lab's production would go down, but the list of Riggers waiting for further implants would grow even longer. Which in turn meant that the odds of an accident during the constant round of construction and adaptation going on all across LaGrange 5 went way up.

Accidents in space could be expensive. Very expensive.

Not to mention fatal.

Though Maeda thought her job routine, it was also important. And rather to everyone's surprise, she was very good at it. Unique, in fact. Which only further contributed to her reputation for weirdness.

She gathered herself in, sinking toward the interior of her mind. Drawing inward from the space behind her eyeballs, she settled her vision on the flashing machine-generated fish that drew the dolphin's sonar.

As Maeda sank deeper into the process the dancing lights stretched away ahead of her as if swimming down a long tunnel. Her perception swam after them.

She *was* the dolphin. She sported among the lights, darting and coursing and twisting, lunging at the elusive glowing streaks as though to swallow them down, only to glide under at the last moment, feeling the ball of light roll over her sphere of awareness, *feeling* the sensation glide back all the way to her tail.

It was all so ... free.

Then a whole new perception jolted her. Seeming to come at once from outside her head and so deep into her mind that it was like a needle of light probing into depths hitherto left dark.

Maeda almost opened her eyes in an effort to bring herself back to the comforting familiarity of the lab. But checked herself.

Something was calling to her.

No, some *one*.

Beck.

Aside from one quick flickering acknowledgement that she might be going mad, she did not pause to wonder how such a thing could happen.

Beck needed her.

Maeda tried to swim down the line of light piercing down, down, down, like a diver pulling herself down a fixed line into the blackened depths.

It *was* Beck. His mind screamed out to her. He was lost. Blind. He needed ... direction.

But what bearings could she provide him?

Only herself.

She understood none of it. Only that Beck needed her. Badly. His cry would not have reached her otherwise.

Down, down, down, Maeda swam. Closing her mind to all but Beck. The joy of their early love, when the world opened to her in bright colors she'd never seen before.

Over the years the stresses of their lives had pulled them back into their own worlds from that perfect unity they once shared. But for Maeda, that link still existed.

Oh Beck, she thought, reaching out to that presence in her mind she could not quite fix. Come back to me. In my world, everything centers on you. Now you must center on me. *Feel* me.

And come back. Please come back to me.

Chapter 4

Beck Egan had first met Elaine Fullerton, the latest in the biannual circulation of EVA department heads, eight months before. The first thing he noticed about her was not her face, but her clothes. A burgundy blouse which he was willing to bet was made out of real silk, not the synthetic fabric spun out of gossamer long-chain molecules here at the torus in zero-g. The blouse's bat-wing collar he thought a deliberate invocation of Dracula.

Her trousers were old-style jeans, or rather an upscale imitation cut so tight as to render the pockets vestigial. Sexual allure might have gotten her promoted into space, Beck thought cynically, but she would find the realities of this world more intractable.

Or were the jeans meant to project an old-time, hands-on, roll up your sleeves look? Not aboard the *Banneker*. Nobody wore jeans. Mostly they wore pajamas.

Or something very like them, simple upper-and-lower garments, loose and comfortable and quick to get in and out of in an environment that could on the instant change radically and possibly fatally. A quick for-your-life change into whatever gear the situation required was regarded as more relevant than fashion. And it helped to have clothes that were easy to clean where water use was always rationed.

As for her face, Fullerton was one of those women doomed to be cute. Rounded cheeks, pert nose, big round eyes, and lips that swelled flapper-style at the center when she was happy to see you, and clamped into a don't-tread-on me grimace if she thought you were wasting her time just existing in the same torus.

The face she generally kept for Beck.

Okay, so she, like most Earth-sent executives, was a newbie determined to command respect. It didn't help her cause slathering on makeup like that. It tended to take on a glossy, rubbery, and generally comic look when the normal three-quarters gravity of the *Banneker* turned your face a touch flaccid.

Her jewelry also contributed to the overall impression of the bizarre. The necklace and matching earrings were undeniably beautiful; with gold blending into blue with repeated detours to red and green, and just the barest hint of stylized faces pictured in the discs. But a journey into the spokes toward the Hub, or down the spindle to the manufacturing sectors, exposed you to different gravities where such artificial appendages could be an irritant at best and a noose at worse.

Besides, there were just too many drills where you had to rush to the nearest life-support equipment and saddle up to withstand decompression, airlessness, hazardous chemicals, or disasters as yet undiscovered. And what if a sector was breached or life support decided to activate its inner child?

Though in fact Elaine Fullerton did not need to worry overmuch about drills. As an administrator from Earth she got to schedule them, then sit around watching the results on her office screens. Like others of her species, she would endure her two years in the boonies, then return to Earth as an expert in space affairs.

So Beck started out admittedly prejudiced, and disinclined to give the new department head a chance to work past the first impression. Why strive to be fair? He played the percentages.

Now here they were eight months later, and without any experience in actually building anything even on Earth, and a scant spoonful of EVAs in the most benign circumstances possible, Elaine Fullerton's favorite hobby was telling the Riggers their job, and finding them forever falling short.

"This is your fuck-up," she announced in clipped tones, biting down hard on each syllable.

She stood at the side of his hospital bed, refusing even to sit down lest it be taken as fraternizing with the enemy.

You could tell that during her eight months in space she'd made only rare excursions from the torus ring because even in the one-quarter g of this section of the hospital she reached out to touch the bedside table bolted to the floor, as if worried she'd float away. Likely she found the room disorienting. Tracks; everywhere across the pasty-beige moonrock floor, walls, and ceiling, there ran inletted tracks. You could convert the space to almost any purpose, conduct virtually any procedure, but any equipment you brought in better be clamped to something.

"I am holding you personally responsible," Fullerton amplified.

"Fair enough," Beck returned from his bed. "But for what, exactly?"

Even the noticeable puffiness of skin at this level of the spoke could not disguise the screwing down of her features from admonitory to downright inflamed.

"Don't try and play games with me," she warned, purring a slight snarl into her voice with a smoothness that could only come from long practice. "You don't have the bandwidth for it."

Beck sincerely doubted that, but he contented himself with looking wide-eyed to demonstrate his innocence. He could tell from the way one leg was cocked that if she'd trusted herself to the gravity, she'd be tapping her foot.

"Look," he said, "I'm in no position to argue who's responsible for what. There was a lot happening, and I haven't seen the vids. Apparently you have. Have you released them yet?"

"Of course not. There are liability issues. These are Earth citizens who were killed. We must also consider," she added with a remarkable approximation of a hiss, "your upcoming disciplinary hearing."

Beck resisted the impulse to shift. Pretty much his entire body where it hadn't been protected by his helmet was one big bruise from the titanium balls. Even in quarter-g resting in any one position for longer than five minutes brought the aches to the fore. The spot where his suit had been breached and they needed to graft on some skin was especially sore.

"I didn't know I was scheduled for one," he said.

"After supervising a fatal disaster? Earth to Egan. Get real. You've undercut me at every turn ever since I arrived on this station. You've acted like a little tin god. Like the Riggers were responsible to you, not me. Made like the habitats were your own private playground, and Earth and all the people who paid the taxes to build them nothing but an irritant. Well enjoy it while you can. A year from now you'll be scrubbing toilets in Colorado. That is, if there's still any job left for you in Space Command at all. Of course there's always the chance you could wind up in prison for criminal negligence, too."

Beck cocked one eyebrow. "Do I sense an interpersonal conflict here?"

***

AFTER HE SOMEHOW FOUND his way out of the pyramids and the shrapnel storm, one of the sleds took him to an emergency aid module. They'd worked him out of his damaged suit, with the help of a rotary chisel and a hand laser. From there a medic travelled with him up the spindle elevator to the Sector Five spoke, which served as the main hospital for the torus because of the easily accessible gradations of gravity as you moved closer toward the Hub. Besides the severe bruising, the flash burns on his right leg looked gruesome.

It was several hours before he had a chance to talk to Maeda. He tried to make a joke out of it. And failed badly, because two people working under his supervision had died.

So strong was his guilt that much as he wanted to withdraw from all the world and pull himself into a cocoon with just the two of them, he could not stop from freezing her out of his shame. He just couldn't get his mind off those screams. Maeda knew that too. And though she understood, at least in the abstract, it hurt her.

Why wouldn't it? Something very serious had happened out there, and though he wanted to pull her down to him, wanted to embrace her, wanted to cry into her lovely black hair, freezing out the world instead of her, the reverse was happening.

He wanted to tell her over and over again, I'm sorry. Not just because he was wrapped up in his own emotions, but because they'd come to this, where the most important factors of their lives didn't pull them closer together anymore, but pointed them away.

And Beck blamed himself. He loved his work, and gave himself wholly to it. While Maida struggled just to get by.

Sitting at the side of his bed, Maeda assumed an imitation of calm. But her eyes, her nervously working fingers, her head swiveling from side to side like she'd just entered a haunted house, showed her to be bubbling over inside. Beck had the impression she was trying to tell him something for which she had no words.

After she left, the medicos put him under local while they grafted new skin over his space burns. They excised some dead muscle, implanting new tissue that would meld in and with the help of some electrodes to stimulate stretch and contract reflexes, replace the loss within a couple of months.

A few more pokes and prods here and there, and they uploaded the record to his personal log and called it a job well done. After a couple of days of observation he could go home. Then they'd schedule exams every third day to see when he'd be cleared to return to work.

Lying alone and uncomfortable, Beck tried to recreate the accident, though his mind wanted badly not to go there. He still didn't understand how the extensor arms could have exploded a titanium-sphere lattice.

One other thing he didn't understand. Going back to his moment of utter disorientation, buffeted by the balls, blind and lost — terrified if the truth be known, though that did not accord with the legend of Beck Egan — he tried to fix on that moment when some impulse had told him in what direction he must go.

Hallucination? False memory? Most likely one or the other. It wasn't like he'd been at his most rational.

Thus he spent the next twelve hours, until Elaine Fullerton came busting in.

Beck knew he was in trouble then. Normally she summoned him. He might be far out at one of the solar panel arrays, the issue might be nothing that couldn't be settled by three minutes conversation over the radio between two relatively reasonable people. Didn't matter. She always insisted he come to *her*. Through all the hassle of returning, going through the airlocks, and getting out of his suit.

Then he'd wait eleven minutes outside her office door while she pretended to be solving the fate of the universe. It was always eleven minutes. Finally he would walk in and sit penitent while she upbraided him about whatever had flitted into her nasty little mind. Almost none of it came down to factors actually in his control. Scotty with his *"But Captain I can't change the laws of physics!"* wouldn't have lasted long with Elaine Fullerton.

He'd sit and look abject, utter a *mea culpa* or two, and wait to be dismissed. Then go through the fifteen-minute process of suiting up again, and sled back to doing some actual work, only to get bitched at later because he'd spent too much time off-site.

Not that she was so very much worse than any of the other department heads he'd been afflicted with over the years. They came chest-pounding into the torus issuing dictats about "streamlined production protocols" right and left, and accusing the Riggers of sabotaging their efforts to modernize the space program.

In fairness, the Riggers *did* sabotage their efforts. Because with the exception of a few administrators who actually took the trouble to learn what they were doing, the new "protocols" were always the same. Reduce the safety checks by half and increase the production quotas by double.

Yeah, sure. Anything you say, boss.

So they blustered and threatened. But what could they do? In the end they were little people, stuck in the classic bind of middle management. Too much responsibility, too little power to carry it out.

Because threaten as they would, the Riggers could not be replaced. Not from Earth. Riggers, unlike middle management toadies, grew in space. And it was a long and expensive process.

This time, though, was different. This time people had died. People from Earth. People under Beck's supervision.

Elaine accused him of sloppiness, laziness, and ineptitude for not personally supervising the placement of the extensor arms.

He wasn't sure just what she meant by "personally supervising" and doubted she knew either, but there didn't seem much point in questioning her. The word "insubordination" came quite readily to her compressed lips.

"I may be guilty of everything you say," he acknowledged. Of course she'd be recording this, and of course she was liable to use the confession against him. But he didn't have the heart for games. "But before you sentence me to walk the plank out the nearest airlock, can we just go over the vids and see what the hell actually happened?"

"You were there. Don't you know? Was your mind someplace else, when you were supposed to be supervising inexperienced workers?"

"Tell you what," he said. "There are numerous records of me making the case that Earth-trained workers need more time and training to be ready for black-space construction. There are even more records of me recommending that no more than one trainee be assigned to an experienced Rigger at any time, so that their training can be fine-honed. Not five to one, which is what I had. Under your direction, by the way."

"And you managed to kill two of them. Why not go all the way and insist on four Riggers for every Earth trainee? That's your real goal, isn't it? To kill the whole Earth worker project by making it too expensive. If you had your way, you'd denying training to all but the chosen few you and your cronies deign to let into your private little medieval guild. Do you have ceremonies where initiates have to drink rocket fuel out of human skulls?"

"Why don't we quit bickering over hypothetical conspiracies, take a look at the goddamn vids, and decide the basic question of responsible for *what?*"

Her lips tightened till they quivered. "You had better be very, *very* careful how you speak to me. Other times I've let such insubordination pass. Not this time."

"You want insubordination? How's this? Why don't we at least try to establish the goddamn facts? Declassify the tapes. Or do you think you can threaten your way out of this? Who has ultimate responsibility for all EVA's?"

Her face veered so far toward red zone he had one hopeful moment where he thought she might drop dead of heart failure. No such luck.

"I am going to recommend charges of negligent manslaughter be filed against you," she said. Then, assuming a shit-eating smile indicative of sudden inspiration: "Unless evidence comes forward of deliberate murder. If your negligence wasn't to blame, then we must consider sabotage. And who else was in a position to carry it out?"

Murder, now.

"With respect," he said, "you have your head up your ass. Which is so tight to start with, you must have worked really hard to jam it up there."

She flared, then restored her artificial smile. "You know, I was hoping you'd say something like that."

Then she was on her way out, without giving him the vids. And issuing so many threats Beck thought of a medieval witch muttering spells.

Left alone, Beck went through the incident over and over again from memory, since Fullerton thought it part of her job to deny him the vids. Probably lawyers for Space Command were already looking them over down on Earth, building their case against him before he ever got a look. Maybe even altering the record. Ten years ago such treachery would be unthinkable. Now it didn't seem so unlikely. Earth had long been on a campaign to strip all autonomy from the habitats.

The effort to relive the catastrophe roused up a new surge of adrenalin in him. And remorse.

But he kept at it, focusing down tighter and tighter. Concentration was one of his strengths; it came from hours, days, weeks, months, and eventually years of trying to meld the neural nets into his own brain circuitry.

At first he'd thought it was the one arm of the pyramid, the one with the extensor arm locked out, that had shattered, the debris from its disintegration and the whirling arm causing similar bursts from other pyramids already in place, which already bore structural stress.

Yet reliving the scene over and over, he thought he detected what at the time his eyes had refused to credit: the lattice being eased into place had actually exploded. Not ruptured under pressure; it had exploded before exhibiting any severe distortion.

No way the extensor arms could cause that. Beck had watched that same operation here, while building the *Banneker*, and in work on the other toruses at LaGrange 5. The exact same process, the exact same materials. Pretty much the exact same extensor arms. Many and many thousands of times.

There had been glitches, of course. A few dangerous. That's what they paid him for. But to explode an entire lattice that way....

What the hell had happened to the bonding agent that was supposed to fuse the balls together?

Something must have gone wrong in the way it was built. Hell. Now construction would have to halt while they not only examined the manufacturing process down to electron microscopic detail, but tested every one of the three thousand or so lattices already anchored in the lower ring.

Heads would fall. His, first thing. A delay like that, the expense, the chain reaction of economic displacements, the whole episode was a disaster of the first order. Guilty or innocent, Beck Egan's days as a Rigger were numbered.

Elaine Fullerton would see to that. But in the end it wouldn't help her. No matter she had as many arms as a Hindu statue, no matter how many fingers she pointed, her career was fully as dead as his.

But how could it have happened in the first place?

Something Elaine Fullerton said came back to him.

Sabotage.

Sabotage? But that was crazy. Who would risk lives just to make a point? Well, maybe more people than he dared admit. But even so, just think of the number who'd have to be involved. Manufacturing, Maintenance, Planning, Riggers ... you're talking major conspiracy here.

No, it couldn't be. Some module jock, maybe. But no Rigger would *ever* sabotage a worksite. That *would* be murder. And a betrayal of everything they'd worked — and died — to accomplish since construction first began.

Could Fullerton have a point, dumb as she was?

Chapter 5

"But *how* did you find your way out?" Maeda asked yet again. She just wouldn't let it go.

"I don't know," Beck told her. Straining to remember, but growing irritated with both of them because the harder she pressed and the harder he tried to recover that moment, the more elusive it became. When he thought back all he remembered was the hard patter of titanium balls off his suit, the wounded Earther squirming in his arms, the fear that one or both of them would get their faceplate shattered, and his wholly disoriented brain searching, pleading really, for some direction out of the trap. Not quite panic, but within shouting distance.

And then ... *something*. Some piece of data, some slice of information filtering through just below his threshold of perception. Perhaps a flash of light across the splintered faceplate that his conscious mind couldn't interpret, but his hyper-aware subconscious could.

"There must be *something* you remember," Maeda persisted.

"Maybe, but it isn't coming to me now. There was a lot going on."

They sat in the living room of their apartment, legs drawn up on bulbous purple sitting cushions, twisted toward each other, their faces inches apart. Maeda had always regarded the purple as somewhat garish. But Beck liked the spray of cushions because they set off Maeda's hair so beautifully, and to his mind, added infinitely sonorous tones to her double-cream *au lait* skin. Which had once compelled his nose to sniff, his fingers to caress, his lips to brush.

And the clutch of cushions offered a number of ways to make love without rising from separate chairs and walking into the bedroom.

Had offered. They were rather more restrained these days.

Twisting this way made his wounded leg hurt, but he ignored it. Maida had shown a lot less interest in his hurts than how he stopped bouncing blindly around the lattices while assailed by a hailstorm of lethal titanium balls, and found his way out. And luck just wasn't going to cut it.

Around them the walls were blank, a uniform shade of blue-gray. In recent years Maeda had acquired a positive horror of the standard mood lights that rippled across the walls and ceilings of most apartments, supposedly adjusting themselves to signals from pheromones, brain waves, and pulse to ease you into calmer or more aroused states, according to pleasure. She said it was like having a voice in your head telling you your emotions were all out of joint.

The screen on the opposite wall was covered over with the same color as the walls because of the relentless newsbreaks about the accident, along with various accusations, and Beck didn't need reminding. And it would disturb Maeda. She'd hear all the gossip in her normal rounds. Such was life aboard a habitat.

The apartment was small, like pretty much all living quarters aboard the *Banneker* except those of the Earth administrators, who though they were allotted three times more space than the citizens, still complained about being consigned to a shoebox.

When Beck and Maeda were newlyweds, it had been cozy.

Now, with Maeda spending so much of her time staring wistfully at nothing at all, Beck found the apartment tending toward claustrophobic. A sensation he resisted because it was a classic symptom of the tube neurosis which affected many of the torus inhabitants to a greater or lesser extent.

Fourteen years, he'd worked in space. Beck Egan, the favored lead suit for the most complex, the most uncomfortable, the most dangerous EVA projects. The man who served as an unofficial but widely recognized spokesman for the Riggers not only aboard the *Benjamin Banneker*, but the four other habitats at Lagrange 5.

He was proud of that. He couldn't let it be taken from him now.

But aside from Elaine Fullerton trying to send him back down the funnel, Maeda was right on the brink. If she got "repatriated" to Earth, what would he do? He'd often reassured her that of course he'd go with her. And believed it when he said it. It was the upright, honorable thing, and he saw himself as an upright, honorable man.

But what the hell would he do on Earth? His life was here. The Big Empty. And Maeda, to tell the truth, was becoming a diminishing part of it. More of a problem than a solution. Sometimes when Beck came back through the airlock it seemed to him that the weight of multiple concerns he could not begin to master all came piling back onto his shoulders in a rush.

And though he knew it to be untrue, he could not help thinking that if only Maeda would try just a little *harder*....

"You know I was working in the lab when that lattice exploded," Maeda said, ending the long heavy silence. "I thought I heard something like a voice. So I strained after it, and it turned into your voice. Not words, just a feeling. You were calling to me."

Beck cast back. "Guess I was. Not calling, exactly. But thinking of you. Yes, I was. Thinking I was going to die, and leave you alone, and that I was so very sorry." Was that true? True enough. Why tell her that the real truth was that he'd been regretting what they'd lost?

"I guess I was talking to you, at that." Though he'd reviewed the incident so many times, he'd glossed over that because it didn't seem important. "Maybe I did call out. Yes, I think I did. Right before I hit the thrusters."

She nodded. Rather dispassionately to his eyes, more concerned with having confirmed a thesis than saving his life.

"At first I didn't know what was happening," she said. "I was afraid I might be having some kind of, well, you know. But then I knew it was you. You were reaching out toward me. And you calling on me to reach out to you in turn. So I, well ... I tried."

"You tried."

"Yes." She looked at him uncertainly, afraid he'd think her fanciful, or manipulative, or insane.

Beck ran his fingers lightly through her hair. Though meant to be an intimate gesture, he felt no intimacy. Just confusion.

"I was blind," he said. "I told you that. Faceplate all cracked to pieces. I had hold of this Earther who kept twisting and screaming. We'd bounced around so much I had no sense at all of where to go. The Earther watching from the sled was no help at all. If I stayed where I was, my faceplate would have ruptured at any moment. If I set off in the wrong direction and ricocheted off a beam, chances were I'd just keep bouncing around. And die. I didn't consciously call to you to show me the way, but ... yes, I was thinking of you. Wanting to get back to you, really. And without the slightest idea how to do it."

Maeda's eyes widened into vast pools deep as space Her lips parted slightly in her softly rounded face, and Beck had an impulse to kiss them.

But he also needed to know what had happened.

"There was so much going on," he said, trying to fix his concentration on that moment. "None of it good. And then this ... sense of direction, call it, came to me. I didn't understand it. Didn't trust it. But I aimed my thrusters at it anyway, and it happened to be the right trajectory. And I lived."

It really had happened just that way, hadn't it?

"So I guess 'thank you' is appropriate. Though I still don't understand."

Maeda shook her head, or rather, it quivered. She looked away. Beholding the soft smooth tint of her skin, feeling the warmth reflect off his lips, Beck thought, as in years past, that she was more than beautiful. She was the whole embodiment of every yearning he carried inside himself. Physical and emotional. She defined the boundaries of his life.

He had been so happy, then.

"I don't understand," she said.

"Me neither."

"I mean, you and I, our minds touching each other in such a moment, that I can believe. I can't think of any scientific explanation, but I believe it. But how would I be able to give you direction?"

How indeed? They both had implants; their minds were not as minds on Earth. A lot of the Riggers were at least half convinced telepathy existed in some indirect form. Beck had long been a skeptic on the issue. But the idea that he might actually have experienced it in no way shocked him.

"Maybe it was just luck," he said. "The direction, I mean. Maybe what I felt was your presence, right where you happened to be, in the lab. So that's what I went for, and it just happened to get me clear."

"Yes," said Maeda. "That would make sense."

She didn't sound like she quite believed it. She reached out to take his hand.

"We talked mind to mind, Beck. I believe that."

"Me too." More or less. "You saved my life."

She kissed his fingers. Then wriggled closer and nuzzled her lips against his neck.

It was a sign she wanted to make love. And though their sex life had tended more toward now-you-see-it-now-you-don't over the last couple of years, Beck was himself seized with the old desire.

He wanted her with a yearning so strong it almost brought tears to his eyes. He'd missed her so badly.

Their minds *had* touched. Whatever had been driving them apart, that which pulled them together was so much stronger.

For now.

Chapter 6

THE INVESTIGATORS FROM EARTH swore to confine him in the Pit of Misery for eternity plus one millennia, without coffee breaks. They promised to make him King of the Universe. They acted like Beck Egan was their oldest and bestest friend. They stared down their noses like if it was a choice between stepping in him or dogshit, they'd take the poop every time.

And of course they kept smugly insisting they had enough evidence to burn Gandhi at the stake, let alone Beck Egan, while Mother Theresa twisted slowly, slowly in the wind from a nearby gibbet.

He wondered if they ever got as bored with the routine as he did.

Early on he realized the interrogators were less interested in pulling out his toenails than in getting him to expose the vast conspiracy they were sure he played a key role in.

Which confirmed what a lot of residents of the habitats believed. Earth wanted to rule LaGrange 5 directly and completely.

Space Command couldn't just order most of the population back to Earth and replace it with loyalists. The skills necessary to keep the habitats intact simply didn't exist on Earth, and no simulators were going to produce them. If Space Command tried to blanket the toruses with Marines against the will of a population notoriously jealous of their rights and prerogatives, sabotage was inevitable.

Maybe not existential, shut-down-the-solar-satellites sabotage, but a more contained and hard to detect industrial sabotage.

Close to half Earth's commerce depended on space production, and three-quarters of the American economy could not function without the work done at LaGrange 5. Even a slow-down would put great big dents in the planet's economy. And you could hardly send an Earth labor force into the habitats to keep things humming along.

And it was that fear that kept bringing the investigators circling back to that same point: the accident had been caused deliberately.

Sabotage.

Ridiculous, Beck kept telling them. Here at L5, living amid vacuum, we don't burn down our own homes.

The idea was absurd.

Wasn't it?

And yet Beck had watched vids of the same explosion his interrogators did.

How could it happen? How could he not see it? He was Beck Egan. Nothing happened at L5 without him knowing about it.

Which was the interrogators' point exactly.

Christ, he thought, I'm getting old. Close to forty; when he first came up into space that would have made him a patriarch. He was more capable than ever, but a whole new generation of Riggers was coming up who though superficially respectful, could not entirely hide the fact that they regarded him as a relic from the glory days. A shade-tree mechanic with no tools but a Crescent wrench and an oil can. A golden oldie.

But could he possibly be so out of touch that such a conspiracy could form without the slightest suspicion on his part?

The Earth investigators didn't think so.

The one time in his life Earth actually over-estimated him, and it had to be now.

Because as the questioning continued over the course of several days, references to the Pit of Misery increasingly crowded out the King of the Universe blandishments.

And were much more specific. As in, sending Beck Egan, and Maeda Rao, back to Earth right now. Keep him out of further mischief while the lawyers from Space Command justified "enhanced interrogation" to a court system increasingly given to finding only religion and the Theron Whitfield administration, now in its sixth year due to "ongoing national emergencies", possessed any rights at all.

So in the end Beck implied that yes, there might be certain elements willing to take illegal measures to contest Earth directives. Especially when, as with the new lower torus being built on the *Banneker*, there was some fear that it would destabilize the habitat, maybe even send the main ring crashing into its radiation shield.

And yes, he might have heard a whisper or two about a few Riggers who might conceivably be involved. But only whispers. No evidence.

But as for the accident that shattered the lattice, he had no knowledge of that at all. Would he have gone charging in to save an Earther if he'd caused the destruction in the first place?

Tell you what, he suggested. Let's pool our resources. Let me circulate a little, keep my ear to the figurative ground, and maybe see if I can't discover something that might be to our mutual benefit.

In the end, they left several charges pending, but did not kick his butt back to Earth.

Yet.

But he better come up with some conspirators' names soon. Else his fate would be too horrible for their sensitive little souls to contemplate.

From first to last, the fact that he might actually be innocent never influenced them at all.

Even given their agreement, Space Command did ground him. No help for that. He had been supervising an operation in which two people got killed. It stung.

But the questioners did impart some interesting facts about just what went wrong. Their original theory of explosives secreted into the binding agent of the lattices proved groundless. Whoever planned the mishap appeared to want to leave at least some plausible deniability on the table. Trying to work explosives into the binding agent would not only prove sabotage, it would be a pretty good indicator of just where and how it happened.

On the other hand, the bonding agent had definitely been diluted with a precision that, while it didn't quite place shoddy manufacturing techniques entirely beyond the realm of possibility, in fact pretty well belied any chance of some purely chance malfunction in the manufacturing process.

So how was it done? The investigators still couldn't figure it out. Every step of every process that occurred in the modules located on the spindle was rigidly tracked. Detailed records were kept in so many separate systems no hacker could jimmy them all.

The most likely hypothesis was that someone had inserted a rogue bit of code into one of the robots, adulterating the bonding agent for just one pyramid. Hopefully. After performing its task, the program had either been removed, or more likely self-destructed, leaving no trace. Neat trick, but one that could have been accomplished from any number of entry points, over a wide range of time.

Now everything that came off the line was being analyzed with all sorts of sonic and spectral devices. Which would cause further delays in construction of the lower torus.

At least the snafu had Elaine Fullerton chain-drinking coffee and sticking pins into her Beck Egan voodoo doll, so things weren't all bad.

And though the investigators could no doubt fabricate enough evidence to pour molten lead down Beck's throat on prime time TV, in the end the most nefarious deed they actually had evidence to was wearing a good-luck charm against regulations.

Two gold ducks with their necks crossed, on an elastic band around his wrist. Maeda had given him that.

But Beck had no doubt that given the right Earth court, they could convict him of assassinating JFK.

But for now they were all buddy-buddy. Everyone loves a turncoat.

As they finally came to an agreement, the chief investigator, a short, cheerful woman with a pageboy haircut and a large golden cross hung reverently about her neck, asked him a question.

"Say you were standing naked in an airlock with a rope tied around your balls. When the doors open, would the vacuum pull you out fast enough to tear them off? You'd have time to know, wouldn't you? I mean, how long can an unprotected body survive in space? Two minutes, three? How long would the rope have to be? All these questions. I always find space so fascinating."

And smiling companionably, she slammed shut the lid of her laptop.

***

IN THE DAYS AFTER the lawboys and lawgirls cut him loose, two-thirds of the torus, or so it seemed, found a way to cross his path to tell him how much they admired him and what a raw deal he'd gotten from Earth. Even people assigned to other habitats found some excuse to visit the *Banneker* and just happen to run into him.

Beck expected it from the Riggers. And really pretty much anyone who spent much time EVA: the spindle workers, pilots, miners in from the moon or the long-haul run to the asteroid belt.

Some of the others, though, they surprised him. The ones who never put on a suit except in a full-scale drill. Teachers, scientists, artists with a thing for space, doctors, nurses, intra-vehicle maintenance hands, even the tourist wranglers — restauranteurs, souvenir peddlers, guides to EVAs, zero-g sports, or purveyors of specially outfitted suites for the big seller, zero-g sex.

Usually those who made their living catering to tourists tilted closer toward Earth perspectives. But it turned out that even a lot of them worried about increasingly heavy-handed interference from Earth.

So Beck basked in his fifteen minutes of being the most popular man aboard the *Benjamin Banneker*. He allowed himself to soak in the praise without taking any of it too seriously.

He knew who he was. A Rigger. And a damn good one. With a strong aversion to getting into situations that took being a hero to get out of. He was proud of his work, and knew that only other Riggers could truly understand what went into it. Not brief moments of super-hero glory, but day after day, year after year of efficiency and concentration. Because space was not a place where you got to do a lot of day-dreaming.

Then the Riggers' worst nightmare came true.

Chapter 7

For years Earth had viewed the implants the Riggers employed to broaden their perception in space with increasing suspicion.

Ever more shrill accusations were made that the colonies at L5 were creating a race of Supermen. Little tin gods, looking disdainfully down on Earth from on high.

Even though the Riggers tried to explain that their actual use of infrared, echo, and visual maps laid out across the inner mind amounted to little more than a new form of Virtual Reality, the implants were not like anything man had ever been born with.

And where would it stop? More and more rumors spread across Earth about the "Singularity" in which a core of humans morphed into something more than human. Beings who would enslave those who clung to the human form, and destroy any religion or ideology that did not worship the New Rulers. Beings who would contend with God himself, as Lucifer had. Only while holding all Earth hostage.

Such paranoia was easily exploited by politicians all over the world.

But in America it took on a particularly virulent form. Because there many chose to answer the uncertainties of the future with a growing religious fundamentalism. This, combined with the "new populism's" hatred for elites, an ever-lowering standard which currently took in anyone who passed algebra, injected a fanatical absolutism to a social question that might otherwise have been resolved through reason and law.

But there existed little scope for either in the American political landscape. To the true believers, God made man in His own image. The Bible said it, they believed it, and to hell, literally, with reason, science and those who looked to such fake sources for guidance. To attempt the least variation from the human form as created in Adam and Eve was blasphemy.

Did God have neural nets in his head? No, and by the time the lynch mob was done, neither would anybody else.

And as to the flow of solar energy and goods from space, still neck and neck with environmental and economic disaster? That, said those who'd learned all the science anyone would ever need in Bible classes, was all a fable created by the wannabe Supermen at L5.

As best Beck could understand, the born-again brigade did not actually command a majority of America's population. But that fact was of declining relevance because President Theron Whitfield had recently canceled all elections due to "national emergencies," and ruled according to his own interpretation of martial law.

There was a theory, or rather a hope, that Beck liked to subscribe to, that all would be better someday. Fairly soon. That only the unending litany of flood, drought, and displacement that turned so many of the population so desperate. Whoever expected to find refugee camps, in practice, full of American citizens? That as more and more saw how technology was reversing the catastrophe, fewer would blame science for bringing catastrophe down on their heads.

At last the age of hate and superstition would give way to a new age of reason and charity.

Well, maybe.

But in the meantime, President Whitfield, who'd never darkened a church doorway till the day he discovered himself miraculously "born again," had just signed a decree stating that no further implants were to be allowed. And that all current research into

"Superman" technologies, as the pronouncement termed the Riggers' enhancements, was to be suspended immediately.

Yet the threat didn't stop there. Because in the wake of Whitfield's proclamation, a significant contingent of congressmen, all of whom regarded any education past fifth grade as the Sign of the Beast, introduced a bill demanding that those who already had implants should be forced to have them surgically removed.

Not that the legislators in question had the slightest idea how that might be done, or what the effects would be on those who underwent it. Didn't care much, either. A sharpened spoon would do.

This was more than a slap in the face to the Riggers. It was a death sentence.

So far the bill hung in abeyance. But everyone at LaGrange 5, even those without the implants, had a question to answer: if Earth should actually try to enforce such an order, just what were they going to do about it?

The word "revolt" was starting to work its way into the vocabulary of the toruses. Compromise had been the watchword for many years. Earth was after all the mother planet. But you couldn't compromise with people who insisted on scooping your brains out.

Accordingly Beck was hardly surprised when an unofficial delegation of Riggers did a little recruiting drive for him.

What did surprise him was that the delegation came from the *Stephen Hawking*. Unlike the other four habitats at L5, all in torus form, the *Hawking* was a giant O'Neill cylinder still under construction. While Beck knew emotions were running high aboard the cylinder — emotions were always running high aboard the *Hawking* — he didn't expect the new generation of Riggers there to give him second thought. Though the age difference wasn't so radical, their experience sorted them into two different generations.

Beck's generation had built the habitats, and regarded them as their home. For the younger Riggers and scientists for whom life in space came as an accomplished fact, the colony at LaGrange 5 was just a jumping-off place. The youngbloods were mainly concentrated in the *Hawking*, that wholly dwarfed the older toruses in size and feel. Though the cylinder's interior itself was yet to be fully completed, already they talked there of building new and bigger colonies around the asteroid belt, or Jupiter, or Titan. With even these being no more than gateways to the stars.

And why take any more crap from a bunch of idiots at the *bottom* of the gravity well?

This was maybe a little further in than Beck wished to venture.

On the other hand, isn't it remarkable how many of life's most significant choices came about when you had no choice at all?

***

THE *HAWKING* CONTINGENT PASSED word via a mutual acquaintance that they'd meet him outside Hydroponics. No qualifications like if he wanted to. The park/arboretum was the most popular site on the torus short of the zero-g facilities at the Hub. They weren't making a fetish out of secrecy.

There were six of them. He recognized them all, more from a professional than a personal capacity. Had worked with some, trained others. The *Stephen Hawking*, had only opened to permanent occupation a couple of years ago. Big enough to swallow the other four habitats whole, it seemed to encourage dreams of a similar scale.

For four years Beck had spent most of his time setting up the initial framework and skin of the cylinder. Spending days at a time away from Maeda. As the scale kept growing and parts were deemed safe for occupation, more and more candidate Riggers came up to speed the immense project. His role moved from hands-on construction into training, because these were not skills you could learn on Earth.

Then three months ago he'd been pulled to work on what he and most of the other Riggers regarded as an ill-advised attempt to add a twin torus to the *Banneker*. Since then his knowledge of the *Hawking* had come mostly through snippets from other, older Riggers still working there.

Even so, he knew about the supposed leader of the most radical faction. Kuende Adebayo was born in Nigeria, educated at Stanford. With only three years' actual hands-on experience in space, which made her a newbie in Beck's eyes, she expressed grand visions for the future of humanity throughout the Solar System and beyond. The only implants she'd had time to acquire were visual and infrared. She was still integrating echo-location into her perceptual field, a process that took months of conscious application.

She was also an outspoken advocate of resistance to Earth.

Yet she wasn't the one who first approached him.

That was a young shaggy-blond man — the older Riggers universally kept their hair close-cropped, shaved heads common with the men and even many of the women — with an easy smile and apple cheeks that gave him an appearance of wide-ranging affability.

"Haines Barber," he said, holding out his hand. "We worked together a few times. You probably don't recognize me without the suit. It's an honor to meet you."

An honor, now. Beck shook his hand. The blonde's grip was firm but relaxed; confident as his grin.

They stood beneath a low tree with overhanging red fern-like leaves and a spiky wooden trunk, on a short path bordered by a shallow pool thick with entangled green vines and spreading leaves. A few feet behind the red-leafed tree some slithery plant that looked like The Vine That Ate Toledo gyrated up along a wall of moonrock colored to look like Earth granite marbled with quartz.

The thick humidity added weight to the heat that nourished the plants.

Overhead a series of rocky platforms, or ore tailings bonded together to look like rocks, extended upward in series, the gap between them widening as the hull opened up from the torus "floor," then narrowing again as it approached the ceiling, two thousand feet overhead, invisible in the mist that filled the air.

For this was the farming sector of the *Banneker*, and the light beamed in from the solar panels over each level of the plant-bearing rock shelves promoted an enhanced level of photosynthesis beyond anything found on Earth. More food was grown in hydroponic pods radiating out on collapsing trusses from the spindle, or free-floating amid the solar satellites around the torus. But it was vital to maintain a substantial amount of plant life within the hull itself to help provide oxygen.

Haines Barber repeated the obligatory lines about how shameful it was that Beck had been grounded by the petty-minded, spiteful bureaucrats from Earth. Beck repeated the obligatory lines of thanks and agreement.

At either end of the path a pair of the *Hawking's* discouragingly youthful Riggers discussed the shrubs and ferns with great interest, effectively blocking the path to the other park-goers. With the pool on one side looking like it harbored an especially virulent breed of alligator and the vines climbing the wall on the other, the whole party stood hidden in plain sight.

A few feet away Kuende Adebayo considered him silently. Weighing him up, making no attempt to hide her perusal. He could read no expression in her brown eyes and face. If there was any, Beck thought it might be other than starstruck wonder at being in his presence, honor though Haines Barber declared that to be.

So okay. She looked a pretty objective type. And considered objectively, Beck Egan was a hoary Rigger legend from the wild and wooly days when pretty much anyone who survived more than three years of EVA got to be a legend. A superannuated space jock, nudging forty and now grounded, who you could just see a little way down the line clamping onto anyone incautious enough to sit next to him in a bar and yammering away about what it took to be a *real* Rigger back when you lived cramped together in pods with a less than stellar safety record, and were only beginning to incorporate the implants. Back when Riggers regularly got squashed like bugs just so the next generation could idle away their time in luxury.

But he could still be useful. Having become the hero of the moment by the simple expedient of, not to put too fine a point on it, tripping over his own dick.

His appraisal of Kuende's appraisal depressed him. Because maybe she was right. Maybe he was past his pull date. Wanting more than anything to stick his life in reverse, hoping the second time through would work out better than the first.

Maybe.

Maybe not, too.

"So the question is," Haines Barber was saying, having recited the usual lengthy list of grievances against Earth, culminating in the recent threat to suspend implants, "what are we doing to do about it?"

"Sabotage the *Banneker*?" Beck suggested.

Barber took a step back, raising his palms before him. "Whoa, whoa. That wasn't us. People getting killed? Hey, we work in space too. At this point all we're talking about is finding a peaceful resolution."

"This point?"

"Before it's too late," Barber said defensively. "You know what I mean. These religious kooks have declared war on science itself. To them, we're all budding Frankensteins. And they won't stop until they set up an Inquisition right here at L5 and tear the implants right out of our heads. Using chisels and pliers, probably, since that's their level of advancement. We're fighting for our survival here, Beck. You know that better than anyone. Unless we get Earth to figure out they need us more than we need them, you know what our future is going to be? Staring at a ceiling sucking our thumbs. The Bible brigade won't stop till they're stirring their grubby little fingers around in our skulls. You think I'm wrong?"

"I think maybe it's not written in stone quite yet, but it's certainly plausible. So what do you want me to do about it?"

Haines gave him a dubious glance. "You don't sound like you're exactly putting your soul into this."

"Hey, you're the one making a pitch. Fine. I'm listening. But don't ask me to press my thumb on 'Confirm order' before I even know what I'm supposed to be buying."

Looking down as if abashed (he wasn't), Barber nodded. "Right, right. You're right. Sorry. Let me spell it out. Right now, you're Somebody."

He raised his hands apologetically. "No disrespect. You've earned it over a lot of years, a lot of hard dangerous work. A lot of friends who died in a lot of real hard ways. But frankly, until this week, nobody but other Riggers gave a shit. Now, well, you're a symbol. Okay? We all know it. Earth set you up. Had you baby-sitting a bunch of people who didn't even belong *inside* any self-respecting habitat, let alone working outside it. The way they made you wear an Earth suit, you're damn lucky to be alive. They screwed you over, then blamed you for their incompetence."

"They did that," Beck agreed. "However, there is the minor consideration of sabotage."

"Do you really believe that?"

"Unfortunately, I do. I've gone over it about twenty thousand times, and there's no way else I can see it happening."

"Well then, that's the shits. *Nobody* has a right to lead anyone to their death in space. Not for any cause. But like I told you, it wasn't us. We weren't here when this sabotage, if that's what it was, was taking place. None of us. Not for weeks. Go on, check. Really. That might make it easier for us to work together."

"On what?"

"On getting L5 to speak with one voice. And not using 'please' a whole lot either. Look. Without people like you, that whole first generation of Riggers I mean, there wouldn't even be a *here* here. And now, because Earth's blaming you for something anybody with half a brain can see you never did, people are starting to see just how far it's gone.

"Most of the people in the toruses have just been turning a blind eye. Hoping it will all go away. Earth keeps pushing and pushing, and they're afraid to push back. But we either stop the train now, or wave goodbye while it heads down the track with half our brains aboard. At the moment you are the most visible symbol of what's happening. You are, pardon the expression, a martyr."

Beck looked at his hands. "I haven't noticed being nailed to any crosses yet."

"Cross your fingers, man. You have been grounded. Is that so very different, for a man like you?"

Barber had him there. Beck had been trying to keep his focus on all the nice things people had been telling him about himself. A hero, a pioneer, a prince among men. It helped him not think about what life was going to be like if he couldn't get back to work. Him and Maeda sitting around their cramped apartment, staring through the walls.

While it lasted. Because being exiled to Earth wasn't that far away.

Of course if he made himself useful like he'd promised....

"Okay," said Beck. "You want the colonies to speak with one voice. So far so good. But what exactly do you want that voice to say?"

"First and foremost," Barber declared, "no one's coming up here and cutting anyone's head open. Past that, the enhancement program is not going to be stopped."

"And if Earth says it'll huff and it'll puff and it will blow our house down?"

"Then there's only one answer. Huff and puff back and see whose house falls first."

Beck did a pantomime of wincing, his palms coming up over his eyes. "And that's the message you want *me* to be the spokesman for?"

"Hey, that's a last resort, all right? Hopefully it will never come to that. But it *will* definitely come to that if we hem and haw and say 'please' every time we ask Earth to consider what it takes to survive up here, then do nothing but ring our hands while they go bury their faces back in their Bibles. That's why we're asking you to step forward. You've got guts, and right now you can be the most unifying force in the colony. I mean, do you see Earth or even most of L5 listening to *me*?"

"And if Earth doesn't listen to me either?"

Haines Barber turned his head sideways to give Beck a questioning look. Not resentful, just trying to figure him out. "What are you trying to tell me? Look, I know you have exposure here. For a man in your position to stick his neck out—"

"Forget my problems. My question is, if Earth decides to, oh, send up Marines instead of talking, what do you all intend to do about it?"

"It won't come to that if we can just convince them we're serious."

"You aren't answering the question."

Barber looked over to Kuende Adebayo, who did not stir from her quiet appraisal.

"I don't know about you," Barber told him, after failing to get an answer to his unspoken question. "But before I'll let any bible-basher come up here and cut *my* head open, I'll fight. The Marines have the weapons, but we're better in space."

"Death or glory, huh?"

"What else is there?" He glanced around in frustration. Still Adebayo did nothing. "I like my brain, man. It may not be good for much, but me and it have grown attached. Before I let Earth fuck with it, I'll fucking throw fucking rocks."

At last it came, the threat Beck had been waiting for.

The colonies had already brought in big chunks of ore from the moon and the asteroid belt. They could bring in bigger ones if they chose to. Ones big enough that nudged toward Earth's gravity well, they'd crash right through the atmosphere with enough mass left to ... what would you like? Take out a city? Targeting wasn't that precise, but launch enough in the general vicinity, one or two ought to score a hit. Or firing blind, you could create tidal waves like nothing Earth had ever seen since the last extinction event. Or kick up enough dirt to turn the whole planet into one big Dust Bowl.

"Yeah," said Beck, "I kind of thought that's where we were going."

"Not," Barber insisted, "if we get enough people making a big enough stink that Earth holds its nose and backs off."

"And is that what you want me to be the front man for, it being such an honor to know me and all? Or am I just supposed to be the smokescreen? The fall guy that catches Earth's attention long enough that by the time they do crucify me, you and your friends can get all your rocks in a row?"

"Man, you *do* have a suspicious mind. What's wrong with Plan A? Uniting L5 in opposition. There's a thousand things we can do short of throwing things. Start rationing their solar energy, just for a start."

"Only you don't believe that will work. Do you?"

Barber started to argue, then gave up in the face of Beck's skeptical look.

"In fact," said Beck, "it may. And I'm willing to put my neck on the line to try it. But not if all the time you and your friends here are getting ready to do to the people on Earth what a rock through the atmosphere once did to the dinosaurs. I'm not going to be anyone's fucking decoy. Have a nice day."

Beck started to walk past him. Haines Barber moved to block his path. Hands raised apologetically, trying not to make it personal. But blocking Beck's path nonetheless. Which normally wouldn't have been such a big thing — Beck tried to think of himself as a peaceful man, though in fact he wasn't — but at this particular point most unwise.

"Haines," Kuende Adebayo said quietly.

The blond cast a glance, asked a question with his eyes, then backed well away. The woman stepped into his place.

She was a trifle shorter than Beck, just enough so that over her shoulder he could see the torus floor curving up to where it disappeared behind the downward-curving horizon descending from above. Citizens wandered along paths through the greenery, lost in the wonder of such organic luxuriance when just outside the hull there was Nothing with a capital "N." As the people grew further away their forms foreshortened, until near the distant horizon he was looking at the tops of their heads.

"There are many reasons you may not trust us," the woman told Beck.

Her voice was water bubbling down a brook. Chocolate, honey, orchids. Snuggling up with a clutch of puppies.

He must be getting older than he thought.

"You may think we're lightweights," she said. "You might not like us because we're from a different generation. You might think we're hotheads, ideologues willing to create what used to be called nuclear winter on Earth just to get our own way. You might," she said, with a slight, oddly patient sigh, "even think we had a hand in sabotaging that pyramid."

"Getting warmer," he said. But for some reason he found himself softening. Because she was pretty? He wasn't yet such a fool that he would let his head be turned by fantasies about a girl almost fifteen years his junior.

Was he?

Because he did find Kuende Adebayo beautiful. Not transfixingly so. Maybe on second glance not even "beautiful" in any conventional form. Her frizzed copper-brown hair bore no particular distinction, her lips and cheeks were not chiseled to any notable fineness of line. Her deep brown eyes were not the proverbial liquid pools you wished to lose yourself in.

She was, considered dispassionately, no more than a moderately attractive young black woman. But she stood with an inherent grace that implied motion even in stillness.

That sort of grace couldn't help but capture Beck's mind. He'd worked long in a weightless environment, where any pressure at all against any object propelled you away and maybe sent you cartwheeling besides. Unless you could master that peculiar sort of lightness that enabled the old Tai Chi masters to hold a bird on their palm because it could find no resistance to jump off against.

Just looking at her, Beck knew how Kuende Adebayo would move in space.

He also sensed a compelling dignity about her. The quiet dignity of one who would always do what she thought right without the goads of rage, vanity, self-righteousness, or ideological blindness.

"We did get our hands dirty on that one," she admitted. "Not directly, but we were irresponsible. We provided a certain technical expertise. All we meant to happen was for a few of the lattices to show themselves defective under routine inspection once they were fused in place. Then they would all have to be reinspected, which might delay the building of the lower ring by a couple of weeks. The people we dealt with, that is what they promised. We hoped that people who talked like us would act like us. And I honestly believe they meant to. But whether by design or mistake, people were killed, and it would be cowardly to deny our responsibility. And a lie. Whatever happens here, I do not want to lie to you. Ever."

Beck stared over at Haines Barber, who didn't seem to mind lying to him at all. Barber smiled, shrugged, and raised his hands in a what-the-hell gesture.

"I am sorry," said Kuende Adebayo, "for what you had to go through. Truly sorry."

"You could all go to prison for this," Beck said, more to test their reaction than with any thought of turning them in. "If I expose you, it will put me in Earth's good graces. And eliminate some people that if what you say is true, shouldn't be up here."

"True," said Kuende. "But you won't. That's not who you are."

"You sound pretty sure of yourself."

"You have a reputation. Some of it is public. That's the part we wished to make use of. And being public, it is not to be trusted. But the other part of your reputation is among the Riggers. And that can't be faked."

Beck shook his head. "Please don't try to flatter me. It only makes me trust you even less."

But it moved him in spite of himself. Because she was right; that kind of reputation couldn't be faked. And hearing of it, Kuende Adebayo had chosen to seek him out, and more, to trust him. With her freedom, and her career in space. That was a testimonial, though he couldn't quite figure out to exactly what.

"You already lied to me," he pointed out. "Even though it was him"— nodding toward Barber — "you got to mouth the words. That doesn't mean we can't work together. But it does mean this. You cannot lie to me again. Can't play me for a fool, either. Try it, and any loyalty you think I may have to you because you people are Riggers, or because we may share some of the same goals, dissolves in that moment."

"I understand."

"And no more shit about throwing rocks, either. I have no doubt at all that some of you are getting together and working out calculations to see how you can do it and miracle of miracles, no more than a few thousand people on Earth get killed. But that's bullshit. You people can't even calculate a structural failure in one titanium beam."

"Point taken," she said. She cast a quick glance at Barber, who gave another shrug, this time at least a little embarrassed. "Beck, every one of us has families on Earth. We are fighting for the future of humanity, not the end of it. I promise we will do nothing to unleash catastrophe upon Earth. I promise on all I hold sacred. And

I hope you will soon know me well enough to trust that what I hold sacred, I hold more sacred than my own life. As do you. Or you would not have gone into the lattice to save those two Earth trainees."

She promised. Was quite good at it, too. Beck had the disconcerting sensation of believing her at the same time he was telling himself not to believe her, just because he did.

What he really needed was for her to promise not to call him "Beck" that way. It had an effect on him that whatever his resolutions about Kuende Adebayo, made him distrust himself.

"I accept your promise," he said. "For now."

"So we can work together?"

"Have we really any other choice?"

Chapter 8

Maeda paused to gather her concentration outside what she called "the jungle," though the only foliage inside was that in the cages for the bats and snakes.

I loved this once, and never took the time to realize it. Always too busy feeling sorry for myself because I thought I was more janitor than scientist. Now I fear it's all going to be taken from me, and beyond that there's ... nothing. Nothing I can see. All gray, and churning, and I'm frightened.

Stop it, she chided herself. *For now you still have a job to do. Do it with love.*

Having ridden down the spindle in scarcely perceptible gravity, she then belted herself to the open-frame elevator that took up half the corridor of the hollow arm leading out to the lab. As the elevator glided silently toward the end at the three-quarter-g radius point, the frame rotated to bring her feet facing the floor, pointed outward into space.

Viewscreens showed solar panels flocking about the torus like witches on broomsticks with silver capes streaming out behind. The moon was close. Too close for Maeda, with L5 equidistant between it and Earth. She had to grab the handholds lest she begin to feel herself falling into it.

Seen from this angle, the other habitats, with their populated torus rings hidden within shields of multi-colored rock, seemed little more than minnows surrounding the great silver whale of the *Stephen Hawking*. The cylinder was so large that the fixed landmarks on its hull — docking stations, temporary construction modules for the Riggers, sensor arrays, metal tracks for external transport, location lights — did not seem to rotate at all as its slow spin mimicked gravity for those aboard.

Something about the huge cylinder called to her. Maeda searched for the source, failed to find it. She'd never visited there. Didn't really want to. Its sheer size, after the close quarters of the *Banneker*, intimidated her. Yet still the *Hawking* beckoned with a promise of uncertainty so vast that if you loosed yourself from the nagging pressures of real life, made all things seem possible.

Holding forth her palm to have her security clearance verified, Maeda stepped inside, to be greeted by an assortment of glass tanks, cages, and of course the pool.

She started, as always, by feeding the Maui dolphins, her favorite task of the day. Naughty as monkeys, they made a great splash and squealing if she ignored them.

Seeing her come to the pool the pod of eight went into their customary transport of delight. Four paired off in teams of two, and starting from opposite ends of the forty-meter pool, charged each other like jousting knights, weaving and twisting as they drew together and zooming past each other by such narrow margins she had to force herself to look. The others leapt from the water in beautiful coordinated arcs. Sometimes one of them would branch off to put on a tail-walking display. The scent of spray merged with the ozone that was always strong in the recirculated air.

She stood at the edge of the pool dipping into her pail to toss out the "fish." Cloned bits of animal tissue actually, treated with some chemicals — to her distress she could no longer remember which — so that as soon as they hit the water they would wriggle violently, shooting off at unpredictable angles, glinting green and silver and gold in the short interval before the dolphins unerringly hit them at full speed and gulped them down even as they did a victory twirl.

It did not seem to bother the Mauis that their food was not live fish, but cloned tissue. Perhaps because they were clones themselves. The species was one of many that had vanished as the oceans warmed. Natural-born Mauis still existed in aquariums on Earth, but it was far cheaper and safer to send samples of DNA up to the colony than live animals. This tank was the only home the clones ever knew, or ever would.

Now with Earth's decree that the implant program be shut down, they would probably go extinct too. As clones, they were listed as "experimental material." Not only did they have no rights, in Earth-think they weren't even alive.

Like the Mauis, all the animals in the lab were clones. The bats for an additional source of echo-location, the snakes for infrared, the sharks for their sensitivity to pressure changes and magnetic fields, the toads for their multi-faceted vision. Clones, every one.

But still alive. *Alive!* And if we kill them here, Maeda thought despairingly, if we murder them so callously as we did on Earth, then in that moment humanity loses one more foothold on an Earth that may be dying beneath it.

Time for those who think it wrong to go somewhere else.

But maybe the Mauis would survive after all. Maybe. Jeanne Chen, the head of experimental technology aboard the *Banneker*, had promised Maeda that despite the expense of maintaining the dolphins, mainly the competition for pods that could be used for the manufacturing quotas Earth kept pressuring the colony to increase, she would do everything in her power to have them reclassified as a tourist attraction, if no other salvation offered. And if not, find a way to embezzle the funds.

When their feeding was done the dolphins crowded around the edge of the pool, jostling for pets. Winken, Blinken, and Nod, Taran and Eilonwy, Ulysses and Penelope, and of course the giant, over five feet long: Gilgamesh.

No one knew their names but Maeda.

So maybe, she thought, stroking their warm slick skin and getting thoroughly drenched as they deliberately tail-slammed up sheets of spray all over her then chittered delightedly at their own wit, you will live after all.

And me? What will I do without you? For everyone in the department will be vying for some way to stay in space, even as animal keepers in Jeanne's projected zoo. And I'm at the bottom of the totem pole.

Ignoring the urgent pushing of the dolphins to be first in line for more caresses, Maeda stood and walked away, silent tears adding to the water dripping off her.

The other animals, she could bear it. As she walked past the shark tank, the half dozen four-foot Portuguese dogfish swimming endlessly in circles did not call to her with their cold, oversize eyes. The bats she'd grown surprisingly fond of for the skill with which they zeroed in on their insect prey — the only species in the lab that was not cloned. But no amount of admiration could render them cuddly. Likewise the toads, perhaps because they always struck her as cartoon characters at heart. The ball pythons, on the other hand, had moved her to an affection not just appreciative, but tactile. She loved the calm way they would loop around her arm when picked up.

She went about her work cleaning and sterilizing the cages. Trying to harden her heart.

What if tourists were less profitable to the Earth economy than the increased production of the spaces the animals took up?

Then they would all die.

For what? Couldn't Earth understand that these creatures were *alive?* What was it about religion that made so many close their hearts and minds to all but killing?

Calm yourself. Or they'll find you standing here in a fugue state. It's happened before.

On impulse, Maeda went over to one of the open-topped glass cages holding a ball python in a comfortable landscape of dirt — or an organically enriched facsimile made from powdered moonrock — twigs, and a small hollow log, genuine because culled from the arboretum. Reaching in, she gently lifted up the snake with one hand behind its head and the other supporting part of its belly. True to form, the striped green and tan serpent wrapped itself around her forearm, bared because she'd rolled up her sleeves to pet the dolphins.

She loved the dry leathery texture of the reptile's skin. Loved the calm unafraid look in its eyes. Even loved the way its tongue flicked in and out so rapidly, searching for heat and scent signatures that were the reason for it being here.

You and I, she thought. Let us go extinct together. I had hoped, like so many of us hoped, that taking the first step into space, humanity would leave behind all the old prejudices and bloodthirstiness and xenophobia of Earth. Would expand into something great and good.

Remember those days? she asked the snake, which regarding her with calm green eyes, flicked its tongue in and out in reply. All of us going forth to the stars bold and unafraid? With love toward all?

How silly we were. We had our brief moment of expanding outward, now humanity looks to be pulling inward again. Back to the same old deadly sins, even as it twists them around into virtues. Destruction as the purest form of prayer.

Smaller and smaller. Shrinking into the past, instead of expanding into the future.

If only we had listened to you, she whispered to the ball python.

And you, she repeated, turning toward the dolphins. For you were starting to show us the way. Into minds fitted to a broader environment.

Into *life*.

A sob broke out of her.

Why, oh why, do we have to be so hungry to take life from each other? What starvation of the spirit has turned us into such dedicated cannibals?

Why can't we *expand?*

She stared into the snake's glittering eyes. Transfixed as a mouse suddenly come face to face with its doom.

You know the answer, don't you, little one?

A vision trembled on the edge of realization. Hints of clarity sparked here and there, but never quite coalesced into one.

In that moment the lab took on a different modality. Instead of an array of individual cages and environments housing individual creatures, among whom she moved as caretaker, the whole fused into a single ... being.

Being.

Life.

A single life force, embodying all of them, human and animal. Cloned and born.

A new vision swept through her. Stark and visual.

Space. Stars. Emptiness. But an emptiness crowded with wonder. With possibilities.

A realm of expansion.

Of escape.

And arrival.

A realm that somehow, in a way beyond her remotest understanding, reflected itself within her own mind.

The snake twisted its upper body restlessly, tightening its coils. Though it had learned to trust her, enough was enough. Primal instincts, warning against being in the grip of another, overcame the bonding that had briefly existed between them.

Maeda placed the ball python gently back in its glass cage. With no particular urgency it slithered beneath the upraised end of the thick branch in its cage, and curled into a coil.

That is the answer, Maeda told it silently. Out there. In space. And in here, in us. The expansion of our minds. The two must be joined.

I don't know how. It is all so far beyond me.

But we must go there. Two directions, one journey.

You and I, dear ones, she told the dolphins, will make it together. I hope. I do so dearly hope. And we must bring all these others with us.

Out there.

And in here.

Chapter 9

BECK KNEW MAEDA HAD need of him. The crisis with Earth pointed directly at her. With no more funding for further research into the implants, how could she keep her job? She needed the animals. Needed the lab.

She even needed him, though their actual contact diminished by the day. Beck was the presence in the background, the man who'd always sorted things, the man who leaned on his abundant network of friends to see that her occasional lapses were overlooked.

But if she was sent back down to Earth as superfluous? He'd said he'd go with her, but if he'd ever truly meant it, which to his shame he doubted, the time was past. Space Command had its hooks into him. Beck Egan could be useful as a scapegoat. A symbol of the revolt brewing at L5 that must be put down with all necessary force and maybe something extra to grow on.

Or he could be useful as a spy.

But to be quietly forgotten, even on Earth? That just wasn't going to happen.

So what was he going to do about it?

Damned if he knew. Betraying other Riggers, that would be spitting on his whole life. No matter how hot-headed they might be.

Aside from that there was ... well, reconsidering this whole revolt business. Only it would have to be one hell of a revolt, to keep him from the clutches of Space Command.

As for Maeda, she might be on her own this time. There just wasn't enough of him left over to go around. If he went through with the betrayal option, he could likely earn enough points to save her.

Only he didn't think he could do that.

Did that mean he was willing to let her drift into whatever hell might claim her?

He couldn't make himself accept that, either.

Meanwhile Maeda drifted around the apartment acting more and more abstracted. Once Beck found her standing at the washbasin, holding a glass of water under the tap. Staring intently at her own reflection in the mirror, but he didn't think she saw herself. Water poured over the rim of the glass and dripped from her hand and wrist.

He called her name, softly, and got no response. He tried several more times, more emphatically. Nothing. Only when he reached around her to turn off the water and gently took the glass from her hand did she give a start and notice him.

When he asked what she'd been thinking about, she either couldn't or wouldn't tell him. In that moment something inside him died. And something between them. Some last harried reservoir of hope.

Loneliness hit like a wave sweeping him into a different life. One where he truly was all alone. Where the ground had washed out from beneath his feet. He'd been a rich man, once. He'd had Maeda. And had his work.

Now he had neither.

What Beck did have was an informal agreement with Kuende Adebayo. Going out among the Riggers and pressing them to state openly just how far they might be willing to go in defiance of Earth. How much crap they were willing to let Earth shove down their throats. Where the breaking point came.

Meaning the real breaking point. Where rather than slink away any further, they would fight. With more than just words.

It was manipulative, and Beck knew it. In a group, trying to impress each other, it was easier to make people swear to bold deeds. And once sworn aloud, it was harder to back out again. And if you could get them worked up a little past their comfort zone to get that declaration....

Well, revolution was serious business.

But for all his rah-rah exhortations, the replies Beck got were too often equivocal. Or downright evasive.

Beck kept hearing words like "bargaining" and "negotiations." He had no problem with them as concepts, except that they were just what the colonies had been doing for years now. And the "bargain" that always got struck, Earth asserted greater and greater control over LaGrange 5, while the colonists pulled back their line in the sand ever closer to the eroding waves.

The younger Riggers, the generation building the *Hawking*, were of course more militant. The older ones, men and women of his generation, had come up when just surviving through twenty-four hours was a victory. Now most were far from ready to retire; they loved working in space too much.

On the other hand, they tended to think the life-risking segment of their lives had retreated to nostalgia.

Beck went from torus to torus, sounding out damn near every Rigger in L5. By shuttle, since as part of Space Command suspending him from work they'd also prohibited all EVAs. He always made his pitch in person. It wasn't so much that he didn't want Space Command to hear; that was just a matter of time. Rather because it's harder to say "no" to someone you're looking in the face. Especially someone you respect.

Often the people he talked to started out sounding pretty gung-ho. But when the emphasis shifted from talk to action, and from the general to the particular, like hand-to-hand combat with Space Command Marines if it came to that, a new whiff of moderation began to scent the air.

"Look," said Merrill Covington, an old friend and a stalwart from the colorful old days, amid a meeting with eight Riggers, "I have family here."

"So do I," Beck pointed out.

"But Doe and I have kids."

Beck showed no reaction, though the remark stung him, as it had in other meetings before. When they'd gotten married, he and Maeda planned to have kids too. Most of the settlers in those early days did. While they were the first real space generation, their possibilities constricted by the necessity of survival, the second generation would live the dream in full. Discovering possibilities that could now hardly be imagined. And eventually coming to glorify the parents whose sacrifices made it all possible. That was the prevailing attitude.

But for Beck and Maeda, the time was never right. Work, you know. And then as the years passed and Maeda began to drift further into dream, Beck realized the two of them had no real family to offer children.

"Don't you think," Beck told Covington, "that your kids, and their kids after them, are just exactly the reason we can't let Earth pull us back into the Nineteenth century?"

A murmur of agreement followed, but Covington was undeterred. His prematurely white hair and craggy face, that looked weather-beaten though there wasn't ever all that much weather inside a spacesuit, gave him a TV-father look that counterbalanced Beck's own tight-drawn intensity and hero status. Or was "martyr" more appropriate?

"You can tell Earth whatever you want," Covington announced to the Riggers clinging to handholds in the construction module docked to the *Caroline Herschel*, which like the *Banneker*, was also being fitted with a countervailing torus. The Riggers had taken off their helmets for the meeting, but left on their suits, which gave Beck a pang that surprised him because of course he was in civvies.

It wasn't just being banned from EVAs that disturbed him; it was being banned from going out and working alongside men and women like these. No matter what his status among the Riggers, and it had grown pretty high over the years, the only thing that made him feel really exceptional, really worthy, was being able to go into space and prove it all over again. Now he felt cut off from them, with nothing justifying his presence here but a reputation that to him felt hollow without the suit to back it up.

"And so long as it's talk," Covington was saying, "you're free to add my thumbprint. We have to make some kind of stand, I understand that. And look, Beck. I agree that talk isn't going to do it all by itself. Not with these yo-yo's running the country now, and President Whitfield virtually claiming to rule by divine right."

"If I have to listen to that asshole quote Romans:13 one more time," muttered a Rigger, "I'm going to puke."

"We all are," Covington agreed. "But he means it. And the crowd who elected him mean it too. And if we do anything that Earth might actually feel, like shutting down some of the solar fields, they'll send Marines up here to start them back up. Now here you come saying, 'let them try it.' That's crazy talk, Beck. We're builders, not fighters."

"We can maneuver in space better than any Marine ever born."

"Yeah, that's probably true. But they've got the weapons, and the training to use them. And if we beat them once, Earth will just send up more. I don't like the idea of starting something we can't finish."

"Who says we can't finish?" Beck retorted. "If they do send up Marines, we only have to beat them once. Then the solar power will be under our control, and at the first sign Earth is sending in the second wave, we pull the plug. On the grid that supplies the launch pads first, but if that doesn't work, we go to planet-wide brown-outs."

"Yes, yes, I know," he said, patting his hands for silence as protests sounded. "Innocent people will get hurt. But only if Earth really wants to carry it so far. And if we back down? I don't care how you rationalize it, every single one of you in this room knows damn well that what we're looking at is first having Marines in the colonies to dictate everything we do, and then having our heads torn open to take the implants out. Why? Because God told them to. Rang them right up on their cellphones and gave them the word to fuck the Riggers over. You say you're concerned for your kids? How are they going to feel with a lobotomized paralytic for a parent? When that's the alternative, then yeah, I'm willing to face up to some people maybe getting hurt."

Covington chewed on that for quite some time. As did the others.

"I don't know," he admitted. "I don't know. Maybe if we can just string it out long enough, Earth will come to its senses."

"How long is that? Far as our esteemed President is concerned, what he demands isn't kind words, but worship. And he's got a whole bunch of violence-prone people behind him who think every time he farts it's God's voice speaking directly to them. You don't reason with these people. And the only way you 'string it out' is if you scare them so bad they're willing to actually talk instead of pontificate. If you're waiting for America to come to its senses and vote him out of office, well, that election is already two years overdue and Theron Whitfield doesn't look like he's planning on having another in this lifetime. Which leaves us with shutting down the power. *Before* Earth sends Marines up here while we're still crying around about how we're builders, not fighters. They may come anyway. If they do, we either fight them — yes, as in real live war, with real live people getting killed — or start shaving our heads to save them the trouble before they rip our implants out."

The Riggers exchanged dubious glances at each other, given a fish-like puffiness by the zero g.

"That's pretty extreme, Beck," Covington observed unhappily. "They can get by on their own grid for a while, but there's going to be blackouts, shutdowns ... we're talking hospitals, nursing homes, air terminals—"

"If it won't hurt, they won't listen. And we have to mean it. Because *they* are true believers."

"Meaning you want to start a massive game of bluff against people who believe God is on their side," Covington countered. "*They're* the real true believers. We're just technicians. We just want to do our jobs and get on with our lives. We can't come close to their level of fervency. As for Space Command's Marines, they have laser and flechette rifles."

"But their suits," Beck pointed out, "are standard Earth issue. And if you don't believe me on anything else, believe me on this, because they stuck me in one. They're shit. And most of these so-called Space Marines haven't spent enough time in zero-g to get any good in them. Not like us. So long as we keep the fight outside the toruses and not in the hull itself, we can win."

"Beck, Beck, Beck," Covington said sadly. "Can you hear what you're saying? Maybe you can't. Maybe you've been spending too much time with your new friends. Kuende Adebayo and that crowd. Just remember, Beck. *They* didn't build all this. We did. Because we're builders, like I said. I remember back, oh, what is it, fifteen years now? When you and I rode up from Earth on the same shuttle. Man, were *you* an enthusiast! I can't remember every word we said. Probably a good thing, because I'm sure it would embarrass us both.

"But I do remember one thing very clearly. Not one single one of those words was about killing anyone. I've made my life here. I don't want to give it up. But if one thing starts leading to another, the way it tends to do drifting into war, then the only thing that will matter any more is who can kill more of who. That's not the legacy I want to leave behind. In fact if that's the best we can do, maybe I'm even willing to let the dream die until future generations with more sense and more humanity come along."

At that point, six of the eight Riggers in the module said that while they didn't fully agree with everything Covington said, they too preferred to explore alternatives, hopefully peaceful alternatives, to all-out war.

For Beck, his whole world was falling apart. He'd finally had to acknowledge that he and Maeda had nothing but a set of rooms that could be called a shared life. Now these people, these friends, that he'd treasured and made the gauge of his own worth, proved to be....

Cowards wasn't quite the right word, but....

What was?

***

BECK WAS STILL ON board the *Caroline Herschel*, trying to inspire another group of Riggers with revolutionary *espirit*, when the call came from Jeanne Chen, Maeda's supervisor.

Maeda was in the lab. No, there wasn't anything really wrong, only ... she wasn't doing anything. Wasn't talking to anyone. Wasn't responding to questions. Should they have her taken — that "taken" seared Beck's soul — to the infirmary, or would he prefer they wait until he could get there?

He went to Merrill Covington, who without a word left work to shuttle him back in a small enclosed sled, since Beck was enjoined from suiting up.

"I'm sorry, Beck," were the only words Merrill spoke to him all the way back.

Beck patted him on the knee. If he tried to talk he was afraid he'd start blubbering. Which was not appropriate to the strong-willed hero of L5 battling the Legions of Darkness.

He found Maeda on her knees staring rapt at a cage containing a green-and-tan striped snake. Jeanne Chen had shooed away the rest of the staff and stood silent at her side. Beck thanked her for calling him instead of the infirmary. Maeda had gone to sick bay with episodes like this twice before. One more and she would be subject to a stringent review by earth-bound Space Command shrinks to judge her fitness to continue on in space. In the habitats you couldn't just have people wandering around playing with the machinery under the illusion they were picking flowers.

When Jeanne Chen asked if he'd like her to stay he shook his head. In a moment he and Maeda were kneeling side by side, alone and silent. Her red jersey was wet, probably from the dolphins, who she'd often told him loved to splash her just for fun.

Beck had no idea what to say. He doubted it would do much good in any case. The two times she'd ended up in the hospital, Maeda had gone totally non-responsive for more than twenty-four hours.

"I used to think," he said at last, "that wherever you went, I could follow. Because I believed in the power of love, and I loved you so much."

Silence.

"I believed in a lot of things, once."

She stirred slightly. A thoughtful look replaced the blankness that had laid hold of her features, and for a moment Beck had hope. But still she said nothing. After a few minutes, realizing how he'd tensed up so much his kneecaps threatened to pull loose, Beck forced his muscles to relax.

"Now I know," he said, talking to himself because it didn't look like he had anything better to do, "there are places I can't follow you. And that just turns me inside out."

The snake slithered slightly higher on the branch it had wrapped itself around. Maeda leaned forward, eyes gleaming. Beck waited for something profound to happen. It didn't.

"It's funny," he said. "You start out, you tell yourself, you're going to do it all. Have everything life has to offer. Not money, not fame, not all that silly crap. Just the important stuff. Like doing something useful." He nodded his head toward the wall, and space beyond. "And with you and me."

No reaction.

"Then things come up. I mean, that's life, isn't it? You and me, we had some really great years. Really great. And I kept telling myself, the best is yet to come. Only, I didn't work on making that happen, did I? I let myself get caught up in my work. I thought, just get through this next patch and it'll be smooth sailing. Just you and Maeda, finally free to take it as far as it can go. To the stars. That's how I thought of it. To the stars."

A sob caught in his throat. "Somehow I never got smart enough to realize, hey, it's all right *here*. Here and now. No, I kept having these ideas of how at some point in the future, it was all going to be *perfect*. And it *was*. For a while. A long time, really. Years. But I don't know, I got my head turned around backwards. I let the work be *now*, and *us*, that was still going to happen sometime in the—"

His voice whimpered to a halt as tears flooded his eyes. His chest pounded with suppressed sobs. The snake flicked its tongue in and out. Beck stared at the white scales of its underside. For some reason they made him and his soulful confession feel foolish. He backhanded the tears from his eyes.

"How does it happen," he asked, in a strained voice, "that one day you look around and that future you had so much hope for, that perfect state you always knew you'd reach, so perfect it would make time stand still ... somehow it's slipped behind you. And what's still ahead of you is nothing but ... a damned hard slog." He paused to swallow down the knot in his throat. "I mean, how does that happen?"

Maeda stared ahead like she hadn't heard a word.

The tears came again, but silently this time. "Now I'm here all by myself, looking at you. I don't know what you're looking at. But I can't help but think there's a big emptiness inside. Bigger than out there, even. And here I am wishing I'd done something more to fill it."

He sobbed aloud. "Oh Maeda, I am so sorry. So terribly, terribly sorry."

Her fingers reached out tentatively. He had a moment of hope. But they moved ahead to touch the glass opposite the snake with its doll's-head eyes.

"Inward and outward," she said. No inflection at all. "In the end, they are the same."

What was this? Zen koans?

"And we must do them both at once. It won't work otherwise."

Suddenly uncoiling onto her feet, she reached into the cage and lifted out the snake. Beck was up beside her, fearing she'd get bitten even though she told him many times how docile the snakes had become. Now, as she seemed to proffer the reptile toward him, he took a step back. He was glad she'd finally come around to acknowledging his presence, but this was getting weird.

"We will build a ship," she said, as the snake wrapped itself around her wrist and forearm with an oddly intimate casualness. "He" — she waved her hand around the lab — "they, will be our guide. It will be a … oh, what do you call it?"

She wrinkled her face in perplexity. Beck hoped that she was easing back toward relative normal, for all the strangeness of her words. "A generation ship, that's it. And he and his friends will nurture us."

Nurture us? What did that mean? The only thing Beck could think of was that the humans on this generation ship — did Maeda have the least idea what a true generation ship entailed? No, or she wouldn't be talking about it — would raise and eat the animals. But that couldn't possibly be what she meant. Maybe something to do with the implants? That was her field, after all. But what?

She stared at him with an exaggerated expression of patience, as though explaining to a small child some principle of behavior that the time had come for him to learn, though the fine points might still be beyond his comprehension.

"Everything moving outward and inward at the same time. We have to find some way to maintain the balance." She pointed the snake at him for emphasis. "Every time we start reaching outward, it turns inward instead. Like religion. It starts looking outward, for a larger God. But eventually turns inward. Compressive. Negative, because the harder it tries to define just what it's searching for, the more it has to protect all these standards it sets up. Until the focus turns to seeing violations everywhere, and decreeing ever-greater punishments to forestall them."

"Yeah, that's an interesting point," said Beck, hoping they were having a conversation. He *kind* of understood what she meant.

"And here in space. We started with this vision of openness, of grandeur. Of expansion. But see how our lives have become contracted. And now people are going to kill each other over it."

"Not necessarily," he said, but his voice lacked conviction.

"Why is it that every time humanity tries to look outward, it ends up turning in on itself instead?"

"Ah...."

Noticing the snake inches from his face, and maybe afraid which would bite the other first, Maeda smiled fondly at it and set it gently back in its cage. Then turned to him with the happy smile of someone who has just resolved a conundrum of some difficulty.

"And over here," she said, shaping a box with her newly freed hands, "machines. Artificial Intelligence. And it is...." She looked confused. Then figuring it out, beamed brightly. "Positive, because it pulls forward. Outward again. But only at first. In the end AI too will turn negative."

"Like religion."

"Exactly!" Her constricted face flowered out into an expression so guileless and happy it broke his heart because Beck could remember that very same look when they were first exploring the possibilities of sex with one another.

"And for the same reason. Humanity keeps seeking *certainty*. And since randomness is foundational to the universe, certainty can never be. So in the end we will tell the machines to build certainty for us. Until instead of looking outward for new possibilities, they will turn inward in a quest to eliminate all those negatives we fear in our souls. It will be as though we have set ourselves for autodestruct."

"Pretty gloomy scenario."

"See? Even machines eventually succumb to a negative feedback loop."

The benefits of a scientific education.

"Maeda—"

"So that's one polarity," she concluded.

"Yes, I see that." Well, he had to do something to hold up his end of the conversation.

"But then...." She frowned so deeply it verged on a pout. "Then there is the other polarity. One that holds forth a continued expansion." A pause while she tilted her head as if listening for a faint sound. "I *know* it does. Only ... I forget how. It seemed so clear, just a moment ago." She stared down at the snake in its cage. "He was part of it. Part of the dream."

"Okay."

Suddenly, urgently, she walked toward the pool. Beck trailed close behind her. Seeing her come, the small dolphins began streaking back and forth and leaping from the water. Maeda went right to the edge of the pool. Beck put a hand to her elbow. If she was thinking about jumping in, he didn't want to have to dive in and get her. He'd grappled with enough desperate people this week.

But Maeda halted. Several of the dolphins took turns to crowd the tile, splashing the water with their tails. Her shoes and pants got wet. She didn't notice.

"They were part of it too," she said. "Only now I can't remember."

"Rest a little. Maybe it will come to you."

"It was so clear!"

"These things happen. It's when you're trying your hardest to remember that it gets most elusive. Let it go for now. Get a little rest, it'll come back to you."

He was so frightened. It was a terrifying thing, to love someone so much, to reach out to them so hard, and to see that all your love, all your reaching, were so completely irrelevant.

"Generation ship. That was part of it. And polarities."

"Maeda." He spoke firmly, with emphasis.

She shuddered, then looked at him in surprise.

"Beck? What are you doing here?"

"We're going home now. You and me."

"But I still have work to do."

"I talked with Jeanne. It's okay. You have the rest of the day off."

"I can do my job!" The despair in her voice tore at his heart, for it revealed that she did not believe her own assertion any more than he did.

"It's not about that. You've got a head full of ideas, but you've lost track of how they all fit together. Now we are going home. You can rest some, and if it all comes back to you, we'll talk about it then."

She peered at his face. "You're flushed."

"It's a little warm here for me."

Suddenly she twisted around as if expecting to see something other than the lab. Her dark brows drew together.

"What have I done?" She was back in Reality Prime, and not liking what she saw.

"Got lost in a daydream, maybe? Sounded like you had a vision. Only I couldn't follow it all. You can tell me later. Let's go home."

She pressed her eyes closed. Pressed her fingers against her temples. "I really did see it. I did! It all fit together. All of it! Only—" Her hands fell away. "Only now it's all iridescent and gauzy."

"Come, Maeda. Time to call it a day."

Chapter 10

Beck spend a day and a night in the apartment with Maeda. Painful, dragging hours, because it soon became evident they had nothing to say to each other.

They tried. Or Beck did. But Maeda refused to be drawn into any further discussion of her vision. Beck promised to do his best to understand whatever she told him, even if the concepts were strange to him.

No matter. She spent most of her time on one of the cushions, chin drawn in, staring at her knees, unresponsive.

He knew the love that once pulsed so powerfully between them was dead. It wasn't coming back, either. He didn't want that to be true, but the single world they used to share had been split in two. His heart told him what his mind still tried to deny.

Emotionally, Beck had that weakness not uncommon among uber-competent people: he didn't deal too well with helplessness. And he had never felt more helpless in his life. How could you love someone so much, try so hard to reach them, and be met only by a blank gaze?

Once Maeda tried to explain: "If I understood it all better, I'd tell you. Only it's like a dream. You wake up and it all seems so vivid. But if you reach back, if you try to picture the details, they evaporate away one by one, until you see that you were standing on a blank stage, with just a few props scattered here and there. I *want* to tell you. But as soon as I try it all falls into these isolated parts so immense, with so many interconnections, I can't find the words. If

I try to tell you anything at all of what I've seen, it will come out all garbled. I know you'll try to be sympathetic, but all the time you'll be thinking I'm crazy. Which okay, I can't argue that. But I can't face seeing it come from *you*."

Could they talk about anything else? He tried that too. Maeda only found it intrusive.

Beck loved the enveloping silence of space. The silence between him and Maeda, though, was churning, demon-haunted, full of smothered screams. So to the relief of them both, after two days he went back to touring the habitats, trying to stiffen the Riggers' spines.

With a fresh aggressiveness. He knew he couldn't fairly blame Earth for all that had happened to Maeda. But it was more comforting than blaming himself, and he didn't remember ever claiming to be a saint.

It was during one of these meetings, held in a construction module like most of the others, that Aran Petrosian, another of Beck's generation, brought up what he called Beck's "new friends."

"Trying to keep up with the youth, are you Beck?" he said, trying to make a joke out of it. "That's a pretty fast crowd you're hanging out with. Kuende Adebayo, Haines Barber, regular fire-breathers, they are. If they could only fabricate fast as they talk, the *Hawking* might stand some chance of getting finished within five years of schedule."

This wasn't the first Beck had heard of lags in the production schedule. It shouldn't have been entirely unexpected. Standing on their seniority, all the more experienced Riggers had returned to their native habitats once the foundational work was completed, the skin slapped on and atmosphere shown to hold. Those who were left were almost entirely of the newer generation, with little experience of working on their own because they'd always been under the supervision of a more experienced hand during the initial work.

"Space Command ought to send Beck over there as supervisor," said Riva Shore, who was of a generation intermediate between Beck and Aran, and the Riggers of the *Hawking*. "He'll slap those shirkers into line. You didn't use to hear any whining and wailing when he was in charge."

"No, just bitching," Beck recalled with a grin. "Most of it coming from you."

"For a while," she acknowledged. "I thought you were kind of a tight-ass, to tell the truth. Until I saw Kevin Harry get pinned between two sections of structural steel." She shivered at the memory. "Then I started thinking, maybe that Beck Egan isn't such an asshole as he acts."

Beck remembered Kevin Harry. He remembered everyone who'd been killed on his projects. Kevin had come up a bit of a hot-shot. Good Rigger, but not quite as good as he thought he was. Beck had grounded him twice for taking shortcuts.

But they were always short of labor, always behind schedule. So Space Command canceled the second suspension and stuck Kevin back out in the steel. Beck saw the accident on vid. About two hundred times. Kevin's white suit speeding through space with thrusters aflame. Like a car trying to beat a railroad train to the crossing. And not quite making it. All they ever recovered was some freeze-dried strands of organic material with Kevin's DNA.

At least it had been quick. Kevin didn't have to watch his own lungs blow out his mouth and nostrils because his suit had been breached and he just *couldn't* hold his breath another moment. Beck had seen that happen, too. Had recurring nightmares of it happening to him as well as others. Maybe he was a tight-ass, but there was a reason for that.

It did bother him that the *Hawking* was running so far behind schedule. Sounded like a bunch of the Riggers over there didn't have their minds on their work. Too busy planning their own little utopia at Lagrange 5. Or maybe the slowdown was deliberate.

He'd have to talk to Kuende Adebayo about that.

Because either way it was sloppiness. And in space sloppiness was the straightest, shortest road to death.

***

THE TWO FACTIONS FILED into their respective conference rooms, one on Earth and the other aboard the *Stephen Hawking*. A study in contrasts: Space Command and National Security in dark suits and knotted ties, and the delegation from Lagrange 5 in, relatively, pajamas.

Beck found it odd seeing himself on the auxiliary screen above the main, showing the Earth delegation's view. Almost always when he'd seen himself it had been in a spacesuit, checking out multi-angle views of construction projects, trying to coordinate with the other Riggers. Now he thought he looked older than he felt.

As for what he was doing in a conference room aboard the *Stephen Hawking*, he'd been one of the delegates "chosen," to use the word loosely, to represent the Riggers. It wasn't like anyone had voted on it. A series of small meetings had been held, and one way or another a body of delegates chosen, a surprising number coming from the more radical faction. Maybe his campaigning contributed to that outcome. Or maybe the fix was in.

The Earth delegation pointedly arranged their archaic papers and their laptops before them with an exaggerated fussiness, considering objects didn't usually float away on-planet. Their dress and their customs made Beck think of dressed-up chimpanzees trying to act dignified.

"Looks like a room full of pompous white males," observed Kuende Adebayo, sitting at his side.

"That's Theron Whitfield's doing," said Beck. "I never much cared for Space Command, but at least ten years ago they didn't dress up in monkey suits."

"I can't live like this," she said *sotto voice.* "I really, truly can't. Having my life dictated by a bunch of flunkies with not one genuine thought between them."

Haines Barber chuckled.

They sat in what would eventually be a lecture hall, with curving rows of benches sloping down toward the central stage, where the images of the teleconference with Earth were showing on split screens. But because the interior of the *Hawking* was still under construction, the chairs to go with the benches had not yet been built, let alone fitted, so that everyone sat on the benches. A limber group, most sat cross-legged, though a few like Haines Barber sprawled out, supporting themselves on an elbow.

Beck himself sat with his legs crossed not because it was particularly comfortable on the hard lunar composite surface, but just to show he still could. Riggers in general had a strong predilection toward yoga, the breathing and concentration exercises as well as the physical poses.

Donald Sims, head of the National Space Agency, cleared his throat and made an announcement.

"We will now say a prayer."

Exclamations of disbelief sounded in the *Hawking's* lecture room.

"You have got to be kidding!" Haines burst out.

Only it was no joke. Another figure — another middle-aged white male, inevitably, in yet one more suit, only blue instead of the uniform gray of the officials — shuffled in from off-camera, and began to ask a blessing from Our Lord. Which included the neutral enough proposition that calm minds and honest hearts would together arrive at a common ground, and the considerably less neutral one that the strictures given by an all-merciful Father — that "Father" brought further jeers from the rebels — would in no way be violated, but that His grateful children would in all ways show their humble gratitude for His guidance.

Kuende could not restrain herself. "That's how you're starting *out*?" she shouted as the prayer concluded.

That elicited a glare from Donald Sims, who'd been bowing his bluff face in prayer. He was a broad-shouldered man, with a wrestler's neck and a crew-cut that all but sang "Onward Christian Soldiers" by itself. Only his face would better have backed up the intimidation he meant to project had a layer of fat not blurred his jaw, neck, and cheekbones.

The ceremony concluded, the minister or whatever withdrew. And the talks, or whatever, began.

Actually, they weren't really talks.

Because Donald Sims didn't start out discussing any of the points which had previously been submitted by the colonists. He didn't even give them a chance to reiterate their written assurance that in turn for delaying an immediate shutdown of the implant program — not cancel, understand, only delay for further discussion — the colonists would bring the construction aboard the *Banneker* and the *Hawking* back on schedule.

Preparing for the meeting, Haines Barber had found even that intolerable. "Fuck, we look like that that kid in *Oliver Twist* saying, 'Please, sir, may I have some more?'"

Though he had no wish to scuttle the talks before they began, Beck tended to agree. The schedule had been set on Earth, by bureaucrats who had no experience of construction in space but an acute awareness of the promises President Whitfield had made to the country about the accelerated bounty soon to rain down from L5, and the schedule for it he put forth.

Where was this speed-up to come from? Longer hours, exhausted Riggers, and a relaxation of safety rules and inspection procedures. In earlier meetings among the broader Rigger population where the petition to Space Command was worked out, Beck had argued forcefully against making a promise that might be hard to fulfill. If they fell short, they would hand Whitfield and the man-in-His-own-image faction a strong argument to renege on such paltry agreements as already existed.

On this, he was voted down. We have to offer *something*, said the moderates. We have to do something aside from make demands.

Now they waited to hear Earth's reaction to their proposal.

Instead Donald Sims began pontificating about How It Would Be.

"Let us be clear on one thing," he remarked in gruff, dismissive tones. "If these construction lags that have plagued both projects are so easy to correct, I have to ask why it wasn't done before. It reinforces the suspicion many of us have that what we're looking at is in fact a deliberate slow-down. Now you ask us to make concessions in return for fulfilling an obligation you violated in the first place. That's not negotiation, it's blackmail."

"With respect, Chairman," began Alvin Honnecker, an astronomer selected as delegation spokesman for no reason Beck could see other than that no one particularly disliked him, "there has been no planned slow-down. The accelerated schedule will require extraordinary effort and—"

"Second, I have to ask by what authority any of you claim to act as spokesmen for L5 or anything else. I don't see a single face from Space Command. Who, I would remind you, are the representatives of a government duly elected by the people. Not some special-interest committee put together by fiat. What makes you think you have the right, the authority, or quite frankly the power, to insist we bargain with you? Go back to Earth and win some elections, if you want to claim any legitimacy."

"Jesus," breathed Kuende Adebayo, as someone else shouted: "hang that jerkwad by the nose!"

Donald Sims ignored that as his eyes focused on the teleprompter.

"However, there is one concession that Space Command, the National Space Agency, and the President are all willing to make.

That is, to table, for now, the word 'mutiny,' with all the legal sanctions it entails."

"With respect, Mr. Chairman," said Alvin Honnecker, in a voice tending more toward desperation than assertion. "I must protest your use of the word 'mutiny.' Nothing that has taken place on L5 could justify your use—"

"Now having disposed of your petition, or whatever, let us proceed."

Kuende sat at Beck's side, staring at the screens, her face alternating between rage and expressions of disbelief. From time to time Beck stole sidelong glances at her. He was finding her more beautiful each time they met. Her sheer vitality was so intense you could feel it like a bow wave shaping the future ahead of her.

What if, just maybe....

No way. Though only twelve years older, they remained separated by a generation gap more of attitudes than age.

Not to mention that he was, in truth, her gofer. But *if* it happened....

He tried to tell himself his answer would be no. He'd never cheated on Maeda. That was important to him. Though standards of fidelity tended to be relaxed in space, Maeda needed to know the sphere surrounding them had not lost its integrity.

And yet....

And yet you're being played for a sucker, he told himself. You think she doesn't know exactly what you're thinking, a woman like that? Probably laughs about it regularly. And maybe not just to herself.

Back on the screen the head of the NSA was cleaning up Dodge.

"All activities relating to the transference of animal qualities into the human brain—"

"A blasphemous and disgusting practice," muttered the head of Space Command, demonstrating that keen grasp of the technical issues that had led to his appointment.

"—will cease at once." Sims looked up from the screen he'd been reading. "In case some of you are unclear on the exact meaning of 'at once,' it means *now*. *Not* after you file another two hundred applications claiming some other purpose to the research. Any violation, and the perpetrators—"

Kuende slammed her fist down on the desk.

"Now we're *perpetrators?*"

"—will be brought to Earth to face charges which, you will very shortly learn when the legislation is introduced in the coming days, could put them behind bars for the rest of their lives."

Beck saw Jeanne Chen, seated a few benches down, put both hands over her face.

"Furthermore," announced Sims, glaring at them like they were naughty children, "there being no further research function for these creatures, and in consideration of the mass and area that has been allocated to them, I hereby direct that all cloned animals — and we have records, remember — shall be sacrificed immediately, and the facilities devoted to them converted to more productive use."

"Mr. Chairman," Jeanne Chen attempted.

"And finally," Sims began portentously, letting it hang there a moment just to scare them.

"Finally?" cried Haines Barber. "You haven't let us complete a single sentence yet, and now you're on *finally?*"

"In regards to the existing implants." The Chairman paused, relishing the statue-like stiffness he had just inflicted on the colony delegation.

"Addressing concerns that have been raised, it is not *currently* the policy of this Administration to require the removal of existing implants, through surgical or other means. Absent evidence to the effect that such devices can be safely removed without risk to the subject—"

"Subject," Kuende repeated bitterly. "We're not even people anymore."

"—no such program shall be implemented. However." Another portentous pause.

"Here it comes," breathed Haines Barber.

"Seeing as how this technology, these implants and neural nets and so forth, appear designed to create a race of supermen—"

"*Asshole!*" Kuende had at last been pushed past her point of restraint.

"—with the possible consequence, intentional or not, of enslaving Earth—"

"If only," someone said wistfully.

"—it has been decided that all EVA suits fitted with any sensors beyond—" He frowned, peering narrow-eyed at the prompter. "Two dimensions of visual?" He looked for confirmation to the head of Space Command, who nodded. "That all such suits be immediately gathered and stored in a secure facility pending shipment to Earth for conversion. Meanwhile a sufficient number of standard Space Command suits—"

Open cries of dismay. Among whom Haines' was the loudest. "He wants us to go out *there* in *those*?" he wailed, pointing in the direction of the outer hull.

"—will be provided."

"We're dead," muttered a Rigger.

"Only if we obey," said Kuende.

And that was pretty much that. The Riggers were still staring dumbfounded at each other when Donald Sims stood and led the others from the room.

"Don't we at least get another prayer?" a Rigger shouted after them. "We're going to need it."

Chapter 11

As soon as the backs of Space Command vanished from the screen and the microphones cut off, pandemonium broke loose in the auditorium as ideas were not argued, but shouted back and forth.

And to Beck's mind, the dumber the idea, the louder its advocates.

Soon the favored policies broke down into variations on two themes. The first was to appeal to some other authority. The Council of Nations, say, or the courts. The fact that the Council had an unbroken thirty-year record of accomplishing nothing at all cut no ice with its utopian-leaning advocates.

As for the courts, the American courts were already fully occupied issuing judgements largely supporting President Whitfield's suspension of the last election on grounds of national emergency. In the meantime he exercised rule by fiat.

To which the dreamers retorted: the overriding principle is to preserve the rule of law. If we fail to observe that mandate, we are no better than "they" are.

To which Beck broke his previous silence to utter an emphatic "bullshit."

Riggers were on the whole a well-mannered lot, and the "rule of law" debate lasted a lot longer than the number of its advocates, scarce a fourth of the whole, would justify. But gradually and inevitably, the arguments, having run out of new ground to cover, broke down into shouting the same lines louder and louder.

Eventually, everyone having paused for breath, the debate turned toward a more widely supported policy; some form of passive resistance.

Leaving aside all the possible forms such resistance might take, the basic idea did possess an underlying logic. The American economy was dependent on the flow of materials and high-value manufactured goods from L5, as well as solar power. By simply stopping work, the colony could throw the nation's economy into free-fall.

And what, it was asked, if Earth reacted by trying to take over production directly?

The answer being that any such idea was a pipe dream. Space Command had a near total lack of personnel sufficiently trained to keep the habitats functioning, let alone make up for the lost production.

Though the last "appeal to a higher authority" adherents kept shouting their views, first blatantly interrupting, then screaming "I'm still talking!" when everyone ignored them, the passive resistance argument was clearly carrying the day. Even among many who before the meeting with Earth and Donald Sims' Stalin imitation, advocated various forms of hat-in-hand appeasement.

To Beck's ear, however, the passive resistance stalwarts never faced the ultimate question: what if Earth simply bypassed all negotiations, all attempts to restore production on its own, and simply came up and broke heads?

And so seizing a moment of relative silence, he jumped up on top of the bench and raised that very question.

He expected to be shouted down. And indeed there were expressions of disbelief; America had not fallen to such depths.

Provoked beyond forbearance, Beck shouted back: "What the fuck do you think the man just told you?" And as the conference room quieted into self-conscious mumblings: "We have only one more decision to make. Are we going to let them take our suits or not? Because if we do, it's the last decision we'll ever make. After that Earth will do whatever the hell it feels like. Including scooping out our brains with a spoon. And there won't be a damn thing we can do about it."

A few voices decried "vigilante justice." This failed to raise much of a chorus.

Then Kuende Adebayo mounted the table at Beck's side. In one motion all the radicals from the *Hawking* rose to their feet and gathered round. It had a quieting effect.

If you'll let yourself be intimidated by this, Beck thought toward the room at large, what are you going to do when you have to face Earth Marines?

"Passive resistance won't work," Kuende announced.

A chorus of voices demanded to know why, though somewhat tentatively.

"Passive resistance isn't just Gandhi and a lot of mellow thoughts. That was one specific situation, not a universal truth. It's a fallacy to think the same tactics can work in all or even most instances."

Of course this provoked an outcry. Those who came to L5 were predominantly liberal in their thinking, in that they hoped for the future more than they feared the present. And whether liberal or not, they were all scientifically trained, yet at the same time tended toward yoga, Tai Chi, and Zen. Being dreamers and builders, they were civilized. The majority firmly believed the pen mightier than the sword. And that Gandhi had "proved" gentleness could overcome violence, that the soft could always defeat the hard.

Kuende just stood there, saying nothing while these opinions were expressed, sometimes indignantly, sometimes defensively. For a good ten minutes she waited in silence. Gradually the fanfare eased.

"For passive resistance to be effective," Kuende told the room, "requires two prerequisites. First, the people resisting have to do more than simply believe in their cause. They also have to know, know deep in their hearts, that they are willing to die for it. And that in sacrificing their lives, they will have at least bequeathed the gift of pride to their people.

"To maintain that faith, to hold fast even when there's nothing in front of you but pain, imprisonment, and possibly death, to withstand all that, you have to have *lived* the oppression you're fighting. Here, the threats we're talking about are still in the future. Horrible enough, for those of us who risk having our implants ripped out by Bible school graduates.

"But will that picture alone sustain you when the Marines start beating us with clubs, jolting us with electroshock, gassing us, and eventually, shooting indiscriminately? Will we still feel so much courage when we see such things happening to the people we love? Few of us have ever experienced violence. And when we do, it will be the most immediate thing in our lives.

"Look how much you still hope for a reasonable response from Earth, despite the evidence before your eyes. When you attempt passive resistance and your own all-or-nothing moment comes, will you hold to your noble principles? Or give up, hoping that once its victory is complete, *then* Earth will finally choose to be reasonable? Remember. If we begin a campaign of passive resistance then cave in, we have the worst of all worlds.

"Because that leads directly to the second requisite of passive resistance. The oppressors need a functioning conscience. There has to be something left inside them that cuts through all the propaganda, all the dehumanization, so that after watching the slaughter of the innocents long enough, they will tell themselves, this is *wrong*. But if you've submitted at the first sign of violence, you confirm the oppressors' opinion that you are cowardly and worthless. Subhumans, who will always give way before a show of strength.

"In my opinion, there is no functioning conscience operating any more in the administration of Theron Whitfield, his more fanatical supporters, and as we have just witnessed, Space Command. Our country let itself fall into the hands of the wrong people. It is no longer the America of which we were once so proud. Yes, many Americans feel much like we do. They will no doubt cringe when we are beaten, imprisoned, and murdered, but their moment to resist has passed. As ours will in turn if we don't fight."

Of course voices of opposition sounded, but to Beck's ear they sounded more rote than heartfelt.

"We resist," Kuende told the room, "or we die. As a people, as a community, as an idea, as a dream, we die."

Then she hopped down from the table and walked away, Beck and the contingent from the *Stephen Hawking* in her train.

Chapter 12

Kuende Adebayo strolled at a leisurely pace down the dirt path, her eyes kept low, glancing at the shrubs and flowers on either side. Not at Beck.

"Well," she said, "Earth's position is pretty definitive."

"I expected to get steamrolled," said Beck. "I knew we were too wishy-washy going in. All that bullshit about 'common ground.' When reason and faith butt heads, there is no common ground."

Following the conference with Earth, she had detached herself from her followers and to his surprise, asked him to walk with her through one of the parks on the *Hawking*. Unlike much of the cylinder's interior, the park spaces were relatively complete because the plants were needed to help generate oxygen.

As always, Beck marveled at the sheer size of the cylinder. Though he had spent a couple of years building it, he'd worked exclusively on the frame and superstructure, his view predominantly that of space. Once the skin was wrapped on and the nuclear generators and helium jets projecting the magnetic field that protected the habitat from radiation running, he'd gone back to the *Banneker* to begin work on the lower torus.

During construction he'd been able to look from one side of the cylinder's frame to the other and know objectively that the structure was immense. But since it didn't contain a whole lot of anything, it bore no more resemblance to an actual habitation than a skeleton did to a living, speaking person.

Now, from inside, the *Stephen Hawking* dwarfed human scale and human perspective. Peering up through the thin layer of clouds that drifted down the twenty-kilometer length of the cylinder, Beck saw forests, hills, buildings one to fifty stories high, and yes, the moving specks that represented people, looking *down* at him from eight kilometers "above."

He lowered his head quickly to douse the sensation of falling that briefly overtook him. Him, Beck Egan. A man who'd spent as much time in zero-g as anyone at L5.

Splitting the walls down the length of the cylinder were three rows of lighting panels that controlled the standard 24-hour transition from light to dark. It was already disorienting enough for people to adapt to this perspective without being torn from the diurnal cycle as well.

At either end of the cylinder deep cups were landscaped into forests alternating with hills that plateaued up in stages around broad green fields, giving convenient access to pursuits in gravities ranging from full to null. Beck's view of the cups was partially obscured by the rolling vistas of ridges and low hills layered atop the cylinder floor, many still bare alloy, designed to provide more visual supports than a flat landscape that curved up and away on both sides, then snuck around back behind your head.

Such a dream.

A long exhalation whooshed between his clenched teeth. "It was my job to get the Riggers fired up. I came up short. Sorry."

"Don't be," said Kuende. "I never believed you'd turn them into a howling mob of revolutionaries overnight."

Thanks a bunch, he thought. Here I've been talking sedition all over L5, making myself even more of a sitting duck than I already was, and now you tell me it was all just for the hell of it.

"Did you expect anything of me at all?"

"Oh, yes. A great deal. Having been slapped by Earth, the natural reaction of the colony would have been to seek further concessions. Now that Donald Sims has kindly made that impossible, the fallback position would have been *talk* of passive resistance. Which the great thing about passive resistance in the mind of the timid, since it's always available, why not wait till tomorrow"

She reached out and squeezed his hand. "But you are Beck Egan. You have a voice. And you have declared armed resistance is possible. So now that is an alternative the Riggers will have firmly in their minds. Even if they do shy away from it at first. The idea of passive resistance now looks less plausible because we have both, in our separate ways, demanded: *think it through.* You did splendidly. There were a lot of people in that room nodding away to passive resistance fantasies. But in the back of their minds they were thinking: 'Beck Egan says we should fight. And he's a man who's earned close consideration.' That voice you planted will emerge front and center when Earth takes steps to enforce its demands. In the end your speech-making — sorry, poor choice of words — your *passion* has helped force them to come face to face with reality."

He should say something self-deprecating. Aw shucks, ma'am. Not out of modesty, but to keep his role in perspective. Perspective, that is, vis-à-vis Kuende Adebayo.

Instead he decided to change the subject because there was only so much admiration from her he could take without at least *thinking* of something stupid.

He waved to take in the whole cylinder. "This is marvelous. When I was a boy dreaming of living in space, this is a lot like what I had in mind. We've been talking of all sorts of possibilities in the colonies since I first came up to L5. But they were always out *there* somewhere. The asteroid belt, the future, something. Meanwhile life was really pretty basic. Pretty cheek-by-jowl. This is one great big step closer to the dream."

"The dream would be even grander," said Kuende, "if we weren't tethered to L5. And Earth."

"Much grander. But that's somebody else's dream. Somebody else's time. My time is past."

"Not hardly," she said quietly. "Your true time is now."

The glance she gave him was difficult to misinterpret.

Unless, of course, he'd just misinterpreted it.

She was still holding his hand. Now she stopped, and pulled him around to face her.

"It's true, Beck. I promise. I know you've been seeing yourself as something of a follower here. But you're not. You're a leader. You just have to accept it."

This is a public place, was his first thought. And I'm a married man. And I can feel the heat from your skin, smell the soft scent of your flesh, and your presence quivers my heart. Your body is so real, so immediate, so very much *here*, it's like I already have my arms around you. All my life I've worked to stay in control of myself. But feelings I really wish I wasn't having are gushing over the dam.

"I don't know what it is," she said. "I just have this thing for capable men."

Then he kissed her. Or did she kiss him? Hard to tell.

Warmth. That's what he would remember later. Waves of warmth flowing from their bodies, to merge and circle in the non-existent space between them. Lips and a tongue that called to him like the promise of space once had. A body firm and lithe and ... capable.

"Ah," she said, as after a long time clinging to each other, clinging to each other's mouths, they eased apart.

Don't think of Maeda. Do *not* think of Maeda. You'll straighten that out later. Somehow. You bastard.

Only he knew that he could never straighten it out. And to his great shame, it didn't matter as much as his lifelong conception of himself and his deep-seated loyalty told him it should.

He was torn. Not between two women; that had been decided by one kiss. But between past and future.

Beck did not delude himself that whatever happened between him and Kuende Adebayo was destined to be love everlasting. Yet she'd opened a new future to him, just by making him realize he'd lost the one he'd long taken for granted. His dreams had been smothered by Earth, and by Maeda's distance.

Kuende offered him new dreams.

Not as noble as the old ones, perhaps, but here and now and churning his heart, his groin, his imagination.

"To be continued," she said, turning and starting up the path again, still holding his hand. The touch of her fingers was miraculous. Like if Adam, or whoever it was, had reached just a little further out on the roof of the Sistine Chapel.

Kuende looked up at the thin broken clouds in the vaguely blue atmosphere. Far overhead there flew a covey of hang-gliders. They twisted and rolled, performing intricate double loops that were in some cases less the design of the pilots than the strange gravitational and Coriolis effects of the rotating cylinder.

"Have you ever tried that?" she asked.

"Never had a chance," he said, appalled by his shortness of breath. "I don't get over here much anymore."

"It's fascinating. Not just the flying, but the way you can trace out the dynamic paths of the atmosphere."

"I'm sure."

She considered him soberly. No emotion he could see, either positive or negative.

"I'll take you," she said.

It wasn't a question.

Chapter 13

Elaine Fullerton called him to her office, no doubt for a good talking-to.

Only when he arrived, Elaine wasn't there. Instead it was the short Earth woman with the page-boy haircut, the one who'd asked how long a rope would have to be for the pull of vacuum to tear off your balls. Probably the Whitfield regime's chief scientist.

Seeing her behind Elaine's desk, Beck started to take a chair.

"I didn't say sit," she said in the same pleasant tones someone else might use for "good morning."

He stood.

"So you had a little meeting."

"You mean that charade with Donald Sims? Yeah. You have the recordings."

"I mean the one after. You and the Riggers. Tell me about it."

Beck described the debate as best he remembered; the gradual switch from "do nothing" toward passive resistance. "And then Kuende Adebayo spoke out against passive resistance, and that was pretty much it except for the usual muttering and so on."

"A long speech, was it?"

Damn. The assholes must have somehow wired the meeting room. The woman wouldn't be asking him such questions if she wasn't looking for a way to trip him up. No wonder she told him to stand. The next stage was to bring him to his knees.

"Longish. She displayed quite a knowledge of political science. As far as I could tell."

"And her alternative?"

"I don't remember her stating one, in so many words. But I believe something along the lines of armed resistance was implied."

"As you've been preaching throughout L5." She sounded like a junior high school teacher threatening to put something on your permanent record, whatever that was.

"We talked about that, remember? You wanted me to sound out the hot-heads. Of which there are a lot less than you seem to believe."

"Or a lot less than you're telling us. And how was Adebayo's speech received?"

"Got a lot of people to thinking, I'd say. But nothing really decisive, not right then. Look, I don't mind standing, but I forgot your name."

"Investigator," she told him with a smile. She was blond, with a squarish face, Roman nose, strong chin. Not wholly unattractive, except for the psycho vibes. You could toss her out the airlock and she might suffocate, but she wouldn't freeze. Instead she'd probably leech the surrounding vacuum of its last Kelvin or two.

"So tell me about your new friends. Kuende and Haines and the others."

Beck told her. Everything he knew.

She took it in with the same locked smile. If the woman did Botox, she was taking it to extremes. "But this is all just talk. No arms caches, no strategies for just how this armed resistance might be conducted, nothing, really, but gossip."

"You told me to make contact. I'm making contact."

"Trying to get into this Adebayo woman's pants, more likely."

Beck sighed.

"Though I'm not surprised you have a wandering ... eye, is it so far?" said the Investigator. "Intimacy between you and your wife getting a little strained, is it?"

Beck held himself in. "And you're accusing *me* of gossip?"

"I'm not sure you realize just how much you — and your dear little Maeda — stand to lose."

Beck threw himself into the chair opposite her desk.

"I didn't say—"

"Fuck what you say. Just so we're clear. You told me to find out how much sentiment for revolt exists at L5 and who's leading it. The answer to the first is, a lot less than you seem to believe. The answer to the second I'm just beginning to uncover. Maybe it's your own career on the line here just as much as mine."

"Don't you dare speak to me like that. Like any of this."

"Maybe you promised whoever's sitting on your head next step up the totem pole that L5 is rife with revolt, and you're going to uncover it down to the last whisper. Maybe now you need some proof whether it exists or not."

At last the Investigator's smile had vanished. She was smoldering.

"Well," Beck continued, "crucifying me over some trumped-up charge of sabotage is going to look pretty pathetic, isn't it? And who are you going to advertise as your next 'inner source then'?"

"You have no idea what I can do to you," she said, close to hissing out iambic pentameter. Her eyes were a slit extending to either side of the bridge of her nose.

Beck made an idle gesture of his hand. "Oh, I know. Rope, testicles, airlocks ... or was it castrating me with your laptop? Can't remember which. But that still won't make good on your promises, will it?"

Pushing back her chair with an abrupt gesture, the Investigator stood. Somehow making herself look tall. "Enough. Consider yourself under arrest."

"Okay."

They stared at each other, their positions from the opening of this interview reversed.

"And of course your addled little wife will be sent down to Earth at once."

Beck held her eyes. "Okay." Not half as calm as he acted, but he had no place else to go.

"Un*less*," said the Investigator, "you can get me some real Intelligence. Very soon."

Nodding, Beck rose.

"What if," he asked, "the whole thing proves to be nothing but a bunch of talk?"

"Then you leave me with a difficult decision," the Investigator replied, her smile at last back in place. "Rope, or laptop? Either way, you can kiss your balls goodbye. And your dingy wife."

Chapter 14

Feeling the faint pulsation on the back of his left wrist, Beck checked his phone. He read the ID with a sinking heart. Another call from Jeanne Chen, Maeda's supervisor.

"I'm sorry to have to tell you this, Beck," said Jeanne. "But I'm concerned for Maeda. I had to cancel her clearance for our facilities today. Orders from Space Command. I have put in applications to move her into other areas of research. But when I talked to the Head of Research to check on their progress, he was, well, unhelpful, to say the least. In fact his tone shocked me. I don't know if it's something to do with your own troubles with Earth, or if Command is planning to send down all of us who were involved in the transference program. In any case, I had to tell Maeda today."

"How did she take it?"

"Surprisingly well. I know how much the program means to her. She loves the animals so much. But she just said 'very well' and started gathering her personal belongings. Of course she was expecting it. Still, she seemed so distant about the whole thing. I didn't get the impression she might do herself harm or anything like that. I really can't say why I feel so concerned. But I thought I better let you know. Maybe you could check in on her. Are you nearby?"

"Aboard the *Banneker,* yes. I'll get over right away. Is she still in the lab?"

"No. I invited her to stay and talk things over. But she wanted to leave as soon as possible. I'm afraid it's become a painful environment for her."

"Okay, thanks for letting me know."

Space Command putting more pressure on him to get his rear in gear and betray some real live fire-breathing revolutionaries?

Have to find them first.

He tried calling Maeda but there was no response. Since they were the official emergency contacts for each other, he used his password to access her locator chip.

She was at the Hub, in the observation ring. Which puzzled him, for he couldn't think of any reason she would be there. The ring catered almost entirely to tourists. But he rode down one of the spokes to look for her.

The observation ring hosted only a sparse crowd. L5 wasn't the tourist attraction it once was. Not after the first wild flush of Earth day-trippers discovered that despite the legends, sex in zero-g wasn't all it was cracked up to be because unless you were already fairly proficient in zero-g, bodies tended to float apart at the slightest pressure.

Following the locator around the ring, Beck watched small knots of visitors rolling by, flailing and giggling and grabbing at each other as they released the handholds projecting from the observation screen and did somersaults and long glides that ended piled into walls or played tag, the games short because the players quickly veered away from one another.

Sticking close to the curved roof, Beck dog-paddled along the handholds. He found Maeda on the far side and swung down next to her.

She stared in something like a state of rapture at the observation "window," which of course was not made of glass but viewscreens providing a much wider range of effects.

Beck steeled himself. He felt totally inadequate to the situation. And the memory of kissing Kuende Adebayo struck a chord of guilt. Though maybe not as strong as it should have been.

The vista Maeda took in with such fascination was nothing but an expanse of blackness spackled with starts. Which was in fact most of what surrounded the habitat.

That wasn't what showed on the screen before most of the tourists, though. To Beck's left a father was pointing out to his two children, aged maybe five and seven, the wonders of the universe. The rings of Saturn, and its satellite Triton, where popular imagining still held life might exist. The red planet Mars, shown in layers of brilliant red and carmine. Venus, shrouded in swirling green fog. Then Alpha Centauri, the nearest star system to Earth. Even the galactic center. All through the same window, though they lay in different directions.

Beck hated it here. Being accustomed to the real thing, he found all these simulations of the space around the *Benjamin Banneker* claustrophobic.

Maeda did not notice as he settled in at the railing beside her. Anchoring herself with two fingers, she just stared at the true reflection of what was out there directly in front of her, which was nothing.

The Big Empty.

For a long time Beck watched her, wondering when she would notice him. But her concentration on the stars — or whatever — was so intense, she barely even blinked.

She looked at once so gentle and so fascinated with everything around her. Fairly flowing over with that probing, keen-edged wonder that had made him fall in love with her.

A warning sign, Beck realized now. But in the early years it had been an endless source of fascination as she her quick-flitting mind linked ideas and symbols in ways he never would have thought of.

During those early years Maeda's imagination was not yet unbounded, in the sense that the associations flew far beyond any connection he or anyone else, including her counselors, could trace. It might seem so to him at first, as she cast her imagination into the mists of the future. But then she would begin back-tracking to what was actually known. It was like a game to them, seeing if together they could find explanations to bridge the gap between now and her far-flung conceptions of the future.

Oh, they had some wild times. It became a joke how they would get to talking, wander so far out into realms of speculation that suddenly they'd both break out in gales of laughter. Then find themselves tearing off each other's clothes en route to bed. If they got that far. Then after lying quietly a while amid the cushions, they'd dovetail right back into the conversation they'd been conducting before, as if the act of love-making had taken them on a tour of space, or the future.

But as the years passed, laughter increasingly turned to incomprehension on his part. The change came so gradually that only in the last few years had Beck looked around and marveled: I've lost her.

Not that he didn't share responsibility. Beck knew that. He shouldn't have left her on her own so much. So much work....

And so much danger. Too many Riggers died in those early days. Maeda tried to hide her concern, but finally she confessed that every time they parted, she had to fight off the conviction she'd never see him again.

What could he do? Either he was a Rigger, or he had no place in the colony. There weren't any free riders. Not in those days.

And Beck had his own concerns. Seeing comrades die, and reliving the scenes in his head over and over for months. Wondering if anything he could possibly have done might have made a difference.

Or waking in the night gasping for breath, having dreamt of a suit breach, of suffocating while he tried to suppress the instinct to gasp for air, which would vomit pieces of his lungs out his mouth.

Or worrying about technical challenges, trying in his restless dreams dozens of solutions that never worked out.

In a way, he'd abandoned her before she abandoned him. Because he'd been giving only part of himself, and she was a woman who needed all.

The love wasn't wholly gone. Beck could still feel it, sometimes. But the gravity that once bound them together like the Earth and Moon, that had faded and left them both flailing.

Funny how all these things you thought you were, the first time they really got tested, you find out you weren't.

"Maeda."

Her head snapped around toward him. "Beck! I didn't...." She appeared to have trouble remembering where she was going with that. "What are you doing here?"

"Looking for you."

"But why? Is anything wrong?" Such utter innocence. That too frightened him.

"Jeanne Chen called. She told me you lost your clearance at the lab."

"Oh that. Yes." She shrugged. "We knew it would happen sometime."

"I thought you might be, you know, kind of broken up over it."

Her black eyebrows, short and thick, drew together as she thought that over. "No, not really. I don't think so."

"Well, ah, that's good, then. Look. Maybe we should—"

An upside-down Earthman tumbled into him, banging his head against the screen. Caught by surprise, Beck shoved him off hard, increasing the man's spin.

"Hey, watch it, asshole," the Earther shouted on his outward trajectory.

Beck clamped down on the surge of anger that urged him to push off and teach the Earther a lesson about the impropriety of calling people names in their own home. Lately his fuse had been shrinking from short to inverted.

The father at the next station over gave Beck a distasteful glance, though it was the other man who'd used the offensive language. He could tell Beck and Maeda were colonists because they were wearing their space pajamas; him the featureless beige that was standard issue among Riggers, Maeda in a deep purple top and blue bottoms.

Maeda gave no sign of noticing anything. "Oh Beck, it's all starting to come clear!" she said excitedly. "You know, about the generation ship and the animals and everything? I've been looking out into space, and I really think I'm beginning to see."

"Really." He veered between asking her to explain this mystical vision to him and fear that once she started she wouldn't be able to stop. For days. "Why don't we go home and you can tell me about it?"

"No!" she cried, eliciting another glance from the father at the next station, who quickly turned away at Beck's answering glare. "It's here, all here. Or I mean ... out there." Spreading her arms, she steepled her fingers onto the viewscreen, and pressed her head between them until her nose flattened against the glass. "Our apartment ... there's too much rock all around. You can't see out. Can't *feel* the space all around."

"Okay." Great. Of course in reality you could see everything you could see here, just on a smaller screen. And if you really wanted to *feel* it, better suit up first. "Tell me."

"It finally came to me. See, the more we try to expand outward, the more we are driven in on ourselves. It's all fear, you see. When you and I first came up to L5, we talked about humanity expanding into space. Only we really haven't gotten very far, have we? We're still at L5. And because the environment is so hostile, we spend all our time holding it at bay. We've bottled ourselves up in these strange circular worlds. Every time you venture outside you risk your life."

Beck wanted to tell her it wasn't anything like that bad. Nor was it. But to say EVA construction was perfectly safe was a hard argument to make, and Maeda was in no mood to hear it.

"It's the same on Earth," she said. "The Christians, those who oppose them, they all try to create these glorious futures. But the more you claim some ideal future as your destination, the more you fear any deviation from the map that will lead you there. So that slight deviation, whether religious or secular, becomes blasphemy even when that was never the intent."

"Okay." They'd discussed such matters before. "Now let's go home and talk about it there."

"But don't you see? We *have* no home! What we call home" — she waved her hands vaguely at the screen, so that Beck reached out to hold her in place — "is just one more place to hide! It drives us inward. Always inward. Not out there" — again her hands waved at space — "like we dreamed."

Beck worried she'd drift into the middle of the corridor, among the tumbling Earthers, "Hold onto the grips, would you?"

Maeda anchored herself in place by the pressure of her toes on the lower railing.

"It's the future that drives us inward, don't you see? *That's* why the animals are so important. Yes, they offer us extra capabilities, but eventually we have to tap into their very consciousness. We need to keep that spirit of exploration while canceling out the sense of future. We have to center ourself in *now*! If we create hopeful visions, we have to accept they are no more than the thinnest film of thought bobbing on the sea of time! We must accept that every chance wave caused by the interaction of *yin* and *yang* will alter them. We must learn to float, not steam full speed ahead!"

Beck's heart was getting wrung out good. She was so far out of reach. "Maeda...."

"The future is a trap. The garden of conflict."

She grabbed his arm, speaking urgently. "I haven't figured out the solution yet. But it has to do with the animals. It has to. And the generation ship. That plays into it somewhere too."

Someone nudged Beck's shoulder, not exactly gently. He turned to see the father from the next station curling his lip at him.

"Do you want to tell your girlfriend to pipe down?" said the man. "Else go somewhere else? I'm trying to teach my kids about the solar system."

Beck took a deep breath to check his first impulse, which was to demonstrate the workings of Selective Pressure.

"Tell you what," he said, reasonably as he could manage. "Me and my *girlfriend*, as you put it, live here. You don't. This is our *home*. So if anyone is going to go anywhere else, it's going to be you." Such was Beck in diplomatic mode.

For a moment the man looked confused. He was big, big as Beck, and bigger around the middle, which may have given him a spurious confidence. He attempted to deepen his sneer, which didn't work so well for him in this gravity, giving him more the look of a blowfish than an angry ape.

"Look, we paid to come here," he said. "And it's our taxes that keep you up here. You *work* for us. Though not very hard, seeing as how you have time to sit around here mouthing off like crazy people. Now shove off and give us some peace."

Beck felt Maeda touching his shoulder from behind, beseeching him to remain calm. So he tried.

"We seem to be having a dispute about who has a right to make the rules here. We could spend a long time arguing various issues, but let's keep it simple. You have intruded on our conversation and called us names. You have said we should knuckle under to your decrees."

"We paid—"

"But see, we *are* here, and we are much better in low gravity. So if you insist on pushing this delusion of authority, we — excuse me, I, in this case — am going to bounce your head off the glass."

The man's first reaction was an attempt to broaden his shoulders and thrust forward his chin. Which started him bobbing up and down, gripping tight to the handhold. His second reaction was to give Beck a closer look, seeing how his body swayed gently as sea grass, held in place by nothing but a toehold.

In that moment the Earther realized just how awkward and ungrounded he felt in this environment. It frustrated him immensely; it seemed unfair. He knew he was going to slink away with his tail between his legs, but still searched for something devastating to say in parting. He looked past Beck to Maeda as if searching for a possible insult.

"Yes?" said Beck. That settled that. The Earther herded his children away, the whole group humping along in an awkward hand-over-hand groping along the railings.

Maeda considered him sadly. "Are you ever going to grow out of that temper?"

"I'm sick of these dickheads. Everyone on Earth seems bent on pushing us around. Well I'm at the point, I'm starting to welcome it."

Maeda shook her head. "Violence is never a good answer."

"No, but sometimes it's the only one."

It was a discussion they'd had before, and they both knew they weren't going to settle it now.

Instead Maeda returned to a further exposition of her grand theory. Which several times referred to something called "the full spectrum of Evolution." (He could hear the capital letter in her voice.) Which was somehow going to be incorporated into human awareness, using the transference program as a starting point but extending far beyond. All this would keep us, the human race, anchored in the eternal Now.

But Beck wasn't listening. Because in telling Maeda he would welcome an attack from Earth, Beck realized it was really true. He'd turned a corner in his own mind. The possibility might still scare him, but the questioning was past.

For him. The Riggers ... God, he was sick of debating ten different variations of a dozen different scenarios of is *this* enough to start a revolt over?

Kuende had called him a leader. Beck wasn't feeling so much like a leader of late, moving from conversation to conversation with no clear result.

But here talking to Maeda about the *Now*, a new idea began to form. Because really, his own personal *Now* couldn't be held off much longer.

If you couldn't lead the herd where you wanted it to go, maybe you just had to stampede it.

Trouble was, just thinking about it scared him silly.

Chapter 15

"WHAT THE HELL DO they think they're *doing?*" shouted Haines Barber, at such volume the tiny speakers of the glider hummed in resonance. At the steering yoke Kuende grimaced. Beck leaned forward to turn down the volume.

What they, meaning Earth, were doing, was inserting a contingent of settlers from Earth into the heart of the *Stephen Hawking*. Quite a large contingent. Looking down on the line of people marching from the disembarkation point, Beck measured off a section against his finger, roughly counted the figures within, then best as he could spanned other parts of the lines.

"Six hundred anyway," he told Kuende. "More, if anything. A lot of children. These are families."

"And no way of knowing if this is the last of them," she said, peering out the window as she twisted the yoke to tilt the glider to an angle affording her a more direct view. "At least they aren't soldiers. If they had been, we'd be well and truly fucked. We knew when the shuttles left Earth, but were we in any position to do anything about it? If part of the rationale for this exercise was to see how quickly we could respond, Space Command is laughing so hard they're pissing themselves."

"We could have made nasty placards, I suppose."

Kuende banked more sharply. Standing on the glider's wingtip as she came around, and inducing irregularities in Beck's heartbeat, she made another pass, looping down to within a hundred meters of the marching flock. Work crews in requisitioned white trucks of the *Hawking* zoomed out ahead of the marching column, converging on a terraced complex of unoccupied apartments. More trucks were being loaded back at the docking point, where banks of elevators carried material up through Interface from the shuttle docked below.

"I don't believe this," said Kuende. "They're bringing their *furniture* up. What's the cost of that, do you suppose? Space Command wants these people here bad."

"Did you know about this, Beck?" Haines transmitted in accusing tones. "'Cause we sure as hell didn't."

Beck ignored him and his indignation. Other work crews, all recruited from Earth because the cylinder certainly had no prior notice, had parked their trucks and were starting to enter the apartments. Or trying to. Squabbles were breaking out between them and a hastily-assembled picket line of some of the permanent residents. So far there was no violence, beyond some shouting and an occasional push. White-suited Space Command police stood by, but there weren't very many of them yet, and no one seemed interested in seeing push come to shove.

But on the far side of the complex, colonists from the *Hawking* were bustling about the apartments, taking out various pieces of gear, some large enough to require four people to carry, some requiring powered dollies and great care in navigation. The equipment was loaded onto small trucks and ferried away in different directions.

"What's all that?" Beck asked.

"Don't know," Kuende replied, catching an updraft to gain altitude. "Squatters?"

"Doesn't look like any kind of furniture I've ever seen. And why would anyone bother squatting there? Two-thirds of the buildings are unoccupied. I wouldn't think there's a desperate scramble for quarters."

"There's some," said Kuende. "Not that anyone doesn't have a roof over their head, but some buildings have been designed to be fancier than others. Earth can't do anything without a hierarchy. So some of the people here have squatted in what they think are the most desirable buildings, hoping possession will prove nine-tenths of the law."

"Not the law here, apparently."

This was the first Beck had heard of such a thing. And the gear being rushed out and piled onto trucks wasn't anything like furniture. Most looked structural, though he couldn't tell for what. And there were bales of some material he could not see, but from the surprising ease with which such large bundles were being handled, must have been quite light. Just the kind of thing that got manufactured in a low-g environment, with a virtually unlimited energy source, a cornucopia of elements available from the asteroid belt, and all the variations in pressure and gravity you could ask for.

"This is an army of occupation," Kuende announced. "That's the God squad down there. A couple more invasions like this, and they'll outnumber us."

"And Earth will send up troops to protect them," Beck pointed out. "They won't even need EVA Marines. Plain old infantry will do. They have plenty of them, and inside the hull, we have no advantage."

She gave him a glum look. "Trying to make me feel better?"

"*Glider B703*," came an announcement over the speakers. "*You are flying too low. Increase your altitude to four hundred meters.*"

"That must be Space Command," said Kuende. "Our people would at least say 'please.' Guess there's nothing to be gained by telling them to fuck off."

Beck expected her to dial in a beam of microwaves from the lightstrips running the length of the cylinder, which would activate the heat thrusters for a brief burst of powered flight. Instead she banked to the right. Abruptly she dipped the nose down to get more speed, then pulled up sharply, all but standing the craft on its tail. Beck expected to die. Instead the glider swooped upward at a dizzying rate.

"How did you know there was an updraft right there?" he asked, trying not quite successfully to keep the indignation out of his voice.

"By watching the shifts in the mist above. You get an eye for these things. Who *are* these people? By Earth standards, it's still fairly primitive up here. Maybe they're poor. Subsidized food and housing? Brand new furniture? That would appeal to a lot of people on Earth."

"Maybe," said Beck. "But poor or not, I'm betting they're hard-core born-agains. Carrying God's word to the stars."

"Or to the heathen, which is us. This is a flat-out invasion."

Kuende tilted the wing for another look. Unlinked from the cylinder's rotation, she and Beck floated in null-g, held in by their seat belts. Which gave the glider what Beck considered a wild ride, untethered by gravity but swept about by Coriolis forces and the wind drafts they created, other drafts from the differential heating over the span of the cylinder, and even differentials in air pressure below the rapidly forming and dissolving clouds. That's why the gliders were all fitted with microwave-powered thrusters, to extricate them from cross-currents they could not overcome. But Kuende scorned powered flight. She appeared sensitive as an albatross to the varying currents.

Beck trusted her, to a point. But he did believe part of the show was for his benefit.

"Damn," she said, looking straight down. "You suppose they have guns in some of those boxes? That would be against the law, but it wouldn't surprise me at all. We are definitely running out of time."

Levelling, she glanced over at Beck, who was working hard to keep his features stolid. "We've been thinking that Earth would send up Marines to control the habitats, but you know, I think they've found a better way. Slower, but harder to stop."

He wished she would look less at him and more at the window, which showed the cylinder rotating around them at an alarming rate.

"Trying to bar settlers by force," she said, "that's not going to play well on Earth. In fact it's not going to play real well with a lot of people here, either. *Shit!*"

She struck the steering yoke with the bottom of her fist, causing the glider to lurch sideways, taking Beck's stomach with it as vistas of hills, forests, lakes, and building complexes danced all across the windows, some seen amid small puffy clouds, some so close they appeared to his perhaps over-heated imagination to be reaching up toward the glider with malevolent intent.

Kuende righted the glider with one hand on the yoke, the other rubbing her throat as if trying to stimulate some solution to the problem.

"Can you think of anything?" she asked.

Her voice was soft. Not demanding, not desperate. Not even cajoling. More like — if Beck wasn't maneuvering himself into a wholly delusional state — expectant. Confident, even. Like Maeda used to be when they faced some problem or other and she expected him to come up with a solution because that's what he did. He was competent.

Can you think of anything?

Nothing sane, no. Nothing that didn't leave him, and likely a lot of others, staring straight into the abyss.

And the alternative?

"Maybe," he replied.

I don't really want to do this. In fact I don't want to do it at fucking all.

But considered objectively, the world had moved way past the point where his wants warranted a second glance.

Chapter 16

Maeda had learned many things from Beck during the thirteen years of their marriage. The basic elements of side-stepping Space Command prominent among them.

So though she was formally barred from the lab, she found her way there anyway. Space Command had worked fast; her thumb, eye, and manual code were all rejected one after the other. So she used Jeanne Chen's override code, that Beck had somehow pried out of the protected systems, to coax the gleaming alloy doors to part. Open Sesame.

First she walked up to the dolphin pool. The animals erupted from the water as one, leaping and tail-walking and slapping up sheets of spray as they tried to soak her head to toe. Maeda laughed in delight.

Then cried, softly and discreetly, so as not to disturb the dolphins.

She'd tried to resist coming here. Her work in the lab, in the entire program, was over. The animals must move into the future without her — if they even had a future. Jeanne Chen had promised to do her best. Meanwhile the routine feedings and maintenance had been assigned to Eamon Doré.

Eamon Doré, from the adjacent lab. The one Maeda never named, never visited, and tried never to think about. She knew Eamon, of course, from staff meetings and occasional shared duties. A bearded, serious sort, who persisted in wearing archaic glasses, and always seemed a little older than his years. A nice enough fellow, she supposed. But Maeda always discouraged any familiarity beyond what was strictly necessary for the job.

The thought of Eamon and his lab partner, Iantha Pettigrew-Jones, feeding *her* animals, made Maeda curl up inside. Not their fault; they were scientists, as she had once been. But....

But in the end Maeda just needed to come here where she had no right to be, to say hello to her only friends.

Everything looked pretty much the same. Exactly, actually. But the way the dolphins frolicked at the sight of her, even when they knew very well it was not feeding time, showed that they had not been getting enough love. Not by Maeda's standards.

Leaving the pool with reluctance, she made the rounds, checking on the bats, the toads, and finally the cuddly little ball pythons.

She had just picked one up out of its cage and was luxuriating in the warm, dry, slightly rough texture of its skin as it wrapped itself around her wrist, when the torus issued a thin metallic wail that rose in pitch and intensity till her entire brain seemed to turn into a chalkboard with fingernails scraping and screeching down.

***

Up in the main ring of the torus, the quake began as no more than a series of rattles overhead. Faint as they approached from clockwise, acquiring a hollow booming quality as they passed directly overhead, then fading away again. Until three minutes and twenty seconds later they came around for another pass.

At the first suggestion of pebbles being tossed against the roof, people walking along the boulevards or riding the multi-tracked beltways looked up, crouching slightly without most of them noticing it. Then they straightened and bestowed somewhat abashed grins at their nearest neighbors. Few of those inside heard it at all.

Such sounds were not uncommon aboard the *Banneker*. Occasionally some rocks from the underside of the radiation shielding enclosing the torus broke off and bounced around between the shield and the spinning hull. After a pass or two around the ring they usually ricocheted back into the shield with enough force to shatter them to powder.

Such disturbances were not enough to warrant the name "torus quake." Which was regarded by Space Command as alarmist language for an event existing only in legend. It referred to the possibility of the whole spinning ring of the inhabited sector becoming sufficiently destabilized to bang into the shield. Such a thing shouldn't happen, and in fact never had, not in any of the habitats. Electromagnetic fields between the two guaranteed that even should a certain amount of destabilization occur, the two structures would never meet.

Nevertheless, it was the specter of a torus quake that the Riggers and others referred to when they warned of the destabilizing effects of building a second torus.

Nonsense, replied Space Command. The effect will be quite the reverse. Two rings spinning in opposite directions will actually be more stable.

Which was true. Theoretically.

Which theory was now being put to the test. Because the pebble-like rattling did not stop. Instead it intensified, with more and more stones bouncing between hull and shield. Louder and louder, until even those inside their homes or offices or shopping heard it. Some knew it for what it was, others wondered. More people began to find their way out into the open, some to see what was happening, others, more alarmist by nature, because they did not want to be caught inside a collapsing structure should some of the more extreme speculations about the semi-mythical torus quake come to pass.

And then the hull *did* slam into the radiation shield. Definitely and inarguably. With a cataclysmic metallic clang, and a jerk that sent most of those on their feet sprawling. And suddenly the sound overhead was not of pebbles tossed against a can. Not at all.

More like a demented giant pounding against the hull, determined to break in.

It sounded like the whole top of the torus was being ripped off up there. Panic began to spread. Because beyond that roof was space. Not a good place to be sucked up into without a suit. Not really a good place even in a suit. Because the gap between shield and torus was by now filled with chunks of rock from the size of your thumb to the size of a house, all caroming off the hull and each other.

The sounds of doom filled the torus. People shouted, people cowered, people cried. But very few people did anything constructive, because really, what was there to do?

***

IF THE NOISE IN the ring was akin to being inside a garbage can hurtling downhill amid a rockslide, the sounds in the spindle were more musical.

At first.

But not a lot less frightening. Because as the upper torus began to swing, even slightly, the spindle descending from the Hub had to swing with it. And the lower torus, still under construction, possessed its own inertia, which lagged behind. Bending the eight hundred meter long spindle holding them together till it screamed in agony.

Later some people in the spindle or the various pods sprouting from it would describe the sound as a banshee wail. Others called it an agonized groan, immense and mournful as if the heavens themselves were dying, so overpowering it seeped into you on all sides, virtually bypassing the ears as it set up vibrations in the eyes, ribs, and groin.

Others contented themselves with calling it the loudest sound they'd ever heard. And the most desperate. Some of those with a religious bent, far from the majority aboard the *Banneker*, compared it to the last trump — only none of them later claimed to be made joyful with visions of the Second Coming.

Maeda had learned enough of space construction from Beck to know at once what was happening. Her over-heated imagination, which in those first few minutes of the quake was far from unique, pictured the long and narrow spindle bending like a bow. She froze, hands unconsciously clasping her neck, while she waited for the *crack* that would mean the spindle was spinning off into space in pieces, structural integrity was lost, and her insides would soon explode into vacuum.

When that didn't happen — yet — her first thought was for the animals. The roiling surface of the pool showed that the module quivered, but the dolphins themselves had vanished to the bottom of the pool. Glass cages rattled all around. The bats were going into a frenzy. The snakes had turned invisible amid the grass and branches of their cages.

What could she do to calm them?

The room lurched wildly.

Maeda hurtled into the bat cages. A yellow hourglass flashed in her vision as the whole room went dark. She tumbled sideways, trying to get her hands up to break the fall but for some reason they stuck at waist level and the yellow light flashed again as pain exploded in her head.

The auxiliary lights came on, flickered, held. They were considerably dimmer, but enough to see by.

The metallic wailing continued undiminished. It seemed to her, lying helpless on the floor, that it was actually straining toward a point so high her human ears could not hear it. And that if it ever got there, the entire spindle would shatter like a glass tube.

Maeda pushed her upper body into the cobra pose. Not that she really wanted to; the floor seemed safer, cozier. But she was responsible for the animals. Her head felt swollen, and detached from the rest of her body. The vertebrae of her neck had jammed together. She could feel blood running down her face, as well as her throat and nostrils.

She saw black dots flitting about the room. Had she gotten a concussion? She realized they were bats; she must have cracked open one of the cages when she slammed into it.

Her hands tingled. Then burned. Around her the universe howled out its death-song in metal tones, backed by the screams of the damned.

Then she realized the screams were real, and coming from the lab next door.

That terrified her as much as the tortured wail of the spindle. Because she knew what they did in there. Tried not to, but knew nonetheless. A heritage from her days as a genuine scientist.

The mindless souls of animals sacrificed in experiments were screaming to have their brains restored.

That's just fantasy, she told herself. Now gather yourself up and meet the situation. Those screams are real. They are human, because they can't be anything else. And whoever's making them needs help.

If she could. The inside of her head felt like it had been occupied by aliens, because it kept trying to push her attempts to think rationally outside her skull.

Cease this self-pity and get up.

She levered herself to her knees. Her hands and wrists burned. Everything hurt. The tiled floor had splotches of blood on it, with more splashing down as she bent her head to look. She shuffled on her knees over to the nearest row of cages, containing the now-invisible snakes. Grabbing onto the metal frame that held them in place, she hauled herself to her feet. It took all her strength, and for a moment as she teetered uncertainly she doubted she would make it.

But at last she was upright. Though cringing slightly from the sound of metal being wrenched out of shape.

The screams continued.

Maeda was beyond thought. She staggered over to the door to the other lab. It was locked. And Space Command had purged all her identifiers from the system.

But she still had Jeanne Chen's override code. What a useful thing! Beck had always been so useful.

Concentrate. *What* was the sequence?

Miraculously, it came to her. Not the numbers in her mind; her brain had turned into an echo chamber. But her fingers unerringly typed out the eight-character code. The door slid open.

Maeda shielded her eyes.

Even in the dim glow of the auxiliary lighting, glass sparkled everywhere. Jagged, broken bits of glass, ominous as dragon's teeth. The cages in this lab were not so thick, nor so solidly anchored as in hers. They didn't need to be. Nothing here was alive.

And what was dead lay scattered across the floor. Heads, mostly, at least of the bigger animals. Dolphins, sharks, even dogs, cats, and monkeys, all of which had been recently prohibited for research even in their cloned form. There they lay, as if beheaded by the monster called up by the torus quake, whose teeth glittered under the lights.

Maeda gripped the doorway, afraid she would fall, possibly even faint. An astringent scent assaulted her nostrils, jolting her into awareness. It came from the preservatives running in rivulets across the floor. The smell turned Maeda's stomach, but helped keep her alert.

The sacrificed animals, their brains awaiting all sorts of imaging before the final dissection, had their jaws propped open. Why, she could no longer remember.

Once more her mind veered away from her and she imagined that the screams were coming from the wide-open mouths of these fleeing, dead creatures.

Only they didn't. They came from Iantha. She lay huddled on her side, knees drawn up and fists pressed to her face. Around her streams of blood merged into the preservatives sloshing about the floor. Eamon knelt by her, an open First Aid kit at his side. He held a spray can of liquid bandage, but every time he tried to pull Iantha's hands away from her face to spray her cuts, she shrieked anew and tried to huddle further in on herself.. She'd been wearing shorts in the lab, and Maeda could see numerous cuts on her legs, which looked ghastly pale in the auxiliary lights. Fortunately they all appeared to be dripping rather than streaming blood.

"Who's there?" called Eamon. He turned toward the door, and Maeda saw his face too had been cut, most notably a long gash above his right eye that had covered that whole side of his face in blood. "Jeanne, is that you? Help me! Iantha's hurt, and I can't see."

"It's Maeda," she said, and was rewarded with a groan.

Once again the room jerked hard as torus and shield slammed together. Maeda managed to catch herself with both hands on the doorframe so that she did no more than spin around onto her knees. The few remaining glass cages broke loose from their frames and shattered amid fresh streams of preservatives.

A cat's head, jaws propped open to make it appear locked in the ferocity of its dying, bounced across the floor to land at her feet. Eamon was hurled sideways. He gave a cry as he landed, and another as he tried to push himself up out of the jagged fragments, then shook shards of glass from his hands. He staggered off toward a corner, where he collapsed sobbing. Iantha still screamed, but her screams were turning weaker, raw-throated and breathy as she lost her voice.

Again the lights flickered, went out, came back on.

Then went out for good.

Chapter 17

THAT FIRST HARD LURCH as the torus slammed into the radiation shield caused Beck the most severe spasm of second-guessing he'd ever experienced in his life.

It wasn't supposed to happen like that.

A moan, that's all he'd envisioned. A minor diversion of the uncompleted lower torus' trajectory, just barely enough force on that end of the see-saw to push the upper, occupied torus against the restraining magnetic fields. That compression should produce enough harmonics to cause an end-of-the-world humming inside the hull, possibly break a few rocks off the shielding as a coda. Hopefully it would all *sound* like doomsday for a few minutes. Enough to remind people that Space Command was shoving the second ring down their throats, and if its rosy predictions turned out to be over-optimistic, they and their families were all going to die.

A small demonstration, that's all Beck intended. And it had taken him several days just to work himself up even that far.

But a full-on torus quake? Where did that come from?

True, Anatoly had warned him this wasn't exactly an exact science. But how could he resist? The security measures protecting the systems on the lower ring offered about as much resistance as a "Keep Out" sign on an open door, with a "Please" thrown in. Anatoly had been close to indignant about lowering himself to hack this "off-the-shelf crap." A whole torus at stake, and that's all Space Command was willing to pay for?

It wasn't like they'd attacked the magnetic fields holding the shield and hull apart. The only system they touched was a single one of the six thruster complexes that maintained a countervailing spin in the lower torus. The others should have kept the structure *reasonably* on course. And the back-up protocols to the incapacitated rocket should have had it back online and doing its job within three to five minutes.

In fact they would have done, had they worked.

Whoops.

That was Beck's first reaction when he got thrown halfway across the module as torus and shield banged together.

His second was: my God, it really *is* unstable.

Of course he, the other Riggers, and most the torus' population had been saying the same thing for eighteen months. While Space Command blew them off with study after study produced by engineers who never once left Earth.

But *that* unstable?

Maybe he should have thought a little harder about that.

Beck dragged himself up from the ground, rubbing an incipient bruise on his forehead. In fact he was having a little trouble forming any clear thoughts at all, between the blow to his noggin and the all-embracing thrumming metal howl of the spindle as it tried to shake itself apart.

Anatoly crawled back to his station, wide-eyed and bleeding from the lip. He was too frightened to resume his seat, staying kneeling on the floor with both hands locked to the desk.

"What the hell....?" he offered.

Beck thought quickly. Or tried to, with that howl vibrating up and down the scale so loudly it reached fingers into his skull, pulling his thoughts into fragments.

The lower torus, though much lighter, had gone out of synch with the upper. With the whole dynamic system destabilized, it was starting to swing past its parameters, pulling the upper ring off-center. He'd known that when completed, the second torus would have enough mass to swing the occupied torus past the resistance of the magnetic buffers.

But the skeleton? That it could produce such effects with just one thruster disabled struck Beck as incredible.

Almost as incredible as the fact that the spindle connecting the two still held.

But for how long?

The second shock, hurling him once more across the guidance-system module, gave him the answer. Anatoly shrieked as the lights went out. Then whimpered as the backup lights came on, as though he'd rather hide in the dark. Beck rose, but no further than a low crouch, because he didn't know when the next shock would come.

If the spindle shattered, then besides killing everyone inside, the sudden release of pressure would slam the occupied torus into the radiation shield even harder.

If the spindle held, the oscillations in the system dynamics would do the same thing, only over a greater period of time.

SHIT!

Okay, okay. First things first. What can you do about it?

"We have to get out of here," Anatoly sobbed from the floor.

"To where? You think there's any place safe in the whole damn torus?"

"But the spindle's breaking up. *Listen!*"

The howl crescendoed. Beck crouched deeper, expecting the structure to be catapulted into space, *sans* oxygen and maybe pressurization too.

The howl eased, slightly, transforming into a series of grunts and moans that for some reason reminded him of whale songs — especially if you were Jonah, hearing them from the inside.

"You can do what you want," he told Anatoly. "In a minute. Only first, you need to help me suit up."

"Suit up?" Anatoly was panting so hard it took him several seconds to get out the second word.

Pushing himself over in the relatively low gravity of the spindle core, Beck unknotted him from the desk. "Yeah. There are suits on the next level down. Come on, man, we did this, we have to straighten it out."

"But—"

"Now, Ant."

***

"Eamon?" Maeda called into the darkness.

For answer there came only a moan, barely audible over the continued wail of the spindle being stretched and strained as it tried to hold the two toruses together.

Iantha's screams had stopped, but only because she'd worn out the lining of her throat. Now she gave off long ululating wails, that faded into a choking stutter as she tried to get her breath back.

I could just stay here, Maeda thought. On my knees, clinging to the doorway. Sooner or later someone will come along and take care of everything. They have to. Don't they?

Probably not. From the way it sounds, everyone in the spindle is having problems of their own.

Like evacuating to the Hub, supposedly the safest location in such a situation. That's what that alarm is telling us to do.

She hadn't even noticed that, the moans of the spindle and Eamon and Iantha being so loud. But once her attention lighted upon it, the klaxon blared forth one more undercurrent of urgency: *wah, wah, wah-wah; wah, wah, wah-wah.*

Maeda told herself she should get out. That's no doubt what Beck would tell her to do.

But was that what he'd do?

No. Not Beck.

But he's, he's ... like some guardian.

Suddenly Beck seemed closer to her, more immediate, more comforting really, than he had any time these past ... years?

She could help guide Eamon to an elevator. If the lights would just come back on, she could do that at least. Tell anyone she found about Iantha. Iantha needed a whole aid team. Or at least several people to carry her up to the hospital.

And where was she to get them?

They'll be there. Trying to reach the Hub, like us. I'll tell them. While I'm helping Eamon.

Maeda noticed she was quivering in fright. It made her neck hurt terribly.

The scenario of getting anyone to save Iantha looked increasingly unlikely as reality intervened.

Whoever you are, she told herself, you're going to define it here and now.

That was a saying of Beck's, about dealing with emergencies in space.

To which she added: do you want the dolphins to see you run away?

Why won't the lights come on? Don't they know what's happening here?

Pushing against the doorway, Maeda dragged herself to her feet. There were flashlights with magnetic clamps stuck to a metal bracket along one wall of her lab. Touching the wall with her fingers — drills had taught her that if the wall bucked while you were in contact it would likely break your bones — she felt her way along.

Coming to a row of counters she remembered as being on a different wall, she had a moment of panic, but swiftly brought herself back under control. All locations in the lab had gotten scrambled in her mind. Whether she knew where she was or not, if she just kept going she had to find the flashlights eventually.

And she did. A whole row of them, all no longer than her palm, with narrow beams because they were meant more to help out in the lab than deal with a major emergency. Maeda stuck two in each of her pockets, then with one in her hand she followed the narrow pool of light back toward the other lab. The warning klaxon still sounded through the thrumming howl of the spindle trying to decide if it would hold together or snap into a thousand pieces.

As she followed the tight-focused beam into the other lab Maeda had to steel herself against the carnage she found there. A shark's head, no more than eight inches long but with mouth open around a jaw crowded with teeth, appeared to lunge at her from a yellow sea of preservative. Heads of cats, dogs, monkeys, bats, all screaming in horror, chased each other around a landscape of broken glass. There was even a dolphin head there, though Maeda turned aside at the very instant she began to recognize it. Its skin had faded to a dull gray with tints of green, and the one staring eye turned up toward the ceiling carried a message of reproach.

Maeda shuffled along. Her slippers, fashioned from long-chain molecules here in the spindle, were tough, but she did not entirely trust them to resist the broken glass so densely cluttered across the floor. She swept aside what she could with her toes, nudging aside the smaller of the heads as well though she cringed at the touch. She could not entirely subdue the image of the open mouths springing up and sinking their fangs into her.

She passed by Iantha on her way to Eamon, who sat in a ball against the far wall. If he hadn't been able to handle Iantha on his own, there was no way Maeda could. She stooped to close and lift the First Aid kit on the way, chiding herself for not thinking to take the one from her own lab while she was in there.

Past the metal benches against which Iantha lay the broken glass thinned out, the heads as well. Maeda had feared to find Eamon helpless. He wasn't, only dazed and overwhelmed. He'd taken off his shirt and balled it up, holding it to the right side of his face in an effort to stop the bleeding. But his cuts were too big for that. He'd lost his glasses in the second lurch, and either they or some piece of glass had opened up a short but bloody cut beneath his left eyebrow.

"Eamon? It's me. Maeda. I'm going to try to stop the bleeding so you can see again."

"Maeda? I thought ... yes. Thank you. I ... it just keeps running down. But don't worry about me. Iantha's hurt bad."

"It will take both of us to help her. So let's just get you fixed up now."

"Oh. Yes. Alright, then."

She needed light. Kneeling at Eamon's side, she reached across his legs and lay the flashlight down by his feet. His shins exhibited numerous small cuts from the glass where he'd knelt by Iantha. Maeda took one of the other lights from her pocket. Opening the First Aid kit she rummaged around and found an injector she could set under the far light to bring its beam onto his face. Ominously, Eamon did not flinch when the light hit him.

She wondered how to control the light she still held; clamping it under her arm was no help at all. Then she remembered the clamp of the First Aid kit was metal. Propping the open lid at the correct angle with a bottle of disinfectant — a moment's consideration told her there was no time for such fussiness as cleaning a freely bleeding wound, at least with Eamon — she clamped the second light on the catch and tilted it just slightly to get the angle right.

There. Just these simple steps made her feel so much more ready to deal with the situation. The sound of the spindle, the sound of Iantha, the broken glass menacing her all around, the heads casting agonized looks, and most of all the picture of herself being catapulted out into space in the next moment, all these she managed to hold behind a film stretched across her mind, across the two-dimensional surface of which she assembled her plan.

Eamon had dropped the can of liquid bandage when the second lurch sent him sprawling across the floor. Fortunately there were two others in the kit. Maeda wanted to wad up some of the fabric bandages to wipe the blood from his cut before spraying on the sealant, but feared she might need all the bandaging the kit contained to deal with Iantha.

Gently she pulled his hands down. A deep cut ran upward from his right temple across to the center of his forehead just below the hairline. As soon as the balled shirt came away it started welling up blood. She did not know if the sealant would work against such a flow.

"Close your eyes, Eamon," she told him, since under all that blood she could not tell if they were closed or not. "I'm about to spray on some sealant."

So much blood! At first she hadn't been able to smell it over the sour astringency of the preservatives, but she smelled it now. He needed stitches, but Maeda doubted she would be able to sew up such a wide cut even if she knew what she was doing and her hands were not tingling and burning, presumably from the shock of the blow to her head.

"Wait!" cried Eamon. "Are you wearing gloves? You should be wearing gloves."

"Yes," she said, leaving it to him to guess what that meant. She pressed the button. A narrow cone of bubbling gray fluid hissed out of the can. A little high at first, so she brought it down directly over the cut.

At first the streaming blood seemed unaffected. Then a few small flaky gray lumps solidified here and there. As the flakes washed away Maeda despaired that this was ever going to work. But she kept spraying with one hand and trying to wipe blood from the cut with the other, or the sealant would all be carried away in the flow.

Eamon winced as some of the sealant found its way past his tight-shut lids. Maeda went on spraying. The flakes thickened. Some began to hold in place. Then crystallized. Maeda held the button down until the stream thinned to a dribble and she heard the little metal ball rolling around inside the can. The right side of Eamon's face, though the active flow appeared to have ceased, was a mess. All that sealant dripping down had thickened the blood into a jagged gray stew.

"I can't open my eye," he said. "Not a fraction."

"We'll take care of that in a minute." She had no idea how. "Right now I need to bandage that cut before it opens again."

But when she went to open some of the bandaging, she found to her dismay that her hands were red with blood. Slick and sticky at the same time. She couldn't possibly work like that. So belatedly she found the packet of thin rubber gloves and slipped some on.

Then did what was no doubt the clumsiest job of bandaging ever seen in space. Butterfly bandages would have been quicker and easier, but Maeda's throbbing hands still couldn't close enough to work them. Fortunately Eamon could help hold the patches in place, but as she tried to bind them down with an elastic wrap her fingers, afflicted with pins and needles so severe it indicated at least a mild concussion, gave her a hard time trying to control the wrap. But at last everything held more or less in place.

The cut over the other eye, shorter and shallower, was easier to close, though by the time she was through, that side of his face also looked like a field of broken ice stained red.

She needed to find some way to wash the dried and crystallized blood away before Eamon could help her with Iantha. They carried out brain dissections in this lab, there must be all kinds of sinks and water or likely something better for cleaning away the red mat.

"Eamon," she said gently.

"Uh."

"I need to wash the blood off your face." This was all taking way too long. Iantha's moans were by now barely discernable above the groans and screeches of the spindle. She might be dying. Likely was, if they couldn't stop at least the worst of the bleeding soon.

"Eamon, where can I find a basin of water and some washcloths? Or anything better, if you have it. Eamon? Eamon?"

No answer. He could not be wholly unconscious; though his head was drooping, he hadn't slumped over onto the floor.

But he wasn't responding, either. Shock and loss of blood had drained awareness of his surroundings right out of him.

And back in among the benches, where broken glass littered the floor in layers, Iantha's groans grew fainter by the minute.

Chapter 18

As soon as he got his helmet on, Beck began transmitting to other Riggers. Usually most of them actually worked not in EVA but inside the structure, controlling drones and robots, so most of the ones actually suited up would be those who were already working on the lower torus. And they had fled up to the shelter of the Hub as the strain of the oscillations began shattering some of the lattices, sending those titanium balls he was so unfortunately familiar with shooting off. But by now everyone within reach of a suit would be putting it on, because the most imminent danger in space was always a hull breach, and you were in no position to do much about it unless you were wearing a suit.

Even as he talked into the radio he went to the nearest airlock, dogged it shut behind him, depressurized so he wouldn't be slingshotted out into space when the atmosphere blew out, then opened the outer door and pushed off, not employing his thrusters because at this point he had no special place to go.

He floated out into space. That first uplift of null-g centered him as it always did, helping to clear his head and blow away some of the cobwebs of remorse and self-doubt. He was back in his world — space. The only place where he truly had complete faith in himself. A faith hard and honestly earned.

Quickly he jetted down toward the lower Hub, at this point little more than a construction shack. Pieces of debris from the ring splattered against his suit, causing heart palpitations as always, but none were big enough to rip a hole or crack his faceplate.

The lower Hub spokes radiated out, still hollow cylinders outlined by a spiderwork of steel, to the torus body. Which at this stage was no more than a series of alloy rings about three-quarters filled with the titanium lattices that would give rigidity and some shock absorption to the hull.

Inside this framework what Riggers called the "plumbing" had been going in. Multi-redundant systems for atmosphere, pressurization, and backup systems of wired electricity and heat transmission. Four of the huge tube-spanning sector seals had also been locked in place within the rings to add rigidity.

Altogether, a lot of mass. Enough to distort the habitat more than the Earth engineers — or Beck, in unfortunate fact — had calculated.

The steel skeleton glinted in the light of the sun, challenging him with its massive solidity. To blow parts of it off would require a lot of explosives, and a lot of skill. But that was the only way to restore stability.

If they had time.

The storm of voices over his speakers contrasted with the quiet, floating peace of space. At first all was pandemonium, as Beck knew it would be. Everyone crying out to know what the hell was going on, where they were supposed to be, what they were supposed to do? Only a few Riggers in the actual vicinity had noticed that one of the ring thrusters had gone offline. And with so much going on no one could be sure if that was cause or effect.

Time to be Beck Egan. Even if he did feel a dreadful imposter.

He managed to cut through most of the chatter in a surprisingly short time. He was, after all, Beck Egan. Clear-eyed, level-headed, and resourceful; a natural leader and a man well worth listening to if you wished to survive in space.

Now to live up to it.

The frantic questions subsided as he fixed the responsibility for what was happening on the malfunctioning thruster. There followed an unruly discussion about what steps could be taken to get it back online with the least delay. Beck squelched that, too.

"We're not going to bring it back online," he declared. "We're going to blow the lower ring instead."

Which of course raised a storm of opinions.

"Even if we could get that thruster working," he insisted, "can it stabilize the system now that everything's oscillating back and forth? Anyone here know exactly *how?* Things have gone too far to waste time playing fiddle-fuck-around trying to restabilize the system. The only thing left is to take as much mass as we can off the lower ring. That will eliminate the strain on the spindle, and allow the magnetic buffers to ease the upper torus back into a stable orbit."

Which pretty much settled the question. Not all the Riggers were entirely convinced, but as soon as anyone came up with some theory about how to stabilize the system, a dozen voices pointed out objections and the idea was shelved. Already giving orders, Beck fixed on his plan, ignoring all alternatives.

More and more Riggers were gathering around the skeletal Hub of the lower torus. Some in sleds, some in individual suits. Some shouted in alarm as titanium balls from the fractured lattices splatted into their suits. But the storm wasn't thick enough here that it was likely to be fatal, and help was nearby.

Beck began assigning specific tasks to specific people. Not that he had any special authority to do so. But he had a plan, and that was the main qualification. Fewer and fewer dissenting voices came over the channels.

Explosives were not in short supply. The *Banneker* always carried a good stock, most meant to be shipped out to the mining stations on the moon or in the asteroid belt. Not all the Riggers had experience in using them, however, so Beck assigned those that did to placing charges and the rest to gathering them.

"Use sleds to approach the ring," he directed, "and the robot arms to fix the charges. There's still too much debris coming off to be safe for suits."

There was some discussion over how to shed the greatest amount of mass in the quickest manner. Beck's original plan was simply to blow off the spokes where they connected the outer ring to the Hub. Others pointed out that while this might be quick, it was also dangerous. If the explosives failed to detach the ring completely, they might leave it dangling half-attached, possibly even increasing the rotational force as more mass swung around in a wider circumference.

Beck thought that if the tangential force increased it would tear off the ring from any surviving attachment points, but since too many of the Riggers were worried about the consequences and he'd proved far from omnipotent to this point he shelved that plan.

"We'll blow off sections of the ring instead," he announced.

Which required precise coordination if some of the Riggers working out there were not to be depressurized and eviscerated by flying shrapnel from shattered beams. Once a piece of metal or anything else acquired a certain velocity in space, there was nothing to slow it down. Charges must not only be properly placed, but properly shaped as well. And everyone still EVA had to find some shelter.

Beck assigned overall command of this operation to Bernice Algarin, a senior Rigger who for reasons of her own, either the extra pay and/or distance from Space Command chickenshit, had spent most of her career in the mining colonies, and knew a lot more about blowing things up than he did.

Besides, by now he had his hands full talking to Space Command. Elaine Fullerton had finally figured out what was going on.

It had taken her a while, since at the first sign of a torus quake she had followed the prescribed procedure for the Earth administrators aboard the *Banneker*. Which was to shag ass out to the Hub, which even if the torus ring knocked itself and the radiation shielding to freeze-dried space dust, would likely hold together long enough for rescue craft from the other habitats to arrive. The administrators could await rescue in their own special hardened module, with its own air supply, that Riggers called "the bomb shelter."

Meanwhile they could call in and get instructions from their Earth-based superiors, who were in Beck's opinion close to the only people even less qualified than they were to deal with a mishap in space.

By now Elaine had gone through her checklist, noticed the flurry of white suits down around the lower torus, and finally gotten around to getting on a channel to the Riggers who were supposed to be her responsibility. Hearing talk about explosives and blowing off parts of the ring, she immediately freaked out.

"What the hell do you think you're doing?" she screamed on Beck's channel. She'd instructed him to open a private line, which he did, but left transmitting in the open for the benefit of any of the Riggers who had time to listen. "Don't you dare touch that ring!"

He didn't give a damn about Elaine Fullerton, but realizing he was playing for posterity, tried to be on his best behavior.

"It's either that or lose the torus. The spindle can't take much more of this. And if it goes, the upper ring goes too."

"Stop this instant! We are working from here to stabilize the system. I am in contact with Space Command on Earth and they assure me it can be done."

"Then they have their heads up their ass," he snapped back. So much for posterity. "The system's too far out of whack to stabilize. We need to get some mass off of the lower ring *now.*"

"We can't afford panic. That's what you're doing. Panicking."

"Okay, I'm panicking. And you know what? All these Riggers here around me with a collective experience of around a thousand years in space, they're panicking too. Know why? Because I'm wasting time talking to an officious fool like you. You've got maybe fifteen minutes before all the charges are set. If you can show any sign of stabilizing the system, we'll hold off. That is, if there's anything still left."

There came a pause. Had she had a heart attack? Oh happy day.

Then she came back on, calmer, with her voice restored to its customary ice-cold snippy mode. "I have just gotten word from Legal. If you do not call off this unauthorized demolition *right now* you will be charged with destruction of property with malice, insubordination, reckless endangerment, sabotage, and under Revised Space Code Article Three, Section A, treason. Meaning, if you have trouble comprehending such a—"

"The *Banneker* is breaking up and you're holding a meeting with *Legal?* Fuck them and fuck you."

He shut down the channel before he could waste more time expressing himself.

"Beck?" Bernice Algarin called in on the general channel. "Come in, please?"

"Acknowledged. Where are we, Bernice?"

"We have one set of charges in place. It should blow off pretty close to a quarter of the ring. We can double that, only it's looking like it will take another ten minutes anyway before we'd have the charges ready. Thing is, if we blow what we have, we have to bring everyone to a sheltered location, so we'll lose maybe another ten or fifteen minutes overall getting them back out after the first explosion. What do you want to do?"

Damn. He'd hoped the charges would be placed faster. "Give me a minute."

Jettisoning one-half the ring would give a whole lot more margin than one-quarter. But one-quarter now might also be better than one-half ten or fifteen minutes later.

There was an old saying among the Riggers: you gotta be right, but you gotta be fast, too.

"Blow it," he told Bernice. "Get your people under shelter fast as you can, and blow it the hell outta here."

***

IANTHA LAY BALLED UP and moaning, red blood from a multitude of cuts leaking into the streams of preservative that glinted yellow in the beams of the flashlight. When Maeda called her name and gently tried to pull one hand away from her face, Iantha just whimpered in protest and stayed locked tight as if rigor mortis had already claimed her. She was a well-built woman, tall and athletic. If Eamon hadn't been able to shift her, Maeda had no chance at all. And with Iantha huddled lying on her side, Maeda couldn't even reach most of the cuts.

She'll bleed to death. She'll go into shock and die.

I need help.

Going back to her own lab, Maeda opened the door and looked out into the corridor.

It was deserted. Of course. The spear-shafts of light she shined up and down only revealed swirling clouds of dust.

Dust? In the near-sterile environment of the spindle?

It meant the walls were being twisted so severely they were beginning to flake. No wonder the spindle groaned so loudly.

Once again Maeda had a vision of being catapulted out into space as the structure broke up around her.

The only reason she'd hoped there would be people there in the first place was that with the groans of the spindle and the warning klaxon going *wah-wah-wah*, she expected to find a scene of pandemonium with everyone rushing here and there like in a disaster movie.

Only there wasn't. Some were probably trying to flee in the elevators, in the unlikely event they still worked, or the near-weightless climbing tubes near the center of the spindle. But most were probably hunkered down in their modules, hoping that if the outer structure of the spindle cracked, the modules might still retain integrity.

She could go search for help. But how long would it take to find it? Would the people in other modules be in better shape than those in this one?

Besides, though she knew her response was not wholly rationale, she would rather stay in her own module than wander the more vulnerable corridors essentially at random.

Maybe Eamon will regain consciousness and—

How? Are you going to put the blood back into him?

You must do *something*.

Maeda went back into the lab, closing the door behind her. Her nerves were thrumming. By now her hands burned terribly inside the blood-stained rubber gloves. It was even harder for her to close her fingers together. Her neck had jammed painfully into a leftward tilt.

This isn't fair! I'm willing to help, but I need my hands.

Whoever you think you are, now's when you're going to define it.

Feeling like she was floating dream-like through the narrow cave of light thrown by the flashlight, she started toward the other lab. Only first she just had to go over to the pool to be sure the strains on the spindle hadn't opened a split and let the water spill out. Not that she'd know what to do if it had.

She shone her light down onto the pool. And felt her heart lift as the Maui dolphins came up. Not frolicking; they just broke the surface long enough to breathe, took a look at her, made some pathetic squeals, then flitted back to the bottom. Only one — she rather thought it was Blinken, but in the poor light she couldn't tell for sure — put on a half-hearted display of swimming backwards before darting down to join the others. It looked less like play than a plea for some sort of assurance.

Standing there in the near-dark with her hands and head throbbing, her fear threatening to break loose at any point, and doomsday noises all around her, Maeda stopped. Just stopped.

It wasn't paralysis. She just felt like she was floating around on the surface, incapable of bringing her mind or her body to bear on the crisis. Like she'd been floating around on this same surface for a long time now. Reaching for something she couldn't see.

There was no clear object, no clear emotional state she strove toward. More a sense of what *wasn't* there. A vacuity into which all her longings had been poured, leaving her surface being, that Maeda she often saw from afar, bloodless as the dried, skeletal husk of some long-dead insect.

Now Maeda felt that vacuity reaching for her beyond these walls. Howling for her to dissolve once and for all. To stop pretending. Stop trying.

So tempting!

No! *That* was not going to define her.

Maeda went to her knees. She knew she must get to Iantha; that urgency still throbbed within her. But there was something else she must deal with right here. And she felt the two were not unrelated.

She reached out to the dolphins with her mind. Not having any idea what to tell them if somehow they answered. Don't be afraid? But they had every reason to be afraid. She was afraid too.

Only one message seemed possible.

I am here.

Rationale thought started to object that this message carried no value at all. What good did that do anybody?

But Maeda felt some impetus driving her, holding forth a sense of direction, compelling and mysterious in equal measure.

Surrendering herself to that impulse, she let it carry her where it would. Dismissing all the old fears that she was rushing only into vacuum, and might never find her way back.

Like an insect emerging from its cocoon, she scraped herself free of Maeda Rao.

And found what she had frequently skirted before, and drawn back from in fear: emptiness.

But this emptiness into which she now sailed possessed a substance of its own.

And here she floated. Not knowing the significance, but no longer fearing the vacuum in and around her, a constant white noise of dread, never stilled.

Her breath, stiff from tension, deepened, then filled her whole body. The pain in her hands eased, though they remained stiff. Body and mind relaxed into a sensation of warmth.

This is death, she thought. Nothing so horrible after all. Just a short walk into another dimension, and freedom from pain.

Maeda came back to the lab. To the noise, and the pain in her hands.

Here in this realm she found her dolphins.

In an acute state of fear. Everything about their world had changed. This new one was loud and violent, and sent frightening currents sweeping back and forth in the pool. They were helpless, and millions of years of evolution told them that helplessness meant death.

Through a gentle prodding, Maeda slid her consciousness around theirs. She didn't know if her own calm could communicate itself to them; it was rooted in indifference toward death, and for the dolphins survival was the one imperative.

But maybe her presence alone was sufficient, because gradually she felt their panic fade into nothing more than discomfort. They still weren't happy with the changes in their environment, but feeling Maeda's presence, they were willing to tolerate it, and wait for what might come.

For Maeda, past and future vanished. She and the dolphins *were*. Together. And in this moment, that awareness overcame all else.

Rising, she went to help Iantha.

Chapter 19

Shining her light toward the back wall of the darkened lab, Maeda saw that Eamon had sunk down and now lay slumped over onto the floor. He couldn't be dead, could he? Surely he hadn't lost that much blood.

If he had, there was nothing she could do about it. Moving carefully, shifting away the broken glass with her feet as best she could, she walked over to him. Stooping, she heard faint, raspy signs of breathing. Not good, but at least he still lived.

She picked up the First Aid kit. Then went over to Iantha, who still lay in a tight little ball with her back pressed again the metal bench, moaning in a steady rhythm.

When Eamon had knelt by Iantha he hadn't taken the time to shift away most of the glass, and had picked up numerous cuts to his shin as a result.

Maeda was willing to risk the same. Yet the idea came to her that it was important to move the glass away to avoid scaring Iantha. So she did the best she could, first with her feet, then kneeling, with broad sweeps of the rubber gloves. The friction made her stiffened hands throb.

Iantha flinched at the tinkling scrape of the fragments against each other. Maeda also shifted aside several heads of cats and toads and bats that still lay in a semi-circle around Iantha. She felt pity for the sacrificed animals, and a sense of guilt that her own work had played a part in their fate. But she was no longer frightened of them.

Needling pains in her shins revealed some of the finer pieces of glass remained. That didn't matter. Iantha was only cowering from the larger ones.

How did Maeda know that?

She just did. And now, leaning over Iantha's huddled form, a vision came to her. So clearly that she first thought it her own. But she soon realized she was seeing into Iantha's dream, Iantha's terrors.

She was surrounded by broken glass. Fields of it, mounds of it, glittering in the moonlight. A narrow path between the threatening mass led down the street. But fitting between the jagged edges was like trying to walk on the edge of a 2x4. Her balance was constantly threatened, and if she fell, she would pitch into the glass. She knew how badly that would hurt, because her skin had already been torn open in so many places.

She was lost. Trying to find her home. The town was her own, yet she did not recognize any of the streets. The rare times a landmark came into view, it stood isolated from any of the familiar sights she expected.

She had to find her way home! Had to get inside. Because it was also growing colder by the minute. The heat was draining right out of her. And when it drained its last, she would die.

At the same time that Iantha pictured herself picking her way down the glass-lined street, she knew herself to be clamped in a ball. Tight as could be. If she unclenched even a centimeter, all the cuts she felt on her face, arms, hips, and legs would be torn still wider open. The blood would drain right out of her, leaving her a bone-white corpse.

Maeda knew Iantha was going into shock. Or rather, deeper and deeper into shock. If it could not be reversed, Iantha would die.

Maeda tugged at Iantha's left wrist experimentally. Iantha just whimpered more loudly, and clamped down so hard Maeda knew she couldn't budge the arm, not with all her strength. And without that, she couldn't reach most of the cuts.

Stymied.

No. She had shared Iantha's vision of terror. That was a start. She tried to return there. To the streets of glittering, tooth-clattering, frozen glass.

As they started to form again around her, Maeda knelt very still, trying not to let her own thoughts intrude. Which was difficult, because the shards of glass were so vivid in Iantha's vision that Maeda had to resist the urge to fold in on herself the same way. She felt herself start to teeter, even though she was kneeling on the floor instead of walking a narrow path.

The cold too cut into her. Maeda began to shiver.

She must reverse that. Maeda did not believe Iantha would bleed to death. Not soon, anyway. But the shock, that was deadly.

Forcing herself to relax muscles tightening against the cold, Maeda sought to raise again the inner warmth she'd felt a short time ago, when she touched the dolphins' minds.

And warmth proffered itself. The imperative was clear; release the tension of trying to bar out the cold. Relax the tension of fear over entering into Iantha's dream.

Reaching out, she set her fingers against Iantha's ribs. Gradually the shivering died.

Now Maeda brought the broken glass to the forefront of her mind. And softly began to sweep it aside, using mental pressure. At the same time spreading a film of warmth over the shards, easing their jagged, frigid menace.

The constricted passages between walls of broken glass widened before her. No longer so afraid of falling, her balance returned, allowing her to walk naturally.

Slowly, careful not to break contact, Maeda brought part of herself back into the lab. Once again she tugged Iantha's left wrist. This time the clenched hand drew away a few inches, revealing part of Iantha's face. Which bore several cuts, from which lines of blood ran down her cheek. Iantha's nose was steadily seeping blood. Since the nose didn't look twisted or bruised, Maeda guessed at concussion.

"Iantha? It's me, Maeda. Maeda Rao."

"Maeda? Oh Maeda, help me. I hurt all over."

"I am going to. Please, just relax and let me get at—"

Iantha shuddered and twisted her head up toward Maeda. But quickly blinked and looked away from the light of the three flashlights Maeda had propped about, though it was hardly glaring. Her eyes were bloodshot.

"That noise!" cried Iantha, huddled once more. "The torus is breaking up!"

"We haven't broken apart yet. Listen to me, Iantha. Iantha?" She shook her forearm gently. "I think you have some kind of concussion. There's nothing I can do about that right now. The communicators aren't working, and the computers are down. But you've also been cut, and I need to stop the bleeding. Please don't clench up, or I won't be able to reach the cuts."

Whimper. "It hurts." Then: "Okay."

Now that Maeda had a better chance to see, the bleeding did not look quite as bad as she'd feared. Deep enough that blood was still leaking out, possibly helped by the preservatives keeping it from drying. There were also pieces of glass still stuck in some of the wounds. The worst cuts looked to be on Iantha's arms, where she'd probably tried to break her fall, and legs, where she'd scraped across the floor when thrown off her feet.

"I am going to pick the glass out of your cuts with tweezers. Then I will spray on some sealer. Then bandage you as best I can. Meanwhile I know you are in pain, but I need you to keep talking to me. We need to keep you from going into shock. Are you ready?"

Iantha nodded.

"Good. Here we go, then."

As she began the delicate work of pulling bits of glass from bleeding flesh, Maeda found that despite Iantha's occasional whimpers and the cacophony from the spindle, she had rarely felt more calm.

Chapter 20

First came another intense jerk. With the lab floor slickened by preservative from the broken specimen cases, it slid Maeda from her kneeling position at Iantha's side almost a meter across the floor. Small bits of broken glass she hadn't been able to clear away cut into her shins, and her right palm as she jammed it down to catch herself.

Following the jerk came a thrumming from the floor and walls. The howling in the spindle rose to an ear-shaking buzz-saw whine.

Maeda thought she, Iantha, and Eamon were all going to die. It disturbed her for them more than herself. She'd found her peace.

Then the squealing passed, and in its wake the spindle's groans and wails also faded.

There now emerged a chittering from the broken glass littering the lab floor as the spindle kept vibrating. Before, there'd been too much noise for Maeda to hear the glass. She began singing softly, hoping to shield the sound from Iantha's ears. Working her way back to the huddled woman, Maeda finished spraying Iantha's cuts with sealant and applied bandages to the worst of them.

Finally the chittering died. Maeda continued singing and humming, trying to convey to Iantha the ease she herself had found.

After some time she heard voices in the corridor outside the lab. She rushed out and found a column of the walking wounded going by, helped by those who hadn't been hurt as badly. Even those not so badly injured walked with an awkward delicacy, as if they expected the floor to fall away beneath them at each step.

The communicators had come back on while Maeda was working on Iantha. She called emergency services and of course spent an eternity waiting until someone answered. Nearly everyone in the torus had some emergency going on. Since she couldn't say anyone in the lab was in immediate danger of bleeding to death, she had to wait for what seemed an interminable time.

Finally a team came down. They carried Eamon out first, a plasma tube in his arm. As Iantha was being carried past on a litter she reached out a hand to Maeda.

"Thank you." Her voice was little more than a croak. "You were splendid."

"I'll come see you," was all Maeda could think to say.

And where was Beck? She'd heard from the emergency team that the Riggers had blown off part of the lower ring to stabilize the torus. Beck would certainly be in the thick of such activities. He'd get in touch with her when the situation permitted.

Rumors were going around about some trouble with Space Command over the demolition. That too sounded like just the sort of thing Beck would be in the center of.

The medicos didn't let her go back to the apartment, because she was bleeding from places she didn't even know had been cut. Since so many people had been hurled around, the medical staff were also checking nearly everyone for symptoms of concussion. And of course they found some in her. They especially didn't like it when she told them her hands hurt; they worried about the spinal cord being jarred or some such thing. So Maeda ended up on a cot among the other casualties lining the walls, waiting their turn at the various overburdened infirmary stations.

No one had actually died in the quake, which was both a relief and a miracle. But quite a number had been injured, and the residents of habitats being overall a pretty hardy group, there was never an oversupply of medics. More staff was coming in from the other habitats, but the ration of wounded to caregivers meant everyone not at death's door was going to have to gut it out for a while.

Before Maeda got to see a medical staffer, she got to see Space Command Security. Right there in the corridor. They were not playing Officer Friendly, either. They demanded to know where Beck had gone. When she asked why they wanted to know so badly, they curtly told her to answer the question or face possible charges herself.

So she turned on her side and made a show of going to sleep. A concussion ought to be good for something. That elicited a number of threats in loud and officious tones. Until Jamaya Underwood, the head doctor in that Sector, came storming out with threats and ultimatums of her own about endangering the health of a patient. Calling them "goons," she ordered them away. They huffed and they puffed, but after a crowd gathered, some holding heavy objects, they left.

The muttering they left behind showed that the habitual contempt many aboard the *Banneker* entertained for Space Command had turned to rage. The Earth administration been warned time and again about the dangers of building a second ring. Ignoring the opinion of all who actually lived here, they went merrily ahead. And *this* is what came of it. Next time might be even worse. Anyone who thought Space Command might learn from such a catastrophe was dumber than they were.

For a while the day blurred. She didn't sleep; she saw and heard what went on around her, but a mist came down separating her from the world in which it occurred.

When she came back to herself the speech-making had moved on, though the wounded still lined the corridors. Though most had been already been administered pain-killers, the moaning up and down the corridor walls indicated the effects were falling short.

Without premeditation, as if moving within another body, Maeda rose from her cot. She began walking up and down the corridors talking to the wounded. They were often eager to share their experiences, relating them in that excited, high-pitched, almost giggly style characteristic of those delighted to find themselves still alive following some traumatic event. Maeda listened for as long as the accounts lasted.

And as she listened, images from the tellers' stories, not so much their words as the visions behind them, began to appear in her own mind. And though she knew right where she was and who she was talking to, Maeda also felt herself partially enveloped by her own experience in the lab. She called up her own sensations as she sought to calm Iantha's fears by seeing directly into them, the cold and the shattered glass and the sense of being lost. How she stared past her own fear to accept the fear. To take it on herself. And somehow ... dissipate it.

Now she tried to do the same with the tales she heard. Seeing beyond the immediacy of the words to the terrors underlying them.

First she tried to dull the freshness of the groans and squeals from the spindle, the pain of hurtling into floors or walls as the torus hull slammed into the radiation shielding, the panic of sudden darkness, and the isolation as the communication systems went down. She tried to gray out some of the red from the blood so many had seen on themselves or on others.

And then she managed, most often, to sink beneath even these horrific memories to take on the terror that underlay them all.

The horror of dying in space.

Such fears were a constant aboard the *Banneker*, but routine generally confined them to the subconscious. Now even though the crisis had passed — probably — that terror kept the wounded cringing and shifting and sometimes whimpering in fear. They didn't want to be here.

Maeda reached into minds to see images of guts exploding out of body orifices. Of bodies swollen to three times their normal size. Of being virtually skinned alive by the sudden flash freezing.

In truth these scenarios, graphic as they might be, were unlikely. What was actually most likely kill you if you were suddenly precipitated into space without a suit, or if your suit was too badly breached to seal itself, was drowning.

Or in point of fact, having your lungs explode. Because the drowning was what happened only while you were still holding your breath. So long as you didn't open your mouth, your lungs wouldn't be exposed to the vacuum.

But then you would reach that magic ninety-second boundary where no matter how strong your determination to hold your breath, the body's reflex to breathe would overcome it. Whether in water or vacuum, you would gulp for air knowing full well there was no air to be had.

When you did that in space, your lungs would explode out through your throat, taking a lot of torn and bloody tissue along for the ride. Which you wouldn't actually see, because almost immediately the vacuum would boil away the liquid on your eyes, searing the surface.

Of course with no pressure around you your guts would expand. Gas exchange in the bloodstream, the sort of thing that gave divers the "bends," could kill you, but not within ninety seconds, so why worry?

Neither would you freeze. You'd feel a cold totally unlike anything in your experience, since absolute zero didn't happen every day. But unlike air, heat didn't blow out into vacuum. It just hung around slowly dissipating. So once more, your minute and a half would all be over before your blood filled with icicles and burst its vessels.

It was just that thinking about that minute and a half took on a haunting quality to those living in space. It became part of the "tube neurosis" that afflicted many of the torus' population to a greater or lesser degree, knowing that beneath your feet, above your head, and beyond the torus walls rising to either side, vacuum lurked. Waiting.

Even Beck thought about it. Of course Beck had seen it happen a lot more than most. Maeda knew it preyed on his mind because she was sometimes wakened by his nightmares. Not often; once or twice a month, usually. When she tried to comfort him he would just make a curt acknowledgement that he'd dreamed about a suit breach, and turn back on his side. Clutching the sheets.

Now in the hospital Maeda found these images of dying in space, many horrific beyond any likely reality, squeezing in on the minds of the patients waiting to be treated. The tension increased the pain from their other hurts.

And so she did what she could to take some of the grimmer edges off such visions. As she had with Iantha, though she herself did not consciously understand the process. Time after time she was battered by nightmare. Time after time she accepted it in all its horror, then gradually calmed it, drawing on the reservoir of acceptance she herself had only discovered in the lab.

It was not easy, and not without pain. Too often, in her own estimation, she flinched away. Then gathered herself together and forced herself on.

She did not succeed every time, and never wholly. But she did leave most of the patients she talked to calmer and in less pain than she found them.

It was the dolphins taught me this, she thought. The realization struck her as profound, but she could not think where to take it.

***

"Is this really the safest place?" asked Beck, as Kuende Adebayo put on another sliding and looping display amid the *Hawking*'s peculiar air currents. She really was an extraordinary glider pilot, possessed of a sensitivity that at its root must always be partially innate.

"You don't think I can handle this bird?" Kuende asked, a smile curling up one corner of her mouth as she fell off to starboard, all but scraping the wingtip against the top of a hill.

In fact Beck was no longer scared of her flying, even though she still exhibited what at first looked to be a reckless tendency to throw the glider toward the floor of the cylinder.

"I mean," he said, "we are in pretty plain view. Don't you think some of the Earthers are using telephoto lens to scope out everything that flies?"

"Probably. Screw 'em. And as far as you're concerned, the safest place would be Neptune. Or maybe Alpha Centuri. You think Space Command doesn't know you're aboard the *Hawking*?"

"Knowing it and putting their hands on me are two different things."

Kuende chuffed. "Since when did you get so paranoid? Blowing half the lower ring off the *Banneker* doesn't strike me as the act of a cautious man."

Beck could not understand how the floor of the cylinder was now right over their heads, in all its tree-sprouting green glory, when a moment before it had been below.

"I did what had to be done. Earth called it sabotage. And treason, of all things. Difference of opinion."

"You saved the torus. Everyone aboard the *Banneker* thinks so. Everyone at L5 thinks so."

Beck thought so too. Of course if he hadn't gotten in way over his head and created the whole crisis in the first place, the heroics would not have been necessary.

Of course Earth saw his actions — blowing the lower ring that is; they still didn't know how the torus quake started — in a less charitable light. The treason charge in particular surprised him. He'd expected malicious destruction, sure. Even sabotage. Which on a habitat, were sufficient to put him away so long he'd need three or four extra lives to serve his full sentence.

But treason? Space Command was taking itself awfully seriously.

Not that he'd hung around waiting to be charged with anything. Elaine Fullerton had tried to have the Space Command gendarmes apprehend him as he came back in, but there were more airlocks than police, and the other Riggers weren't cooperating at all, shutting down so many systems it must have looked to the cops like mice were chewing the wiring. Not to mention that most of them could hardly find the spindle, let alone anyone dodging around inside it.

The one redeeming feature of Space Command was their absolute incompetence. They appeared offended by the very idea that they should actually know anything about the environment they were supposed to be supervising.

Getting to the *Hawking* had been only a little trickier, even though all traffic between the habitats was monitored. But when there was a sudden flurry of inter-habitat traffic, all very natural as the damage to the *Banneker* was repaired, Space Command found they couldn't track all vehicle numbers and routes. They'd installed the system ten years ago amid a lot of self-congratulation, and spent more time since defending it that trying to make it work.

Beck had come to the *Hawking* partly to keep anyone aboard the *Banneker* from getting caught trying to shelter him, and partly because there was just such a cornucopia of places to hide. Besides being huge, much of the cylinder, especially the interior, was still under construction. If there was one thing Beck knew, it was how things actually got built in space. Space Command might have blueprints up the yin-yang. If anyone actually got around to making a systematic search for him using those plans, they'd think they just stumbled into an alternate universe.

"But what I really like about you," said Kuende, not that she'd been talking about anything particular she liked about him before, "it's not easy to find people who are at the same time so competent and so hard-core born-again wild-assed insane. I mean, we are talking like bug-fuck crazy here, you know?"

Her language, usually so restrained and precise, rather shocked him.

"Thanks for the endorsement," Beck replied. "If I do go to trial, I'll be sure to use you for a character witness. But what exactly are we talking about?"

She beamed, exposing strong white teeth in a smile that simply reeked of exuberant self-confidence. "The way you started that torus quake. *That* was one gutsy move. I don't know that I'd have dared. Haines was going around saying you were too cautious, you'd never move the habitats to line up behind us. I offered to bet a month's salary, and he quieted down. But even I never dreamed—"

She broke into laughter. Whole-hearted, deep-throated, irresistible. The sound, so at odds with her customary reserve, tingled along his nerves from head to toe, though that wasn't where they centered.

Then caution bit down hard. Was this conversation being recorded, by any chance? It was a cynical calculation, and no doubt unworthy of Kuende Adebayo, but Beck tried to make the calculation: how much was he worth as a man who had already played his best card, as opposed to the concessions they might wring from Earth by handing his ass over to Space Command?

"I didn't have anything to do with that," he announced, strict in his enunciation. "The torus ring, yeah, that was my decision to blow it. But it had to be done."

And when Kuende's smile did not abate a centimeter: "You think I'm crazy enough to risk a torus quake? Hell, Maeda was in that spindle." Not that he'd known about that. "If we'd blown that ring ten minutes later, she might have been killed. Along with about five hundred others. More, if the torus hull got breached. My friends. Believe me, I don't have that many to spare that I get so casual with their lives."

Maeda. He missed her. Hadn't been time to say goodbye. He didn't know how all this business would work out, but the odds looked to be at least fifty-fifty he'd never see her again. The odds that in one month he'd either be dead or in prison were even better.

And the funny thing about it, he wasn't sure now how it had all come about. He supposed history was like that. Events roared along, things that at the time we can't see or understand. Until something that might look fairly small at the time pushed you onto one track or the other. So softly you didn't realize you'd just made the biggest choice of your life, and from here on it was destiny that ruled, not you or your preferences. Your personal life, your personal inclinations, your hopes and fears, your dreams, no longer mattered. You were no longer a shaper of destiny; you were its tool.

But Kuende was still grinning ear to ear. Much more ebullient than was characteristic of her.

"You know, it's funny," she said. "You and I don't really know each other. By conventional standards, that is. I mean, obviously we share a broad dream, but how to get there and what it will finally look like, we haven't had time to talk much about it. Not like Haines and the others; we've been talking about nothing else for three years now. And to tell the truth you come across as less of a dreamer than, oh, a pragmatist. A real here-and-now guy. But right now I feel closer to you than any of the others. I've been trying to figure out why, and what I came up with, after all these years of talk, someone finally made something happen. And it was you. Not the talkers, not the idealists and the grand visionaries, not even the Machiavellian types you get hanging around the fringes of any revolution. You. All these radicals I've been gathering around me, most are brave, and most are smart, in their way. But they just don't have that same quality. Not like you. For a long time I wasn't so sure I did either. Now I'm beginning to think maybe I do. Particularly so long as you're around. And having you around, I feel so much less ... well, alone. That surprised me."

Well, that was good news. Wasn't it?

"Because I'm so crazy and all, you mean? Or would be, if I was crazy enough to do something as crazy as what you think I did?"

"Don't you trust me?" she asked.

An awkward moment. "Let's just say trust is a relative concept. And while I'm glad we're getting to be such great pals and all, the thought persists that maybe you take your dreams *relatively* more seriously than you take my survival."

Kuende's head snapped around toward him from her consideration of the viewscreen. "I'm not that way," she said. "It's not about which I take more seriously, you or my dreams. I would never betray a friend and ally. Much less a man I...."

Wait for it.

"Love." She shrugged. "Well, sort of. More than anyone else anyway, these last few years. Don't look so surprised. I always knew I had a thing for capable men. And you, you" — she thought about it — "make me feel capable too. So I guess it's as much about narcissism as love."

"Well.... I'll take it. And yes, of course I started that quake. So if this is being recorded, that's my confession, right there. Only I never thought it would get so far out of hand. And while I seem to be in a confessional mood ... I love you, too. Sort of, since that's the standard. And I'm not proud of that."

"Because of Maeda?"

"Yes."

"But you do anyway? Or think you do?"

"Pretty certain, actually."

"So what are we going to do about it?" she asked levelly.

"That's up to you. My own thought is, let's go with it. Let's go with the whole thing. Us, fighting Earth, all of it. Live the dream or die with it."

Kuende looked up at the viewscreen and the incredibly wide-open vista of the cylinder it revealed, a not-quite-finished world you might make yourself believe was ready to be fashioned into a new Eden, especially if such visions were in the back of your mind when you first came up into space.

Out of nowhere she laughed. "Like I said, you're a man who makes things happen." She reached over and squeezed his knee. "And now I want you to make something happen for me."

Reaching to the console, she flipped the switch to call in a microwave beam to start the thrusters. Then fiddled with a dial on the yoke to set automatic pilot. Finally she twisted another dial and the windows of the glider went opaque. The tone and light didn't change, but something like a thick sheet of glaze ice appeared to have settled over all the glass. Beck stared, trying to convince himself this was really happening as they waffled up toward null-g. And that it was right and proper that it should.

Kuende unhooked her seat harness. Floating free, she fish-wriggled over the seatbacks into the cargo compartment, which was empty.

"Coming?" she said, as her feet glided back out of sight.

Beck thought about it. For all of about half a second. Which was plenty enough time to tell him his old life was gone, and his new one, scary and short as it would likely prove, should at least be well worth living.

Chapter 21

Maeda did not know how it happened.

In the days that followed the torus quake, she started to grow into a legend.

Beck became a legend too. But his legend actually started on Earth. Where the name Beck Egan became synonymous with sabotage, treason, insurrection, and a threat to Life As We Know It.

Most of L5 was surprised to learn they were in a state of active rebellion against Earth. Of course for many years there had been no love lost. Finally the torus quake proved what they had long maintained. First, that adding a lower ring that never figured in the original design parameters would destabilize the system. Second, that no one in Space Command seemed to grasp the central fact that L5 wasn't sited in Peoria, but out in an environment where incompetence and decisions based on politics rather than science equaled death.

Fact: the *Banneker* had indeed been destabilized. Fact: once the Riggers blew off half the lower ring, the system came back into equilibrium. For that Beck Egan was a criminal? What should he have done? Let the torus shake itself to pieces just because Space Command insisted it wasn't really happening?

Having been proved wrong and endangered thousands of lives, was a charge of treason really the best Space Command could do to reward the man many thought had saved the *Banneker*?

Apparently it was. And while the Earth-bound bureaucrats were at it, why not declare L5 in a state of rebellion as well.

Why? Because they wouldn't hand over Beck Egan.

Beck didn't emerge from the quake a full-fledged hero. That he was the first one to come up with a plan, and commanded sufficient authority among the Riggers to carry it through, only demonstrated what everyone already knew about him; that he was a fast-moving, quick-thinking, rock-steady man. The sort you wanted around in a crisis. Just as he'd always been.

What actually transformed him into a hero, as opposed to a respected figure, was Space Command. If Beck Egan was their definition of a traitor, a lot of people started thinking, then sign me up.

Then when Space Command added insult to injury by putting a price on Beck's head, implying the habitats were rife with informers who would gladly betray their own people for money, that really drew a line in the sand that forced every resident to stand on one side or the other.

If any stood on Earth's side, they either kept very quiet about it or took the shuttle down to Earth.

Then when President Theron Whitfield himself declared that if Lagrange 5 didn't surrender Beck Egan "we'll come up and get him," the pretty unanimous response in the colony was, try it. Because if we allow this, we are no better than slaves. And no one in the colonies except perhaps the born-again newcomers in the *Hawking* were ready to call Theron Whitfield "massa."

So when Earth readied a force of three ships full of Space Command Marines to carry out Whitfield's threat, the solar satellites serving the grid that would power the Earth-based lasers needed to lift the craft into orbit all malfunctioned at the same time.

Immediately Earth tried to set up a new grid. And seventeen million people lost power when the system went down.

Realizing the consequences of jury-rigging another grid to lift the shuttles two or three miles above the surface and *then* having the lasers fail, Space Command scrubbed the mission, even as the President proclaimed a "new dawn" in space.

Victory. For now. But new power networks were being cobbled together from Earth's own remaining power generating facilities. It might take a few weeks, but once completed, nothing could stop the Marines from coming to L5.

The colony debated its response. After a number of meetings, a so-called Lagrange Council told Space Command that if the marines come up, the solar satellites would go down. All of them.

Yeah, people would probably die. Your people.

Be resolute, the President told the nation, standing with his arms crossed above his ample gut and his lip puffed out in his best Benito Mussolini imitation. Once the Marines are launched, the power will be restored within a few hours, a day at the most.

Many on Earth took heart from his declaration, though his record on fulfilling his declarations would not inspire faith in any rational mind. Yet even among the true believers some waffled: 24 hours was an awful long time to go without television.

Among more rational minds, none of whom happened to be part of the administration, it was pointed out that even assuming the Marines were victorious, it had taken years to build the existing network of satellites with an experienced workforce of Riggers. Should the colonists actually resort to the sabotage they threatened, would the damage really be repaired in twenty-four hours? By whom?

So for now a sort of standoff prevailed, in which despite Theron Whitfield's boasts of delivering Shock and Awe to the colonies, and L5's counter-threat to reduce the United States to a third-world economy, a lot of people in both camps hoped the parties would stop beating their chests and find some way to talk themselves out of war.

Needing some short-term victory, Space Command doubled down on its initial demand. Give us Beck Egan. *He's* the traitor. *He's* the leader of the to-the-death rebellion. Turn him over, and we can talk.

To many of the colonists, it was a major victory. With but two worms in the apple.

One, giving up Beck Egan left an awfully bad taste in the mouth.

Two, no one knew where he was.

Somewhere aboard the *Stephen Hawking*, in all probability. That was a big area. Full of radicals and Earth-haters now making the rounds of the toruses, addressing crowds and winning more support than formerly for the position that any attempt by Earth to send troops into the toruses must be regarded as an act of war.

Real-life, yeah-people-are-going-to-die war.

But who sits at the top of the gravity well?

A lot of people who would have found this sort of talk horrifying a month ago were now finding it starting to make sense.

Maeda couldn't help but be aware of all this. But only as background to visions that increasingly took her further afield. That field being deep space. For her imagination was carrying her to more distant vistas.

And some of her ideas were starting to take root in the colonies.

***

IT ALL BEGAN IN the aftermath of the torus quake. All sorts of stories circulate following any such life-changing event, as the survivors seek to elevate the experience into legend.

Many of the stories centered on Maeda Rao. How Beck Egan's wife, barred from research by Space Command, had defied their order, slipped into the implant program labs. And when the quake hit, how she saved the lives of her badly injured co-workers, though herself suffering severe injuries. (Maeda tried to deny their actual severity, but since a week after she had bright red eyeballs and still couldn't close her hands completely, that was regarded as typical Rigger stoicism. They grew 'em tough, at LaGrange 5.)

Then after telling the Space Command storm troopers who questioned her about her husband where to shove it, she walked about the hospital bringing relief to one injured and/or traumatized person after another. Many swore her presence had been more effective than any of the pills they'd been given.

In fact, it began to be said that Maeda Rao had accomplished something like a laying-on of hands; that the panic that came perilously close to swallowing many of the injured had been banished. Even the physical pain eased.

Nor was it a mere dulling of sensations, as might happen with drugs. Many of those Maeda touched felt themselves transported to an elevated state. A feeling of warmth, and of acceptance into a larger universe.

Many used the word *belonging*, though belonging to what remained obscure, no two expressing it alike.

In the aftermath of the quake the population of the *Banneker* was primed to search for inspiration, even miracles. Feel-good tales, a cynic might scoff, with a ratio of one part reality to ten of wishful thinking.

Yet confined within the tube-like hull of the torus, with rocks from the damaged shield still banging their way around the roof in a constant low but threatening thunder, even cynics were not wholly adverse to thinking — wishfully, no doubt — that something new and beneficent was arising in their midst. That the expansion into space, if they could just protect it from Theron Whitfield and his crowd, was leading them to a higher plane of existence. That some sort of expanded consciousness, for want of a better word, did beckon.

And that the dreams of space that had first brought them here might take them even further than they'd imagined.

Maeda was bombarded by appeals to make public appearances, to become a spokesman for the colony, to give interviews that would take up all her time for the next two years. Even to preach in the streets.

She resisted all these requests except those to visit the hospitals to comfort those still in pain or mental distress. Which took all of her time, because following the quake there were quite a few.

As for issuing statements or proclamations, that was all too alien. Nor could she find the words to express the vision she felt inside her, even though the power of it expanded every day, lifting her to a state of positive buoyancy.

But she did talk to the people she visited. About space. About out *there*. About where she felt their destiny lay.

And though she had to speak in generalities, she soon found many of her utterances, groping and uncertain as they were, transformed into abstruse theories advancing whatever idea or philosophy the commentator favored. Building semi-coherent systems out of the sayings of Maeda Rao became quite the cottage industry throughout the colonies.

A new mood had come to L5. Space evangelism, the more cynical called it. An outpouring of ideas about moving into the further reaches not only of the solar system, but the galaxy itself. Such visions, free from scientific limitations, had always before been more popular on Earth than aboard the habitats, whose residents had their hands full just trying to survive, let alone challenge the laws of physics. Now, however, plans circulated among even the science fundamentalists about how traditionally accepted boundaries might be challenged.

Other visions strayed further into the realm of the mystical. Maeda had several times been heard saying how humanity must escape the tyranny of the future. An ambiguous statement not much clarified by her assertion that the antidote was to be found in Evolution.

But whatever she meant, her remarks loosed a flood of theorizing on those subjects. Among which were included multitudinous takes on the "group mind." Not because Maeda ever mentioned such a thing, but because many were saying that she herself, with her miraculous powers of communication transcending traditional ideas of telepathy, represented its early stages.

Maeda was appalled that anything she said could unleash such storms of discourse. The answer, she would sometimes say when pressed, isn't in me, it's in wherever your own mind can take you.

She wasn't wholly sure just what that meant, either. But by putting the onus on her questioners, it did relieve the constant pressure on her to give bullet-proof definitions. And oh yes, just how *do* you do that mind-reading thing?

Maeda saw herself being transformed into the Idiot Savant of L5.

And this, she thought bitterly, is the woman they're starting to call a prophet.

The poor future, if so.

Chapter 22

THE EARTH VIGILANTES CAME on in a bunch, assault rifles and shotguns ready in their hands. Kuende watched calmly, standing at the far edge of the park as the vandals crossed the grass from the apartment building they'd just finished searching and trashing.

Fleeing residents told of being shoved and threatened, and beaten with rifle butts and kicks when they objected. Those too fearful to open their doors watched them knocked in with battering rams. Theft and destruction were the order of the day. In the name of the Lord, no doubt.

Kuende didn't need the report of the residents to know what was happening in there; she could see and hear the windows being broken out of the terraced building. Sheer vandalism.

The Space Command police, sent up ostensibly to protect the Christian community, should have stopped it. Instead, three of them walked on each side of the vigilante group, looking more like an escort in their white suits than a containing force.

The park, one hundred meters to a side, consisted of a grassy field dotted with wading pools and small sand-filled playfields with swings, slides, and climbing cages for the young children who were only recently beginning to come to the *Stephen Hawking*. A knee-high border of rocks surrounded it. Kuende stood there with Haines Barber to her right and Jessica Firth to her left. None of them displayed weapons, though laser rifles were laid at the base of the rocks at their feet.

"Twenty-eight," came a voice in her ear. "Not counting the cops."

"I think we have to count them," Kuende replied, without moving her lips at all. One of the neural nets in her brain had mapped out an extensive vocabulary, which she triggered by thought alone. She sent and received through small earpieces. "They're sure not on our side."

"I thought there would be more," Haines transmitted in the same manner. "Earth sent up more than six hundred of the bastards."

"There's a difference between being religious and being a fascist thug out to intimidate anyone you think will knuckle under," Kuende replied. "What surprises me is that this few of them would dare go stormtrooping around this way."

"They think we're unarmed," Haines reminded her.

"Yes, of course."

Firearms of any sort were not allowed aboard the cylinder, except for the police, and they didn't usually carry them. These six did, though. And the vigilantes sent up from Earth had obviously laid in an ample store.

"This is likely some attempt by Earth to create an incident," she said. "What have they got to lose but a bunch of thugs, and those are hardly in short supply these days. Why these guys volunteered, though...."

"'Cause they're dumb," said Haines.

"Because they think they can get away with it," suggested Jessica, another Rigger and like them fitted with the vocabulary mapping neural net and earpieces. "After all, if they believe we're unarmed, where's the risk? Especially with the Space Command whiteys backing them up."

"They probably think we're all wimps anyway," Haines added. "That's the image Whitfield's been putting around. Everyone with a college degree is a wimp. Anyone willing to talk instead of waving a gun is a wimp. So what do you think? If they shoot first, can we kill them?"

"It will come to less trouble in the end if we don't," said Kuende. "No one start killing anyone unless I say so or there's no choice."

The group came ambling across the playfield, swaggering, taking their time, showing off. Dressed pretty uniformly in black or camo, heavy on the leather. Heavy boots, a fair sprinkling of chains, and a lot of very prominent knives, men and women both. Lots of tattoos.

At fifteen meters Kuende held up her hand to signal them to stop. They ignored her.

Haines bent and picked up his laser rifle. Five other Riggers who'd been lying concealed behind the rocks rolled up onto their knees, laser rifles shouldered but not leveled. The thugs slowed, looked at each other, then stopped as the figure in front, a squat, extremely broad-shouldered man with a bald head and a short beard, held up his hand.

Several of them set the butts of their weapons to their shoulders, but did not aim. Though as far as they could tell they outnumbered the blocking force four to one, it is still disconcerting to be standing in the open while your foes are sheltered behind rocks. Aside from which, Kuende thought they were genuinely surprised to find the opposition armed.

"Better step aside, lady," the squat man in the front of the crowd opened as a conversational gambit. "We ain't dinkin' around. You don't want a load of 12 gauge buck up your ass, tell these jerk-offs to back off."

He carried a shotgun with a long magazine slung over his shoulder, a holstered pistol on his right side, and a hatchet on his left. His right hand rested a on a thick metal-studded belt a few inches in front of the pistol. His broad, fleshy face lent a piggish look to his features. His best feature was his voice: deep and resonant, with a definitely threatening rumble to it. The ideal voice for a fascist street-fighter.

"I have a question," Kuende returned calmly. "What makes you think you can go around ransacking our homes?"

The man pulled the pistol out of its holster. Kuende held her arm out to the side to tell everyone not to shoot him.

"This, first off. Second, we're a *posse comitas*."

"He means *comitatus*," Haines remarked in her ear.

"You're harboring an outlaw," the squat man went on. "Beck Egan. And President Whitfield has called on all able-bodied citizens to aid in catching him. If we have to, we'll tear this whole place apart brick by brick until we find him."

Kuende sighed, then waved her hand around, taking in the torus. "That is an awful lot of bricks. It also happens to be our home."

"Tough tit, snowflake," called a weasel-faced woman among the crowd.

These, Kuende thought to herself, are an extraordinarily ugly group of people. Ugly in thought, ugly in looks, ugly in speech. Recruited not for their religion, but their violence. The real Christians were probably relieved to be rid of them.

One of the Earth police stepped forward. "It is forbidden to possess firearms within the cylinder. I am ordering you to surrender them at once, or be charged with a serious violation of the law."

"What about their guns?" cried Haines, unable to keep silent any longer. "They just slip your notice, maybe?"

The Space Command cop ignored him. "I repeat. Surrender your weapons or face the consequences."

Kuende normally had excellent control of her temper. The thugs didn't bother her that much; that was simply who they were. She did not respect them as human beings, and was therefore equally indifferent to their insults or whether they survived the next ten minutes. Earth's hypocrisy, however, had long been a sore point, and never had she seen it displayed more blatantly.

Backup she transmitted to the Riggers and others waiting in reserve.

The second floor of the apartment complex behind her was set well back from a broad patio fitted with chairs, benches, and play stations. Its front was a blue-gray wall of lunar rock, looking rather like Earth's exposed-aggregate masonry. A line of Riggers, twenty-five strong, now stood up from behind the wall with lasers aimed.

Some of the thugs aimed their rifles in return.

"Don't shoot!" screamed the cop, whether to the thugs, the Riggers, or both, Kuende didn't know. Maybe he didn't either.

The moment hung heavy, and she relaxed her knees, ready to dive behind the stones. The squat man turned and waved his hands downward, telling his followers not to start anything. It took him a moment to realize he still held the pistol. He returned it to its holster as he turned toward Kuende.

"If any harm comes to anyone here," he snarled at her, "I will hold you personally responsible. Got that?"

"Kuende Adebayo," she returned. "Just so you know. Now you can all consider yourselves under arrest. That applies to you jokers too," she told the cop.

"Arrest by who?" exclaimed the leader indignantly, while threats, obscenities, and jeers broke out behind him. He pointed, gun still in hand, to the white figure standing beside him. "*These* are the cops."

"Really? Thanks for telling me. The way they were backing you up, I thought they were just more fascist jerkoffs with their heads stuck up Theron Whitfield's ass. I was going to *ask* ... y'all" — that was pretty good — "to put down your weapons. Only you know, you are just the *stupidest* group of people I've ever come across. I just know you'll fuck it up and people will get killed."

Do it she transmitted to the glider channel.

"So we'll handle this the safe way," she told the thugs. "Look up."

Caught by surprise, they did. And saw half a dozen gliders drifting slowly overhead.

"You mean to tell me you really missed that?" Kuende asked. As she shook her head in disbelief, she reached behind her neck. She'd been carrying a small mouth and nose mask there on a rubber strap slung across the front of her neck. All the first-line Riggers had. Now she, like them, yanked the mask around and clapped it over her face, at the same time dropping to her knees.

"Gas!" yelled several of the thugs. A shot rang out, then several.

Do not return fire she transmitted as she ducked low. Gunfire followed her, the bullets spranging off the rocks, stinging her face with flakes. Knowing better than to look over the top, she wriggled sideways and peered out between two sloping rocks. The squat man was charging her position, shooting as he came. His legs were unsteady; the gas was starting to get to him.

Would he fall in time? Kuende gripped her laser rifle, torn between shooting back and taking her chances.

A stream of light from behind and overhead lanced into the center of the squat man's chest. He staggered and bellowed as dark tendrils of steam rose from the wound. The light held, producing more steam. As the squat man fell the light cut up through his shoulder. Kuende heard the blood hiss as it turned to steam. She turned her face away. Then lifted it above the rocks.

The squat man lay face down, blood running from his body to be quickly absorbed by the ground. Kuende told herself vaguely that she'd tried to avoid all killing, but right now she just didn't feel that much about it one way or the other.

Beyond the dead man, thirty-three bodies lay prone, heaped atop one another across the playfield.

Chapter 23

"Sorry," Beck said. "I couldn't take the chance the gas would down him in time."

He knew he didn't sound too terribly broken up about it. He wasn't. The man was an asshole.

Kuende didn't seem too upset either. "That's all right. Better him than me, which is what he was trying for. And I had this feeling as I said 'do not fire.' It was like there was a clause in there saying, 'anyone but Beck.' I knew you'd make your own decisions."

"So what now?" Haines asked impatiently. "We've killed one of the people Earth sent up here. He may have been a fascist thug, but by the time the eulogies are done he'll be looking like Mother Theresa's saintlier brother. Not to mention I don't know if you two can take enough time off from admiring each other to notice, but we just staged a coup. You ask me, Earth will be coming soon."

"Very likely," Kuende agreed.

"This is not all going quite according to plan."

Beck raised an eyebrow. "You mean you people actually had a plan?"

"Until you came along," Barber retorted.

"Damn, too bad you never told me. But then, I was just the guy who was supposed to inspire the toruses to revolt, wasn't I? You were going to be the leader. Once I secured your revolution for you."

"Fuck off."

Beck knew they were both feeling nervous in the aftermath of dealing with the thugs, but he was having difficulty containing himself. The bad blood had been building between them for a while.

"Would you like to reconsider that statement?" he suggested.

Kuende settled the boys down, putting a hand on Beck's arm and shaking her head at Haines.

"Stop pretending like everything was in control," she told him. "We had a sort of a plan, more or less, only no way of achieving it. Did you really think everything was going to run according to some schedule we set up?"

Haines stewed, then sighed and raised his hands. "Sorry," he told Beck. "I'm trying to see how all this is going to come together, and it keeps looking like shit through a fan."

"Let's just forget it."

Nevertheless, something in Kuende's statement he couldn't quite put a finger on intrigued him.

A little later he and Kuende stood at the command station of the *Hawking*'s equivalent of Hub Central, a rising disk projecting from the outer hull, fifty meters across. Residents called it the flying saucer. The Admin center consisted of screens, screens, and more screens. Huge, inward tilted screens looking down from the sloping walls, smaller screens two meters on a side lining the circumference, and row upon row of the screens of personal workstations. The center of the curved ceiling appeared to be made out of glass giving a sweeping view of Earth and the stars beyond, but of course it was a digital projection looking down from a well-reinforced wall.

"Does anyone know how to change the picture?" Kuende shouted down from raised platform at the center of the room. "It looks like Whitfield's staring down our throats."

"I'll work on it soon as I get a chance," someone called back from a workstation below.

They were here because they'd marched in and taken the place over. Not that there was much resistance. Most of those who worked here were permanent residents, working under a few Earth administrators who didn't do much but sit and look on. When Kuende walked in with Beck and a few others, all armed, the residents had been interested more than alarmed, some of them amused, some of them guarded.

The four Earth admin types were terrified. They'd watched the fat thug sliced through by a laser. Though they didn't know it was Beck who fired, they, like everyone else in the colony were by now well familiar with his face, broadcast throughout the colony at regular intervals along with a fresh denunciation by the President along with the promise that "time was growing short." The Earthers could not be sure they weren't going to be sent back to the home planet via the nearest airlock.

When Kuende calmly told them that due to a breakdown of order aboard the *Hawking* caused by renegade elements from Earth she meant to assume "temporary" control of the cylinder, the Earthers waited to see if part of that control included pulling out their fingernails. When it became apparent that wasn't on the program, one of them stated a formal protest in equally calm terms, then they all scurried off to their living quarters.

If Beck had just witnessed the Lexington and Concord of the first revolution in space, he thought it a bit anticlimactic.

As for the thugs and their police companions, before they could wake from the gas the rebels cuffed their hands behind them with plastic restraints. Then marched their groggy prisoners to the holding pens between outer skin and interior. There'd been some resistance at first; the thugs staging a sort of sit-down strike and saying they'd have to be carried. Kuende put Haines in charge of the detail and walked away.

Now when she called up a view of the cell blocks on one of the large disc screens she saw some bloody clothes and bloody faces and a bunch of sour looks, and everyone where they were supposed to be.

"I'm beginning to like Haines better," said Beck.

On the screens monitoring the interior of the cylinder, everything looked peaceful enough. A number of gliders swooped like swallows over the complex where the newcomers had settled in. There had been a few outdoor prayer meetings, but no one displayed firearms, and no one called for taking over the torus.

Instead, people bustled like ants across a playfield in the center of the four apartment complexes the newcomers had taken over. They had asked for and Kuende had granted bonding agents, steel girders, wiring, piping, and scaffolding, along with some large machinery. All the hand tools they needed they had brought up themselves. As for the raw material of their construct, they were tearing down one of the apartment complexes piece by piece.

They were building a church. A big one, from everything Kuende or her representatives had been able to make out. Hopefully that would keep them from mischief.

Kuende did contact some of those they'd identified as leaders to inform them of the imprisonment of the thugs, and warn them not to make trouble over it. They protested the incarceration of what they claimed to be members of their "flock." But Kuende got the impression they were more embarrassed than indignant. And not one made any threats.

"You know," she told Beck in an aside, "I don't think they like those thugs much more than we do. Wouldn't surprise me if the so-called posse was forced on them by Whitfield's flunkies."

When she brought up the subject of guns, the leaders first debated her account, then when presented with the pictures, looked dismayed. They protested ignorance. They couldn't have been quite as ignorant as they pretended, but overall they did leave Beck with the impression that they'd rather attend to their church-building and leave the thugs to Kuende.

Haines arrived just as the conference call ended.

"Let 'em rot," was his suggestion for the thugs.

"There's a problem with that," Kuende pointed out. "If Earth calls them martyrs, it gives Whitfield one more excuse to send up the Marines. He can call it a rescue mission instead of an invasion. Call on the country to endure power shortages for the sake of the innocent hostages."

Haines put his palms over his eyes in a show of suffering. "Man, we are *so* far past that point. It's not if, but when. Anything else vanished in the rearview when *he*" — pointing at Beck — "staged that torus quake."

Beck went cold. "That was a very stupid thing to say."

Once again Kuende intervened as the two men drifted closer to chest-to-chest. Gently she pushed them away from each other.

"Hell," said Haines, "It's not like I'm even saying it was the wrong thing to do. Only that after it happened — however it happened — we lost control of the schedule. Preparations aren't going to be as timely or complete as we were hoping for. We need to accept that. Our own actions may not be as neat and humane and righteous as we planned. Speaking of which, what *are* we going to do about the God squad? If the Marines do come up, do we really want these yo-yos at our backs? And how many more guns do you suppose came up in the Christians' 'furniture.' We just going to let that go?"

"Haines, the Christians have their children with them," Kuende protested. "The vast majority of them are families. You and I may not care for their beliefs, or how they want to force them on us. But do they really look like commando teams to you?"

"Kue*n*de ...." Haines glanced sidelong at Beck, hesitated, then continued on. "Think about this. Please. Say everything comes off just as we hoped. Those people are *still* going to be here. Think about the implications of that. Not just for today, or next week, but out into the future. Does that sound like some minor glitch to you?"

Kuende took the question in stride — pretty much. Just a slight widening of the eyes timed with the slightest one-sided nod of her head to let Haines know he was out of line.

Meaning, that this was not a matter that should be pursued in front of Beck.

But Haines just couldn't keep his mouth shut. "If we don't do something about those people now, then when? *How?*"

Kuende punched him playfully on the shoulder. "First things first, Haines. You worry too much."

"Think so?" he returned sarcastically.

"Yes. Because there are problems we can solve, and problems we can't. Not in the near term. We can't evict those people. If nothing else, we haven't the means to return them to Earth."

"Then demand that Earth send up arks or whatever the hell else they use."

"That's not going to happen, Haines. So let's concentrate on not messing up what we can actually do something about. Eyes on the prize, okay? Winning the prize doesn't mean that for the first time in the history of the universe everything's absolutely perfect. Only that we win."

She turned a dazzling, shake-you-down-to-your-socks, but not quite convincing smile on Beck. "So here we are in a state of armed insurrection. It's all come sooner than we wanted, but that can't be helped. The question facing us now is, what to do about it?"

And so they talked about future possibilities, the three of them, just like they trusted each other.

✳✳✳

As Beck jetted along on gentle pulses of his thrusters, the sheer scale of the *Hawking* continued to amaze him. Though he'd spent several years working here, no one vantage point could give you a truly comprehensive idea of the scale.

Now the actual cylinder lay behind him as he moved further into the external frame extending beyond the end cap. Unlike the toruses, where most manufacturing was carried out in modules extending out from the spindle, here the modules were mounted on a giant cylindrical frame extending four hundred meters out.

Beck stayed near the center of the external frame, where any rotation imparted by the structures was close to imperceptible. Along the outer frame, rotating to provide three-quarters gravity, you had to watch yourself. Impact with the structural members was unlikely to break any bones through a suit, but it could throw you in a direction you didn't mean to go, and possibly damage your thrusters enough to prevent you from recovering. It could even smash the connection to your oxy-tanks.

That was one reason it was so helpful to have infrared, radar, basic echo location, and a 360-degree field of vision in the suits. Even so, with a number of objects moving around at the same time, as was common in construction, you did not feel at all like Earth's dreaded "Man Plus."

From his position near the center of the manufacturing cylinder, the more distant spider-web of girders all but disappeared beyond an occasional blue or golden glint where lighting illuminated it. This even though the longitudinal pieces of the main frame were sixteen meters thick, as he well knew from jockeying so many of them into position during construction. The starfield beyond, so brilliant as to provide an illusion of casting its own light, was sectioned like an abstract painting with black lines where the girders cut through it.

All through the frame a maze of modules, silver or white-surfaced to make them more visible, resembled a crowded city of squares, lozenges, spheres, cylinders, and an assortment of seemingly random shapes, like the spiny urchin just above him or the nautilus slowly revolving in the distance, adapted to some particular industrial process.

To his back was the outward-bulging end of the cylinder itself, with a circumference greater than any of the torus rings. Beck had a sensation of himself as a very small and slow-moving minnow about to be gulped down by Megalodon, in the midst of a dark and endless sea.

It wasn't safety that made Beck stay close to the weightless part of the frame. This was where he expected to find what Kuende Adebayo wanted to keep secret from him.

Though many of the modules within the manufacturing cylinder could be reached through pressurized passages to avoid the need for EVA, those passages would presumably be monitored. And the numerous seals meant to provide safe compartments in the event of a breach could also be triggered to trap him. Beck didn't know if Kuende thought that whatever secret she was guarding was worth more than his life. His heart told him it wasn't.

His mind was not quite so sure.

Anyway, if it was him hiding something, he'd stick it in one of the modules only accessible by EVA.

So far he'd restricted his search to the larger modules. For one thing, there were just too many for him to check them all out, and the longer he poked around, and especially the more airlocks he tried to jimmy, the greater the chance that he'd be detected.

Besides, he figured he was looking for something big and heavy, which would nonetheless need to be quickly deployed should Earth make its move. And more likely to be kept in a storage rather than a manufacturing module. And so he swam through the complex, occasionally calling up the schematic to guide him. The diagram would cross his vision as a sort of semi-transparent film across his faceplate, through which he could still see his surroundings.

He knew he would be intercepted eventually. Kuende, Haines, and the others weren't half such clever-clogs as they thought they were, but they weren't stupid. They wouldn't leave the crown jewels unmonitored. If there were any crown jewels, that is. Beck didn't know for sure. But they were damn sure hiding *something* from him.

Coming to the airlock of his twelfth large, low-g storage module, Beck entered the general-purpose access code. First-line security on the modules was mainly *pro forma*. Standard philosophy was that it was more important to offer quick refuge to a space walker who might have a breach in his suit than to guard every last item of manufacture like a dragon's gold. Besides, the population of L5 was probably more law-abiding than your average choir of angels.

The other modules had all opened at once to the general code. This one didn't.

In fact it made no response at all. Didn't even flash the red-lettered "screw you, idiot" code common to machines contemptuous that you didn't understand all the nested menus, subroutines, and special exceptions as well as they did. It just acted dead, dead, dead. Like maybe it was one of many that had not yet been rendered operational.

Ah-ha.

Beck did not regard himself as a thief. Slip a thousand unearned credits into his account, he'd report it at once. It was just that he had this compulsion to acquire access codes, stray bits of info meant to be restricted, back doors into security systems, classified communications between Space Command's torus administrators and Earth, general decryption programs, things like that. He used to tell Maeda it came from working in space, where if he needed to invoke overrides in some emergency, he did not want to wait two days for his request to go up the chain of command to see if it fit Earth's anal-retentive idea of need-to-know.

Maeda maintained he was just sneaky by nature.

And for all Kuende Adebayo obviously didn't fully trust him, once she let him a certain way into her life, she'd gotten lax about cordoning off the rest. Not that she knew. She'd undoubtedly be shocked at what could happen when you left Beck Egan alone for fifteen minutes with your personal computer.

Now he made use of his explorations to activate and open the airlock, with a not inconsiderable flash of "so there" satisfaction.

Once inside the airlock he did not have to wait for pressurization because the interior held no air, just heat. He glided into the vast darkness of the module. His contact with surfaces in the airlock had been minimal, not enough to absorb any of the rotation that the schematic informed him provided one-tenth gravity.

It was the perfect gravity for storing big, heavy items you might need in a hurry. Just enough to make it easy to strap or bolt them into place, yet still be possible for two or three people with thrusters to lift and maneuver them through the cargo doors.

Below him and stretching away on all sides as far as the light from his headlamp could reach, was an array of some kind of bales. With a quick burst from his thrusters, he glided down to investigate.

Just bales, covered with tarps of some plasticine material. Grommets around the edges of the tarps were hooked to short elastic cords run through bolts in the floor, then looped back and hooked on at the other end. The bales were quite large; around fifteen meters long, five wide, and three or four high. How heavy they were remained to be seen, but heavy or light, in this gravity they'd be easy to move.

Beck cut his thrusters and glided against the top of one of the shiny plasticine tarps. There was just enough slack in the covering to give him a handhold. A trill of anticipation hummed inside him. He loved this secret agent shit. Loved showing people who sought to mislead him that Beck Egan was not as dumb as he acted.

The material beneath the tarp did not feel hard as metal, but had no give to it. Now rotating with the bale, picking up the light gravity, Beck slipped over the side, grabbed one of the hooks, and loosed it from the grommet. Though he was a strong man, he had to use the logarithmic power of his suit. He then unsnapped the rest of the elastic cords on this side, careful not to let the hook smash into his suit.

Finally he raised the edge of the tarp. His head lamp glared off some shiny fabric. Very tight-packed; with his gloves on he couldn't work any of the edges loose from each other. Of course not. The fabric was so incredibly thin it formed a vacuum between layers. Even in this marginal atmosphere the pressure over such large surfaces was too much to budge.

But he didn't need to examine it closely. Beck knew just what he was looking at. Vast sheets made of carbon nanotubes. Try to get any thinner, and you'd violate the laws of physics. Yet thin as it was, it conducted electricity, which gave it a very high emissive rating. Most useful in certain applications.

It was one of those moments in life when all you could say was: *Shit!*

Beck said it twice. Once for himself, once for Kuende.

Not that he was totally surprised. He'd already thought of the possibility. Just hadn't been able to make himself believe anyone would be crazy enough to actually try it.

Which meant that okay, maybe he *was* as dumb as he acted.

Refastening the hooks, he jumped up ten meters, proned out in the direction of the green light marking the airlock, and triggered a short burst of his thruster.

All his implants flashed in at once.

He cut his headlamp. Not to hide himself; that was futile against Riggers with implants and full-spectrum suits. Just to make himself a less obvious target if they started to shoot.

Chapter 24

As he floated above the bales strapped to the floor of the module Beck couldn't see the newcomers.

Not on visual. But they showed up bright as you please on infrared; fuzzy flashes of crimson from their thrusters against the dull-copper glow of waste heat being ejected from their suits. Five figures closing in on him. The semi-conscious pings of echo location rose in pitch as they approached. ETA forty-three seconds, if anyone cared.

Beck didn't see all this as an overlay on his visuals, which saw nothing at all until at twenty seconds away the newcomers cut in their headlamps. The better to shoot by, if they were so inclined. Instead he watched, or more accurately *sensed*, a schematic form somewhere near the center of his brain. Had it been an actual diagram as presented across the viewscreen of Earth helmets, visual would be null. And radar would still need to be processed through his eyes, along with the associated readouts for range, mass, inertia, etc. And if the newcomers split up, he'd only be able to concentrate on one at a time.

Now the neural nets implanted in his skull processed the input for each separate sensor modality in the instinctual working of the species that first formed the circuitry. The nets then fed the result to another neural net that coordinated the whole and fed it to separate parts of his brain, so that in the center of his skull a coordinated awareness of all the inputs formed. That awareness remained even as most of his conscious thought was turned from perception toward planning.

Coaxing such abilities into existence, forming the relevant networks and teaching the native parts of the brain to interpret and merge them, took hour upon hour, then day upon day, then month upon month. Outside the lab the process still continued, every time the suit sensors fed information to the implants. In a man like Beck, who had spent so many years working in space, those abilities were honed to a most exacting edge. But even among less experienced individuals, the Riggers' brains were in their way the most highly trained and specialized organs the world had ever known.

Beck sank down onto the top of one of the bales. He wondered if they'd kill him. He didn't think so, but he wasn't sure. He'd be very disappointed in Kuende if she gave the order, but that was her karma to work off.

He was surprised to find himself so unafraid.

Two of the five pulled up and sank onto the opposite end of the bale on which he stood. The three others lined up on a bale to his left, so that the two groups would remain outside each other's lines of fire if it went down that way. Those three carried laser rifles. One of the suits in front of him held a circular vibra-saw on a three-foot pole, a weapon some of the Riggers had been experimenting with to use against Marines in ultra-close combat.

The other, who Beck knew from its catlike ready grace to be Kuende Adebayo, bore no weapons. Their five headlamps pulled the forefront of his conscious thought back onto visual, though instinct kept tracking the other channels.

"You know," said Kuende, "I expected something like this."

Her voice didn't float out into the space between them. Rather it came through on one of his communication channels. And while it did tickle his ears lightly — anticipation reflex, it was called, like a dog licking the air in response to some learned signal promising food — the sound, like the other data, seemed to originate more in the middle of his head.

"So did I," Beck replied. "It hurts my pride, but I did think it a little strange how no one else ever thought quite so much of me as you did."

"Oh, now he's feeling all sorry for himself," came Haines Barber's voice. He was, as Beck expected, the one with the vibra-saw. "You tried to join us of your own free will. You started that torus quake of your own free will, too. You could have knocked the whole habitat apart. So don't try and come across as the injured party."

"You know, Haines," Beck said calmly, "I am going to advise you, strictly as a friend and ally, to shut up."

Haines blustered visibly, rippling his suit.

"Or what?"

One of the three with laser rifles raised it.

"Everyone just settle down," came Kuende's voice. "Dara, lower the fucking gun. Haines, take the man's advice and shut up. I don't need you turning a difficult situation irretrievable. And Beck, stop sounding so put-upon. Yes, I kept secrets from you. The situation was moving so fast I couldn't keep up. It wasn't so much I was deliberately keeping you out as trying to figure out the right time to bring you in. If it helps, I'm sorry."

She waited a moment to give relative calm a moment to settle. "Alright then. I suppose you know what you're looking at," she said to Beck.

"Solar sails. And I'm thinking that if I keep nosing around, I'm going to find the material for frames, and mounting points on the hull to attach to and control them with. I was wondering why you missed your production schedules so badly. But I still don't understand. To move a small ship somewhere beyond reach of Earth, it's arguably doable. But this much nanomesh, it must cover an area the size of, I don't know ... Texas?"

"In the initial deployment. Later on, close to twice that."

"You're planning to move the whole damn cylinder?"

"That's the plan."

"But just to deploy a system like that — not that I've ever done it, any more than you have — my God, it will take three weeks at least. And then to move something like the *Hawking* out of range of Earth destroyers, with the initial velocity about the pace of a languid ant ... I presume you've done the calculations, but what are we talking here? Three months? Best case?"

"Good guess," asserted Kuende. "Deploying the sails, though, that part we should be able to complete in seven days. That is, if we can get pretty close to every Rigger in the colony working on it."

"Which was where I came in."

"Originally."

"And when were you going to tell me?"

"We didn't know if it could even be done at all."

"You still don't."

"No, but the more we go over the figures, the more we think we have a good shot at it. *If* we can get the labor force, and *if* we can keep Earth from stopping us. We didn't know how long it would take you to get the Riggers ready to cross the line. We didn't know if you'd go along with it at all."

"And so you decided to put me in a good mood." Well, he had allowed for the possibility.

Of course Beck couldn't read her expression behind her faceplate with five headlamps shining in her eyes, but he got the expression Kuende winced.

"Can we talk about that part in private, please? Look, Beck, it's all happening too fast. You did get the Riggers fired up, but you got Earth fired up too. None of this is happening according to any schedule we could have planned. We've been trying to play catch-up, and coming up with a lot more bold declarations than concrete plans. In truth I kept things from you because, well, I didn't know what I needed you to do."

You seemed sure enough in the glider, Beck thought sourly. "This is great. You started down the warpath with no idea in hell how it was going to play out. Was that why you sabotaged the lattices? To force me to join you?"

"It seemed like a good idea at the time. But I swear we never expected anyone to get killed."

He shook his head. "And these are the people who are going to take an unfinished cylinder out of orbit. So do I have this right? You were counting on me to accomplish what you needed done without even telling me what that was?"

Haines couldn't hold himself in any longer. "Hey, *we* didn't fuck up the *Banneker*. That's what threw everything off schedule."

"Haines!" Kuende snapped. "All of you. Listen. If it wasn't for Beck, the toruses would still be saying that even passive resistance needed a lot more debate. That we can even talk about the things we're talking about here isn't because Haines was so snide, or the rest of you struck brave postures. It's because Beck *did* something. In the real world. Don't blame him if reality doesn't always live up to your grand declarations. It didn't for us, it didn't for him."

Beck eased back from his contemplation of grabbing Haines' saw and cutting his head off with it. Kuende probably wouldn't like it.

"So how was this supposed to work? You wanted the Riggers to fight off the Marines. While you were deploying the solar sails?"

"Something like that."

"And then they'd be left behind to deal with the consequences."

"That was one of the parts we still haven't quite worked out," Kuende said uneasily.

"But leaving that aside, just where would you go? The asteroid belt? If Earth could take over the toruses, it could still reach you there, eventually."

"The plan was actually to slingshot around the Sun and head for Jupiter. We can be there in one point three years. With its current range of taboos, it will be decades before Earth can possibly reach us there."

"Maybe."

"And in the meantime we can fit the *Hawking* to move further on."

Beck was incredulous. "Further on into what?"

Kuende waved her hand above and behind her. "Out there."

"You mean space? The Big Empty? That's insane. You're talking about a generation ship. The *Hawking* was never meant to be that. You'll all die."

"What the *Hawking* is now and what it could be in fifty or eighty years are radically different concepts."

"And that's the dream you want the Riggers to sacrifice their lives for."

"No," Kuende protested. "We're hoping they'll come with us. There is more than enough room. We need their skill and their ingenuity. We need their *dreams*. Your dreams, Beck. You know they've been stifled here. Share your dreams with us. With me."

Be very, very careful here, he warned himself. "Why do I think you're still lying to me? Is it just because you're so damn good at it?"

"Beck please." She sounded genuinely distressed, but who knew what that meant? Not him, apparently.

"Beck please what?" he prompted.

She hesitated, then shrugged her shoulders. Which through the suit with its several layers showed as barely a twitch. "All right. We have fitted rockets to masses of—"

"Kuende!" cried Haines.

"He already knows, Haines. Or is it just a suspicion?" she asked.

"In your case, suspicion is enough. Aside from Haines showing an obsession with rocks, the *Hawking*'s inventory lists a number of heavy-duty thrusters that I noticed aren't where they're supposed to be. Sloppy record-keeping?"

"It's not what you're thinking," she insisted. "We've attached rockets to clumps of ore waiting to be processed and spread them in a wide orbit, yes."

"To bombard Earth?" Beck asked incredulously. "To produce another mass extinction?"

"No! What do you think we are?"

"You don't want to know."

Kuende made a gesture of appeal that in the bulky suit produced a rare appearance of clumsiness. "The ore, the only bodies we attached thrusters to, are clusters of smaller rocks. The clusters will start breaking apart almost as soon as they start moving. None of the individual rocks has enough mass to make it through the atmosphere. But when they burn up they will create the most spectacular light show you can imagine. Just a warning. How does Earth know we can't send down anything larger?"

"How can I?" Beck interrupted.

Kuende ignored that. "The display will draw off any destroyers Earth chooses to launch. They'll have to use their firepower to break up the clusters, to be sure some larger rocks don't get through. That should keep them busy until they can no longer reach us. Even after the last cluster is destroyed, how can Earth be sure? I tell you, Beck, this can work. The plan isn't fool-proof, but it's not simply foolish, either."

He heard Haines sigh into his helmet. "Any more secrets you'd like to tell him, Kuende? I can't think of any offhand."

She ignored him. "I've told you everything. Now in turn I'm asking you to swear that you're still on our side. Or *my* side, if that still makes a difference after the way I misled you."

It made more of a difference than he wanted to admit to himself.

"What she means to say," Haines interjected, "is knowing all this, are you going to go running to Space Command and try to get a pardon for selling us out? Because if you are...."

Beck couldn't help himself. He'd been using his thrusters to hold himself tighter to the bale than he needed, in case of trouble. Now he launched himself at Haines. Caught with his mouth typically open, Haines didn't have time even to decide if he'd really use his menacing saw. The impact knocked him tumbling into the darkness. The saw stayed in Beck's hands.

The three with laser rifles swiveled toward him.

"No!" shouted Kuende. "No shooting!"

But that wasn't really an issue because the two further away had their line of fire blocked by the third, whose rifle was spinning off following a backhand blow from the saw. In an instant Kuende was upon them, grabbing the barrels of their guns and pushing them up.

"Everyone *stop!*"

Grudgingly, everyone did. As Haines came jetting slowly back, Beck handed him the saw. For a moment the scene went very tense, then Haines looped the weapon over his back by its sling.

"So how about this for a plan?" Beck suggested. "Why not kill me — shouldn't take more than fifteen or twenty of you — turn my body over to Space Command, and tell them you're good responsible citizens who won't have your pristine environment contaminated by a saboteur? All of President Whitfield's boasts about how he's going to come up and get me will suddenly prove true. He'll be too busy admiring himself on television to give you a second thought for weeks. It would buy you some time. And since I'd be dead, I couldn't reveal your deathwish — excuse me, plan — to spirit the *Stephen Hawking* away to the deeper reaches of the solar system."

Haines turned toward Kuende. "Am I missing something here? I mean, it sounds good to me. Bit of a cheap shot on our part, but oh well. Only, why is *he* suggesting it?"

"To show us that there's grounds for mistrust on both sides," Kuende explained. "Okay," she told Beck. "Point taken. Now tell me something. Me, personally. Are you still on our side? I know we may have disagreements over this and that, but in the plan itself, the dream, are you willing to help us?"

Man, did that ever come with a lot of fine print.

On the other hand, Kuende was asking him for his promise to her. Personally.

And at the moment that counted for a lot more than it really should.

"Yes," Beck replied. "I'm on your side."

"Kuende...." Haines whined.

"That's settled, then. All right everyone, back to the cylinder. Beck, you're with me."

Chapter 25

THE TWO OF THEM said nothing as they swam back through the open channels amid girders bristling with modules and the immense gantries and motors of the manufacturing cylinder. They entered the *Hawking* at close to the center of the bulging endcap. Coming through the airlock, they shed their suits, oxytanks, and jetpacs, which would all be recharged and held ready. In a habitat, even one so vast as the *Hawking*, you were never far from a suit.

Kuende, more familiar with the layout, led Beck with a purposeful dogpaddle along the handholds to a series of rooms familiar to the zero-g sectors of all the habitats. The doors and walls of the corridor glowed with shifting patterns of lights in a sinuous, rhythmic interplay.

Of course Beck knew what their destination was, and his only reaction was an urge to get there faster. Trust and mistrust, pie-in-the-sky visions and all too realistic obstacles ... Maeda ... all that that was relegated to a world he could deal with some other time. Kuende was *now*. All other considerations had to fit themselves around her.

Kuende slid her ID card into the lock and a door clicked open. Inside was a compact room with cushioned surfaces of light purple fabric. Scents could be set to a wide range of natural and perfumed fragrances. Kuende punched in Ocean Shore. The slightly salty tang and hints of sea breeze melded with the swaying motion from nets of silk-textured ribbon shifting through all the colors toward the red end of the spectrum.

The internal air currents could be set to a greater or lesser turbulence, according to how many random shifts and turns you desired in your sexual encounters. Kuende swung the dial all the way up. Almost by the time the door clicked shut behind Beck, she was out of her clothes. Swinging off one of the nets, she knocked him back into the cushions, where she soon had him out of his.

She was sleek as a fish, and nearly as flexible. Rays of light swung across the room, turning sections of her brown skin mauve, golden, sea-green, and an infinitely deep and beckoning shadow.

The two of them were at each other like hungry sharks. In free-fall they twisted around each others' bodies, making full use of touch, taste, and scent. The air currents bounced them gently around the nets. By the time they got themselves aligned enough for him to enter her, there was very little of Kuende Adebayo left unexplored.

They clung face to face, kissing, as they ground around each other, their groins pressed as tight together as their mouths. Zero-g intercourse ran to the circular, since too exuberant a back-and-forth motion could bump you toward opposite sides of the room.

But after she bit down hard enough to give him a bloody lip, Beck backed his face away. A few drops of red blood smeared her cheek. He found it erotic, not that he needed much more in the way of stimulation. The rest of his body seemed to gather itself in his groin. Where his *hara* was supposed to be there churned a concentrated ball of sexual urgency.

Kuende pushed her upper body back from his chest, locking herself in place with her legs around the backs of his thighs. She uttered repeated moans, all ending on a sudden deepening close to a snarl. She gripped the flesh over his ribs. Beck made a point of keeping himself in shape and hadn't thought there was much there to hold onto, but the strength of her grip plucked loose enough to anchor her.

They were drifting, turning, bouncing off the cushioned walls, sliding along the nets, but never once ceasing the now tight, forceful orbits of their sexuality. Beck wished her upper torso was nearer because he had a sudden desire to bite her shoulder.

And then another random wind moved them. The top of Kuende's head bumped into a wall or ceiling or floor, he couldn't tell. Just hard enough for him to feel the impact transmitted through her body into his groin.

That did it. For some reason the impact released her into a shuddering, stuttering, body-waving climax that set off his own. As well as bouncing them around the walls and nets like billiard balls.

For a long time, it seemed, Beck floated in another dimension. An enormous energy had built within him, then been discharged like lightning from a storm cloud. Now he felt a deep, massaging relaxation spread from his groin throughout his body.

Then she was kissing him again, and that was alright, too, sore lip and all.

***

"WHEN YOU SAID 'LOVE'...." Beck began tentatively.

"I think I did say 'sort of.' The part about more than anyone else in the past few years, though, I meant it. Come on, don't tell me you were picturing us growing old surrounded by worshipful grandchildren."

That brought his spirits down a notch. The idea of growing old, with anyone, was looking distinctly naïve.

They floated side by side, naked, their toes hooked in the ribbon netting. Kuende had dialed down the air currents, but an occasional zephyr stronger than the rest would lift them from their predominantly horizontal position and stand them up straight, so that they would have to extend their arms to fend off the cushioned wall. Despite the airflow, the scent of sex still dwelt comfortably in the room, merging into the ocean tang.

"I seem to remember you saying something about love yourself," she pointed out. "And that was even before we screwed in the back of that glider. Of course, men are always a lot freer with expressions of love when they're still trying to get into your pants."

"I actually think I might have meant it at the time. Sort of."

And that was true, though not greatly to his credit. New dreams, life on the edge, the admiration of a younger woman — not that twelve years was exactly Spring and Autumn — a seasoning of fear, always heady stuff, and....

And face it. A change from a life you felt closing in on you. Including Maeda.

"And now?" asked Kuende.

Yes, exactly. And now?

"You know, I think I really do."

"Well don't get carried away with it. We still have a job to do."

"I haven't forgotten."

Unfortunately. And maybe that too was part of it. The way his life was now, Kuende Adebayo looked to him like a liferope. Not to drag him free of the shoals and reefs surrounding him; such passivity was alien to his nature. Just the one single thing he was sure of. The one center around which he would arrange everything else.

She might possibly betray him; she might be lying to him even now. That didn't matter. What Beck held onto was that he knew what he felt about her. Maeda, his problems with Space Command, not to mention President Whitfield, getting the Riggers to revolt, sailing the *Hawking* free of L5, every one of these subjects came with mountains of problems, conflicts, and indecision.

Whereas Kuende, yeah, he loved her. She could pull a pistol out of the clothes still waving around in the breezes from the ventilators and shoot him right now, it wouldn't matter. He'd be disappointed. But he'd still love her.

And that was just so luxuriantly simple.

He swung sideways and kissed her. He'd meant the gesture to be affectionate, but she turned it into something else. Which was fine too.

"Getting ready for the rematch?" she queried.

He was about to demonstrate his affirmation when an antic idea crowded in on him.

Dammit, *nothing* in his life was simple!

"In a minute, yeah, I'd like that. Only about this job you tell me we still have to do."

"Yes?" She appeared surprised he'd change the subject. He was himself.

"There's no way you're going to get the Riggers to stay behind and cover your retreat from Earth. If that's what you were counting on me to do, forget it. What you're telling them is: your dreams don't matter. Only ours. And *those* dreams you should be willing to die for, because we're the future and you're the past. You really think I can sell them that? Hell, if I even began, I'd stop being Beck Egan on the instant. They'd all see me as a sell-out."

Kuende looked abashed. "I suppose you're right. See, our perspective tends to get so narrow. Once you start telling yourselves that you are the future of humanity, then if you aren't very careful, everyone else starts having no purpose but to help you achieve escape velocity. It's not like that hasn't occurred to me. It's even occurred to Haines. But we couldn't see any way around it. So we...."

"So you seduced me to see if I could come up with something."

She pushed him away. "No. We may have flattered you, but as for seducing you ... whatever else you may think of me, I do *not* fuck anyone just to manipulate them. Not ever. That part of my life I keep for myself alone. When I make love to someone, I damn well mean it."

"That part," said Beck, "I believe. So okay, I'm sorry. But look at the rest. I remember when a lot of you first came up to help construct the *Hawking*. You forgot how expensive it is to transport anything up out of the gravity well, so you brought a whole big bunch of attitude along. Like you believed Newton's laws would change themselves just for you, since the fact that you all had the same ideas proved you were so much smarter than anyone was or had ever been. It took a few fatalities — way too many, and I remember every one of them every day of my life — before anyone would start to listen. I suppose you thought my generation were just lackies to Earth. Too small-minded."

"Too small-minded, no. We, most of us anyway, didn't think that. That's not fair. Subservient" — he heard her sigh uncomfortably — "well, don't you think you were?"

He grimaced. "Yeah, maybe we were. But that doesn't mean you should have tried to manipulate us with one set of dreams while holding onto another. You had no right to write us off that way. Nor to cast us as sacrificial lambs good for nothing but to help you escape Earth. You never earned that. You may have had your heads in the stars, but your feet were standing on the structures *we* built for you."

Kuende shuddered, an action he found erotic despite the circumstances. "We got too wrapped up in our own fantasies. Too clannish. That's the danger with conspiracies. Once you reach a comfort zone, it looks too dangerous to widen them. So what now?"

"So now you have to accept the Riggers as full participants. You have to tell them straight out you mean to sail the *Hawking* out of L5. And if they won't go along, you either have to leave them out of it or try to fit your plans to theirs. Even if that means delaying the grand plan. No, be quiet. You already lied to me once, so that I'd lie to them. Now I'm going to tell them the truth. So you either find some way to live with that, or you kill me."

"I would never do that. Or allow anyone else to. No matter what."

"There is one way for this to work. And that's for everyone concerned to know the truth, and be equal participants. Meaning, we *all* fight to hold off Earth, if that becomes necessary. Your people don't hold back while they fit solar sails. And we *all*, everyone who wants to, get to leave on the *Hawking*."

"But how many will agree to that?" she protested. "To venture into space in a habitat never designed for it? The Riggers, most of them, have families. They'll never agree."

"Maybe, maybe not. But the offer must be made. And they will decide on their own just what they want to do about it."

"And so we'll end up with you and ten others on our side? Beck, you are dooming this plan to failure."

"Your plan was doomed from the start. Because you never even *tried* to sell your dream. You tried to con me so that I would con the Riggers. And it almost worked, because Theron Whitfield and Space Command have been working overtime to push them, and me, over the edge. But to make it work, you had to *inspire* them. Only I'm not an inspirational guy."

"You're the closest thing to a hero in L5," she countered, rather sulkily. "Where else were we supposed to turn?"

"I'm *not* a hero. I've been doing a lot of redefining lately—"

"You never struck me as particularly the introspective type. No offense."

"I mean in actual deeds, not what I thought about them. Call it another generational difference."

"Do we even still *like* each other?"

"Incompetence, indecisiveness ... betrayal ... no, I'm no hero. No dreamer, either. I see them, maybe reach for them ... but in the end I'm just a grease monkey with a lot of time in a space suit. Dreams always float away from me. Except maybe this one right here." He stroked her arm, but though she did not pull away from him, neither did she make any response. "But no matter. What you need is a true dreamer. One who can inspire others with that same dream."

She stared at him curiously. "Any idea where we can apply?"

"As it turns out, I may."

They drifted side by side in silence for a while.

"*I* thought you were a hero," Kuende said at last. "I've seen better in vids, but...." She twisted around as if trying to survey all the habitat, perhaps all L5, easily shifting her toes in the ribbon netting to hold herself in place. "I needed one here. For me, just for me. Because I've been trying to be a hero. And you know? It gets lonely."

She considered him. He awaited her verdict.

She leaned forward. They embraced. His penis stirred in her public hair.

"Oh hell," she said. "I guess you're at least as close as I am."

Chapter 26

It had been some time — exactly how much she was surprised to find she couldn't remember — since Maeda last left the *Banneker*. Several years ago Beck had urged her to see the *Stephen Hawking* as it was being built, but she always put him off. With so much of the structure still being framed out, it looked too open. A spider web about to get parted by the stars.

In truth she had developed a fear of open space.

Now, however, as the transport sailed toward the *Hawking* she stared out the window from her mesh couch and was exhilarated to find flying through space in a small craft no longer frightened her. No longer made her feel that her flesh was slowly evaporating into the vacuum, leaving her more and more transparent.

There was still a sensation of expansion. But mental rather than physical, and it carried with it an ebullience of infinite possibilities yet beyond naming. Even though Maeda knew she as an individual could not live to see a fraction of the wonders that glinted in her mind, just seeing, *feeling* them made her part of a quest. Immortalized, in a way, by destiny.

For the first time in years, she felt she belonged. Where, she couldn't exactly say. But somewhere. Somewhere, or something, vast and alive.

The transport docked at one of the spaceports built into the skin of the cylinder. Coming through the airlock Maeda found herself easily adapting to the mild spin that moved her as soon as she touched a surface.

Beck met her in the waiting area, along with a tall, willowy black woman with an unusual mix of determination and gentleness in her eyes.

Maeda knew at once that Beck and the black woman were lovers. Was she jealous?

Not that she recognized. Nor resentful. In fact it struck her as odd how far the distance between her and Beck had opened that the fact that he had betrayed her, if it could truly be called betrayal at this stage of their marriage, did not seem in any way significant.

Though she found himself wishing him well, Maeda did not wish Beck happiness. It came clear to her now that happiness had never been at the center of his quest. Only striving.

They'd grown so far apart. And yet Maeda still felt a twinge of anxiety at the thought that Beck would no longer be standing behind her.

She did wish him that ease she remembered love-making — and love? — could bring.

After a quick awkward glance at each other, Maeda and Beck did not hug. Well, friends did not always hug in one-eighth g; it could be embarrassingly awkward to get unentangled again. But lovers always did, and married couples most often.

The willowy woman shook hands, careful not to start Maeda bobbing up and down with her obviously greater strength. She introduced herself as Kuende Adebayo. Which Maeda already knew; Kuende had not yet grown quite so notorious as Beck in the toruses, but her name was still frequently heard.

"Another craft followed us," she told Beck and Kuende. "It wasn't marked, but I'm assuming it was Space Command police. They've been trailing me nonstop. Should you even be here?"

Kuende displayed a gentle smile modulated by soft, full, lips. She conveyed an extraordinary sense of warmth and unconcern. She was one of those women who somehow bypassed all conventional ideas of pretty to achieve a distinctive and extraordinary beauty.

"They won't dock," Kuende assured her. "They will demand clearance, but it will be denied. They will try to lock on to airlocks here and there and jimmy the codes, but they will fail. It's become routine. If they try to force the locks with explosives, well, we are prepared for that too. Hopefully there won't be any fatalities. And the Space Command police who were already here before the *Banneker* quake, those we didn't send back to Earth with the thugs, have learned to keep to themselves."

They took an elevator through Interface to the interior surface of the cylinder. As the doors opened Maeda gasped, even though she'd told herself not to act overwhelmed like some Earth tourist.

She'd seen vids, of course. And looked out from the viewscreens aboard the *Banneker* to see the *Hawking* lurking at the center of L5 like a whale amid mackerel. But nothing could quite prepare her for the true immensity of the cylinder. Earth might offer vast expanses, but they were all open, not enclosed and folded back on each other. Seeing the opposite floor so far above through a sprinkling of clouds, Maeda instinctively searched for something to grip onto, lest she float up into the sky.

The landscape itself was remarkable only in its immensity. About two-thirds consisted of forests, lakes, and meadowed hills. Amid them apartments and community centers and sports pavilions and office buildings rose in series of plateaus meant to merge into the curve of the floor. The curve itself was too vast to notice except at a distance.

All this was not, could not, look natural, no matter how many trees and lakes you filled it with. The vastness of it made a mockery of the very human scale the landscape was designed to emulate. Maeda would have much preferred to see a more exotic, even alien landscape, rather than this distortion of all that was natural trying to mimic normality. It kept her unsettled, like a disturbing, repetitive dream that never quite rose to nightmare.

And all those people directly overhead, even if so distant!

She forced a smile. "It's all very grand."

Beck and Kuende Adebayo cast half-hidden looks at each other. She wasn't fooling them.

Catching that conspiratorial glance, she knew they wanted something from her. When she'd received the original invitation from a messenger, she'd assumed that since she and Beck had parted so unexpectedly, he wanted to see her. If only to regularize what they both knew to be true: that their time together had come to an end. He couldn't very well come to the *Banneker*. The *Hawking* might reject Earth police, but the torus, though filing complaint after complaint, had not been so resolute. People muttered darkly about a police state, and Space Command did not trouble itself with denials.

But this was no friendly parting gesture. Beck, who had always been so concerned for her, and Kuende Adebayo, who came across as wanting nothing more than to be her beloved, protective sister, could not hide their conspiratorial air.

They meant to make use of her.

***

"Is THIS WHERE YOU live?" Maeda asked, as Beck ushered her into a sculpted chair and pulled up another opposite. The chairs were red and purple, which jangled her. The walls of the apartment, once Beck turned the mood reflectors off, were a beige just crying out for something to relieve their heavy dullness, but the only picture to be seen was an old NASA print of colliding galaxies, standard issue at L5. Most settlers replaced them with some style of Earth scenes, locally produced, generally dripping with sentimentality for forests, now largely dead, and ocean beaches, which these days were as likely to break on the deserted borders of flooded cities as sand.

The near-bareness of the room was most suitable for a fugitive, which certainly fit Beck's status. The most wanted man in space or Earth, from what Maeda gathered.

"I don't generally stay in the same place more than a day or two," he told her. "Mostly I'm down in Interface somewhere, with all the pipes and flues and filtration stations. Fascinating place, really. I remember building some of it. I don't surface all that often in case there are some Earth agents among all those cathedral-builders. Not that they're likely to dare try anything, but we're trying to avoid trouble. For now."

Beck leaned forward in his purple chair, forearms on knees with hands steepled, the very picture of calm reflection. "You've been creating quite a stir aboard the *Banneker*."

"You didn't call me here just to say hello, did you? Let alone try to get back together."

The steepled hands spread philosophically. "No. You're here because in a few days at the most you would have been arrested for sedition and sent back to Earth. Among other reasons."

"And you and Kuende Adebayo? Or am I just imagining things?"

"No, you're not."

Strange how much that could still hurt her, when she knew she'd lost Beck long before. "Well ... all the best."

"Thank you. You've been creating quite a stir over on the *Banneker*. In all the habitats. Healing the sick and calming the fearful. And starting up all sorts of dreams and speculations. Which Earth was not going to tolerate much longer."

"That's all been exaggerated. It's nothing I wanted. It just came to me, during that torus quake. And now people are making up whole philosophies, half of which I can't even understand, and attributing them to me."

She saw him wince, wondered if he'd been involved in all that terror and carnage of the *Banneker* quake. It seemed like the sort of thing he'd get involved in. For a man famed for his cool-headedness in crisis, Beck had never lost that reckless, violent streak.

Now he wanted something from her, and Maeda guessed it would be something of the same nature. His love for her had always rendered him the most gentle of men. But now he loved someone else. And looked at objectively, as Maeda was seeing him now, Beck Egan could be downright scary.

"I still don't understand it," she said, trying to make light of what had happened. I don't know what it is, or how long it will last."

"You can't run away from it, Maeda. Between Earth thinking you're part of the grand scheme to subvert L5, and more colonists every day seeing you as some kind of healer and prophet, you've lost control of your own fate. Like I have. To try and hide at this point would take a hole so deep it would swallow you up."

Even more frightening, because undoubtedly true.

"Oh Beck, I was just trying to ease people's fears, that was all. I had concussion, and the quake had just struck and everything was very strange. Now I'm being told I have psychic powers. I *don't*."

He cocked an eyebrow. "You sure about that?"

"Yes!" Pause. "Or if I do, I can't control them."

"Nonetheless, after the quake, an awful lot of people *felt* them. And still do, from what I hear."

"Only some. And I can never tell who it will be. Sometimes I know I won't get through. With people like, well, you. People who either don't have fears in the first place, or have grown so used to living with them, I just sort of slide right off."

They stared at each other, realizing what she'd just said.

Beck abandoned his air of imperturbable logic. Placing his fingers to either temple, he began rubbing like a man trying to dispel a headache.

"I have fears. Only, I always tried to keep them to myself. Still do. I was kind of a cold fish, wasn't I?"

"No, Beck. Not at all. In those early years I felt like we'd melded together. I was so happy."

"Well, I'm proud of that, anyway." He gazed wistfully at her. "You were so sensitive, like there were these hidden currents all around bearing parts of life I'd never seen before. So beautiful. I guess maybe I hid behind the role of protector. Instead of, well

...." To her utter amazement, a sob broke out of him, quickly suppressed. "Husband. Lover. Friend. I've always thought I was so loyal. Like that's just who I was. But the truth is ... I've betrayed you." Wistfully, but not with love.

"Don't think of it like that. This, us, ended years ago. You still tried to play the protector. And I'm grateful to you, because I came to need that. But I ... I don't know, really."

"You had other places to be."

"Yes. I suppose that's true.

Taking in a great draught of air through his mouth, he blew it out through puckered lips. "Okay, we both played our part. It was still a lot to lose."

"Yes." This was too painful. "What do you want from me, Beck? You and ... her."

"Kuende?" Closing his eyes, he gave a quick shake of his head. "What I want, is to use you. There. Short and sweet. I, we, Kuende, the rebels aboard this habitat, we want to use you. There's a movement growing aboard the toruses, and like it or not, you're at the center of it. Right place at the right time, or wrong place at the wrong time, I don't know. I recognize you didn't start it. That is, you never did anything but try to help people. It was others who made it into something mystical. Something ... epochal. But now you are the living symbol of it. Like I'm the living symbol of resistance to Earth. I chose my fate, and yours has been forced on you. For that I am sorry. But what we want for ourselves has become immaterial."

"You're frightening me."

"Yeah, my blood pressure's nudging up there too. But here we are. What we, my friends and I, *want* for you to do, is to spread a vision."

That "my friends and *I*" sent such waves of loneliness sweeping through her she instinctively reached out a hand to steady herself.

"I think," Beck continued, "that it's a vision you already have, in some form or another. But for our purposes it needs to be more focused. In fact it has to fit a sort of schedule. And for that, you have to believe. Because there is simply no falsehood in you. Damn, there's so *much* of you I let slip away."

A low moan scraped through his lips. "But to return," he said, calming himself with that cold efficiency that had once both attracted and intimidated her. "That intrinsic honesty, that sincerity of yours, with all that's been going on around us, it has become a force in its own right. Kuende understands that. So I'm going to tell you the truth. And if having heard it you don't believe in the vision behind it, then well and good. You're free to do as you will. Except return to the *Banneker*. Go back there, and you are days from an Earth prison. Maybe hours."

"You say you want me to promote a vision. How? By preaching in the streets?"

"No. Just by believing in it, like I said. If you can. And let nature take its course."

"What are you talking about?"

Beck looked profoundly uneasy. "A lot people think that you are influencing the way people think throughout L5. Just by having your own visions."

"That's crazy," Maeda protested. "Beck, I don't even *have* a vision! If I was some kind of prophet, wouldn't I know it? Right or wrong, wouldn't I be convinced I saw the future?"

"You've had your moments. In fact I believe you actually are, in some form or another. I don't know how far it will reach. But Maeda, understand. We're coming up fast on the sharp end here. Earth has to be repelled. I don't know if we can do that even with your help. But I'm pretty sure we can't do it without."

Her mind filled with a kaleidoscope of possibilities. All the ideas that had risen up within her ever since the quake, or even before. Half-formed, seeming to contradict each other often as not, ideas about the future of the mind, the future of humanity, vague glimmerings about evolution and AI, however disorganized the mass, it all pointed in one direction.

The future.

Space. Not L5. Deep space. The Big Empty.

All her disparate ideas sparked into coherence in one blinding flash.

And vanished almost as quickly. Because taken as individual strands, they didn't fit together any better than before.

But some overarching, all-inclusive idea that lay behind each jumbled fragment, some urge, some yearning, some *hope*, still bound all the rest together.

Maeda knew with absolute certainty that the whole grand scheme, when it finally coalesced according to whatever form chance, passion, possibility, and even a modicum of reality, would mold it to, could only occur here and now.

It was all so simple, really. So terribly simple.

"Do you love me, Beck?" She became aware of their hands still clasped, left them that way. "I don't mean can we start over, anything like that. You and I have had our day. I only want to know … do you love me?"

He went to one knee at her feet. Considered her face carefully. Honestly, she thought, even though with Beck that could be a tricky quality to assess.

"Yes. Yes, I do."

Maeda nodded. She clasped his hand and kissed it.

"That's important to me. It doesn't change anything, but it's still important. I'm scared, Beck. Lonely, and scared. I know you love someone else. That's all right. Just so you'll be there for me."

"To my last breath."

"I will do what you ask, as well as I can. Even though I'm not totally sure how." Even as she said it, a burden of dread lifted from her. So long as you kept trying to hide, so long would the fear hound you. Stop hiding, and all that was left to face was reality.

"Thank you," he said. Still on his knee, he looked about the bare walls as if there was something more he wanted to say, but couldn't quite find the words. "Thank you."

"Oh, wait," said Maeda. "One more thing. Not a condition, but if it could be done, it would make me very happy."

"Name it."

"Can I have my dolphins back? I know it will be tricky getting them here under Space Admin's nose, but that's just the sort of thing you're good at."

He nodded solemnly. "You shall have your dolphins."

Chapter 27

IN THE DAYS FOLLOWING Maeda's arrival aboard the *Stephen Hawking*, the cylinder became a mecca for visionaries and dreamers from all habitats of L5. It all happened with what Beck found astonishing speed and intensity, even though he was the one who'd arranged for something like this to happen.

Many factors went into this widespread expansion. President Whitfield's increasing bellicosity was convincing many that the days of living their own lives as they had always done at L5 were closing fast. Then the torus quake aboard the *Banneker* reminded everyone of the fragility of the environment in which they lived. And how allowing Space Command control of it must inevitably lead to disaster.

The living symbol of all this was Beck Egan. Few colonists believed Beck guilty of anything more than taking the action necessary to save the *Banneker*. Now Theron Whitfield was not only threatening to send troops to remove him forcibly from the *Stephen Hawking*, he also foamed over about reinstating the death penalty, long a pet project of his, and sending Beck on its maiden voyage.

To which he added a new charge: that Beck Egan had so many implants in his brain he'd been reduced to an "animal."

Which meant to the bulk of the population at L5 that in the President's estimation, they were animals too.

So the population of the habitats was primed.

But for all Beck had become entrapped in the hero legend Kuende Adebayo and the *Hawking's* Riggers had hoped he'd assume, he was not in fact the figure who could convince the mass of those currently living at L5 to cast their fate to the solar winds and venture forth in a vessel built to stay in one place.

Because at root, Beck was a Rigger. Long widely respected and now even venerated by many, but a Rigger still. A man who projected courage, competence, even an improvisational flair in novel and hazardous circumstances. All qualities vital for surviving in space. The pragmatic backbone of any dream of radical, solve-it-when-you-come-to-it venture into The Big Empty.

But not a man to inspire such dreams.

In contrast to the fast-spreading legend of Maeda Rao.

She inspired grand dreams.

As to the exact nature of those dreams, as more and more people flocked to the *Hawking*, that became a subject of much debate. For in her private utterances, Maeda could be as frustratingly obscure as the oracle at Delphi.

This did not necessarily work against her. Because while arguments naturally erupted over the meaning of this pearl of wisdom or of that overheard exchange — was she speaking literally or symbolically? Were those her real words or somebody's interpretation? — there came to be a general understanding that these were in fact oracular announcements. Their very ambiguity seeded profundities that could not be expressed in more straightforward language, and were therefore harder to refute.

To that diminishing group of spoil-sports (not to mention 'fraidy-cats) who demanded specifics, her supporters replied: describe transcendence. Describe orgasm.

Some things were better done than debated.

Besides, how detailed a map of the future did you want? Because this future involved the deeper potentials of the human mind. If you demand proof, talk to the people she soothed during and after the *Banneker* quake, and whose pain she lessened.

From this vantage point, implants and all, we could not possibly even guess what the end point might be. That we must leave to our descendants.

But first they must be free. Free to dream. Free to venture where they would.

And free not to have their synapses excised by fascist scum who believed that God invented the AR-15 to render thought superfluous.

So for them to be free, we have to be free.

Throughout the *Hawking* a far-reaching ebullience took hold about the whole idea of the future, even while the present looked increasingly grim.

Maeda herself did not follow much of this. She was coming to think of her role as meditator-in-chief. To concentrate as deeply as she could, and let her subconscious thoughts bubble up. Or possibly, just possibly, disseminate throughout L5. After all, if even now we couldn't know if light was a particle or a wave, how could we define something so ineffable as pure thought?

Unknown to Maeda, Haines Barber and some of his ilk kept pressing Beck and Kuende to impose a more coherent philosophy upon her. One which could be more directly tied to the their idea of revolution *now*. Or at least the day after.

Patience, counseled Beck. Things are going our way. Don't throw crossties on the track.

There was more to Haines' urgings than just a schedule. He wanted to set the groundwork for what Beck could only call a junta.

"Look," he told Beck and Kuende when Beck called him on it. "If we do take the *Hawking* out of L5, we are going to have to achieve total self-sufficiency from Day One. While living in a habitat that hasn't even been fully built yet. Some people are going to say do things this way, others, do them the other. There will definitely be emergencies we haven't planned for. And some of them are going to have to be solved immediately. Without extended debate followed by a vote. When the shit hits the fan, we will need some central authority that can get everyone aboard to move in the same direction, at the same time. Besides, what about the Christian squatters? I accept that we can't offload them without starting a war the minute we tell them to pack their things. But once we're on our own we can't stop everything for them to hold a prayer meeting asking God to tell them what to do."

He had a point.

"The trouble is," Beck countered, "that's just the kind of bullshit that will stop us from ever moving the *Hawking* from L5 in the first place. Right now the dream is spreading. It may not be the same dream in all cases. And yeah, there may be frustrations when we're in a big hurry and different factions want to hold a philosophical discussion. But these are sensible people. They've survived in space a lot longer than you have. When it comes to sticking thumbs into dikes, they move quickly and efficiently. You just have to stop scorning them. Because I tell you this. More and more Riggers are ready to fight the Marines. For the colony. For the dream. *Not* for Haines Barber and a few close friends."

The discussion happened more than once.

And always Kuende sided with Beck.

"All along," she said, "we've refused to trust anyone but ourselves. We did a lot of talking, hatched a lot of plans. And never got any closer to where we wanted to go. Beck's right. We didn't trust the rest of the colony enough to actually talk to them. So we schemed and maneuvered instead. Now you want to add shouting to it. That won't work, Haines. Right now we need quiet. Quiet enough for Maeda Rao's ideas to spread."

"And just what the hell *are* her ideas?" Haines shouted in exasperation. "If there's five hundred people listening to her at any one time, you get five hundred different explanations. And she's such a head case she probably believes every single one of them herself."

Silence clamped down. Kuende put a hand on Beck's shoulder. But Beck wasn't going anywhere.

He saw no point debating it, which was all he was going to do in front of Kuende.

But then one day while out pulsing through the manufacturing sector together inspecting preparations for mounting the solar sails, Beck found himself knocking Haines' head against a flange, pausing only to send two of his friends spinning off into something hard. Though in vain, their attempt at intervention did save Haines' life, because Beck was right on the point of ripping out his air tube. The slight pause for thought gave him time to reconsider.

So he drifted back and allowed Haines' suit, detecting a state of unconsciousness, to administer stimulants to bring him to. It only took a few seconds; though such forced immediate revival produced quite a shock to the system, drifting unaware was not a good survival strategy in space.

As Haines spasmed back into awareness, Beck patted him companionably on the shoulder.

"I think it would be best if we left Maeda out of the conversation," he said, and jetted off.

Whether Maeda truly possessed some quasi-mystical force that inspired all aboard the *Hawking* to turn their thoughts away from Earth and L5 toward a more expansive future, or whether she was just a convenient symbol for an idea whose time had come, the effect was irrefutable. Riggers who had before been reluctant to join with Beck in his attempts to organize resistance to Earth, now accepted it as the only course open to them.

And though no official announcement was ever made, realization began to spread that the *Hawking* was destined to leave L5. Exactly when and how remained vague. Risks and possibilities were debated with fervor, but the ultimate goal itself began to take on all the trappings of revealed faith.

Of course even as this idea spread, many people who journeyed to the cylinder retained doubts and fears. And that was where Maeda's physical influence exerted itself. She could calm almost anyone. Those who interacted with her reported that their fears, hitherto murky though causing a high level of generalized stress, took on clear visual form in their minds.

And just as their terror climbed toward an unbearable pitch, those pictures began to blur. Like having the sharp edges taken off, reported several who'd been through the experience. Until eventually the image would shimmer, and thin, and lose much of its potency.

The report of such experiences confirmed the belief growing through L5 that something unique was occurring here in space. To them.

And damned if Theron Whitfield or a hundred like him was going to strangle it in the crib.

Chapter 28

"It's come," Kuende told Beck.

They stood together on the command platform of the *Stephen Hawking's* main control center. The room itself consisted of three platformed, six-sided levels of screens and workstations. The lower two levels were currently manned; the top consisted of floor-to-ceiling screens. From the raised central platform Beck could see the whole room.

The announcement that Earth vehicles were being readied for launch had come twenty minutes ago.

Watching schematics of the grid powering up, Kuende shook her head. "They finally feel confident enough about their power supply to launch. Space Command admin aboard the *Banneker* has been notified that lift-off begins in forty-eight hours." Space Command computers had long been porous to the Riggers. "Forty-seven, now."

"And President Whitfield hasn't yet started his King Kong routine? I'm amazed."

"Maybe he's watching television and no one dares interrupt."

Who's coming?" Beck asked.

"Six personnel carriers. Assume twenty-four Marines in each."

One hundred and forty-four. Not all that many, really, though plenty enough to produce a tightness in his throat. In fact Space Command probably couldn't muster over three hundred on a good day. Marines were extremely expensive to train and maintain, and until now there had never actually been a clear purpose for them. Most of their training still took place on Earth.

"Any word on whether they'll occupy the toruses, or come straight for the *Hawking*?"

"Sounds like they're looking to board us and take control. Admin at the other toruses has been told to stand by to provide additional supplies for the attack if needed, or to take in damaged ships and the wounded. The main purpose of the warning was to give them a heads-up to have their police ready if there's a demonstration aboard the toruses."

"Any destroyers?"

"Not that we have word of. But they wouldn't necessarily tell L5 Admin. There'd be no point to it. My guess is that they'll launch a few, but only after they're damn sure they've got enough juice on hand to laser the Marines up out of the gravity well. And if we need to we can distract them with a bouquet of middling rocks lighting up the atmosphere."

"Are you ready for this?"

Kuende grinned broadly. "No way. You?"

Beck returned the grin. "Hell no."

Yet they'd known this must happen. As soon as the Riggers started deploying the solar sails out from both end caps of the cylinder, Earth must act to stop them. Whether they were absolutely sure of the power grid or not. Better in Theron Whitfield's view to risk dropping a few carriers full of Marines five or six miles out of the sky then have the *Hawking* sail away while he stood around with his thumb up his butt. Definitely not the way the Duke would do it.

As for the rebels' "plan," Beck had convinced the others to simply start deploying the sails. Riggers throughout the colony didn't need to be told what was going on. Many had already been informed and made their plans. Others took transport craft over from the toruses. The majority brought their families.

It was the moment of truth.

Beck figured the pilgrimage to the stars — well, Jupiter, for a start — might still grow. On the other hand, it might cool off, too. Much of the current idealism was based on idealism. Let Maeda Rao's supposed "vision" get debated too long, and it would break down into factions, some groups refusing to help just out of spite. Right now a sense of wonder still prevailed. So many people feeling they didn't want to wave the dream goodbye, and not yet having sufficient emotional coolness to recognize all the very good reasons they should.

Besides, what was to be gained by letting Earth take the initial action then having to react to it from whatever position you found yourself in? Theron Whitfield's much-heralded attack must come while enthusiasm was still at a peak. That initial surge of indignation would propel a lot people into strong actions they would not subsequently have time to regret until after it was too late to turn back.

That was how Beck saw it.

And by the time he finished talking, the rest of Kuende's hot-heads, who had trouble seeing any strategy outside the context of themselves, were prepared to accept it, though a few like Haines Barber rather grudgingly, as well.

So now they'd see.

Up on the command platform, Kuende checked the screens all around. A few, satellite fed, were turned to the Marines' launch site. No signs of any more activity than usual. The Marines were still in their barracks. The personnel carriers, no more than medium-sized craft that could be towed out and launched quickly, still nested in their open sheds. The real action would be taking place in small offices integrating power grids all across the United States, trying to assure a reliable supply of electricity would be there for the lasers when the time came.

"Not much for anyone to get excited over," Kuende observed. "Should we shut the power sats down now, maybe give Space Command second thoughts?"

Oh, so tempting. "No," said Beck. "We need to get this done while feeling's still at a height."

"Well, the Riggers are doing a splendid job deploying the sails. Are you confident they'll fight once the Marines arrive?"

Was he?

"Yes," he said. "Because they're Riggers. And the dream lives or dies right here. Give up, lose … they won't be Riggers anymore. And there's no longer any way to fool themselves otherwise."

Chapter 29

The Marines had finally launched.

No one knew just where they would attack the *Stephen Hawking*.

Some thought they'd cluster around two or three airlocks, using explosives to force entry.

Beck didn't think so. The locks were mined, and Space Command wasn't quite so dumb they wouldn't have figured that one out.

"They'll attack the sails," he told Kuende, standing in the command center of the Hub, checking the array of screens. "Send the Marines in through the manufacturing cylinder to destroy the anchor points and the motors." Rocket fire would be useless against the sails because it would just punch a few fist-size holes in the giant spread. "Their immediate task is to anchor us in place. Then they can send more Marines up to take the *Hawking* itself. Maybe even ground-based infantry, once they force a lock or two."

"That's not exactly the Marines' most favorable ground, fighting us at close-quarters in zero-g," Kuende pointed out.

"But it's what they have to do."

Kuende grimaced. "This is going to be a bloody business."

"Having second thoughts?" asked Beck. The idea that Kuende Adebayo might be intimidated amused him. Beck himself was fairly humming with energy. Win or lose, he was eager to go into space and fight. Eager to be finished with his old life and get on with the new.

"What good would they do if I had them?" Kuende replied. She gave him a considered glance. "You mean to lead the counter-attack, don't you?"

"Got anyone better in mind?"

"No." She shook her head sadly. "There is no one else. It's just … if anything happens to you, I am really going to miss you."

Beck shrugged. "It's not a call we get to make." He reached out to stroke her face. "You and me, we started something I'd really love to finish. Someday. Over a lifetime, for preference. But we also started something else we have to finish first."

She took his fingers, kissed them. From the corner of his eye he caught Haines Barber sneering at them.

"Well," she said, "let's just believe, okay? In all of it."

A call came up from the control pit, echoing the message flashing across the screen immediately in front of them:

"Solar grids are down. They're lifting on Earth power now."

Beck watched the six troop carriers rise. He tensed, hoping for some of the lasers, that provided the propulsive power by boiling off fuel in a jet chamber, to fail, sending the craft tumbling back to Earth. He felt guilty about wishing such a death on anyone. The Marines, trained in space operations and well harmonized to their equipment, were in most ways closer to the Riggers than anyone on Earth. He could not help scorning that part of himself that wished to see them tumbling and screaming back to Earth in a long, terrifying fall.

Have to get over that, he told himself. Quick. And hope the rest of the Riggers can bottle up any such sentiments as well. We're at war. And if we're going to stand any chance of winning, we have to make ourselves deaf and blind to anything else. Experience *may* give us an edge. But if it doesn't, it will come down to attitude. And those people are warriors. We're builders.

Suddenly he was scared. How did that happen? But still eager to go destroy those invaders who threatened his home.

All six of the silvery, minnow-looking ships made it up out of the gravity well.

"Has she got any impulse at all?" Beck asked Kuende, as the great spread of sails, wider than the cylinder itself, rippled with glints of red and green and yellow under pressure of the sun's photons.

"Hell yeah. We're accelerating toward a thundering hundred meters an hour. Almost."

"Guess we won't outrun them, then. I better suit up."

"I'll go with you."

He stopped, blocking her path. "Kuende, it's all been decided, remember? You're the leader. You have to be someplace you can lead. If we fail, you'll have to hold the people together and assemble the best defense you can. If we succeed ... the *Hawking* will need a true leader. One who can inspire people. And one who will listen to them, too. That's you. Not me, not anyone else."

Haines Barber would make an attempt at it. And doom the whole project.

Kuende had to survive this. He didn't.

They faced each other awkwardly.

"If I ever meant that 'sort of,' I don't any more," she said. "Let me just say straight out I love you."

"Yes. And I never meant that 'sort of' at all."

"Come back," Kuende urged. "Please, Beck. Come back."

"Do my best." There were other priorities, and they both knew it. It still felt good to hear her say it. "Good luck, Kuende."

He turned and walked away before they could say anything more maudlin or, God forbid, kiss. He had too much on his mind to spoil a good kiss. Already his perspective was shifting.

He was going to war.

First time for everything.

Just do your job, Beck told himself. You're Beck Egan. You came by your reputation the hard way. You're strong, decisive, and at least as brave as the next fellow. You're as good in space as anyone, and better than most. And these people who'll be fighting next to you, they're first-rate. Stay alert, and why shouldn't you come back?

Kuende is certainly all you could ever want to come back to.

Meanwhile, that nausea you feel is just your body mobilizing its resources.

***

AFTER MARTIN LAHOYA FINISHED helping him suit up, Beck sat on the bench running along the back of the module with the eight other Riggers, a magnetic clamp on his tank to keep him in place in the near-zero g. They all carried laser rifles or rocket launchers recently fashioned in the manufacturing modules. In addition their suits were variously fitted with shrapnel bombs, vibra-saws, and knives. They fixed their eyes on the screens lining the hull above the row of helmets opposite.

Instead of the usual silver-white, their suits were coated with a non-reflective black, in the manner of Space Command's Marines. It wouldn't help a whole lot, as the Marines had infra-red and radar, just like the Riggers.

But the Marines had to read the data visually on their faceplates, instead of feeling it in their neural nets. And that left them prone to data overload, and maybe a second or two's hesitation.

We can win this one. We can.

Though the module was pressurized everyone wore their helmets. Fitting the exterior mesh that transmitted data from the suit sensors to the Riggers' pigtails was a process best not rushed.

No one said a thing as the screens showed the steady approach of the Marines' white, short-winged personnel carriers. Getting larger and larger even as the magnification shrank.

Beck wouldn't have said he was scared, but he did experience a distinct tightness in his lower abdomen, an elevated pulse rate, and tingling in his joints.

But he was also very, very angry, and growing angrier by the minute. When he'd first watched the Marines' carriers launch from Earth, he'd experienced fellow-feeling even as he hoped the power grid Space Command had cobbled together would fail and drop them a few miles back to Earth.

Now they were of a wholly different species. Demons. Vermin in space suits. To be not defeated, but squashed and exterminated.

He wondered if the approaching Marines felt the same way. Maybe they didn't think in those terms. They were trained as warriors. Likely they had their own ways of coping. Maybe as the craft approached the Marines were telling themselves, it'll be just like another training exercise.

Maybe some of them were looking forward to it.

For all Beck's mounting fury, he watched in near-disbelief as the Earth craft drew closer. There had never been war in space. They were about to cross a line into a totally different future.

I'm not frightened, he told himself, not really.

He repeated the mantra every thirty seconds or so.

It just seemed incredible that in a few moments both sides would pour into space and actually try to *kill* each other.

The white numbers at the bottom of the screens showing the ETA of the approaching ships hit 5:00.

I am not frightened.

Well maybe a little.

He'd so much rather be making love to Kuende.

Right on cue, her picture flashed on the central screen.

"All right, my brothers and sisters, here it comes. You all know what you have to do. Good luck to each and every one of you. Beck? Do you want to say anything?"

She spoke straight into the screen, having no idea which of the two hundred and forty-three black suits spread across the screens of the Command Post was him.

He didn't have anything to say. He'd never been a big rah-rah guy. Work is work. But he got to his feet anyway, looking up into the screen above the workstation.

"We're all Riggers," he began.

Profound. He let the moment hang, watching the viewscreens that showed the Marine personnel carriers skimming along just outside the framework of the manufacturing complex, heading straight for them. The solar sails had been deployed at both ends, but the Marines apparently meant to concentrate their attack at this end. Take out half the sails, the *Hawking's* chance of escape was nil.

With half their people stationed on the other side, the Riggers would start out outnumbered. But as soon as the Marines deployed from their ships, reinforcements would be hurtling down the tramways from the other end.

Beck waited one moment longer, to be sure the Marines' approach wasn't a feint, and they meant to zoom over the cylinder and attack the other endcap after all. But they slowed, rapidly and in unison even though widely spaced around the circumference of the manufacturing cylinder. Good piloting. The craft dipped their tails down toward the frame, giving the impression of snakes rising up to strike.

The bay doors on the bellies of the craft began to clamshell open.

The attack was here, all right.

He addressed the Riggers through their mental channels.

One more job to do, guys. A big one. I am so proud to have spent my life among you.

Then he swung along the handholds toward the door of the module, transmitting on audible:

"Let's go."

Chapter 30

Eight Riggers followed Beck through the outer, airlocked door of the module. Riding the vacuum, they spread out, then glided forward with a spurt of their thrusters. Three hundred meters ahead and above them, twenty-four Black-suited Marines sprang from their acceleration couches to pour like a witches' coven from the upright belly of their personnel carrier, speeding along with the craft's momentum.

Beyond the Marines glittered the brilliant starfield of L5. Beck perceived it with a new freshness, almost like he could breathe it in.

As the war parties closed to two hundred meters Beck couldn't actually see the Marines in their light-absorbing suits. Not on visual. But their thrusters left bright red flares on his infrared, his radar traced their position in wisping lines of green, and the rising ping of echo, quicker to interpret at close ranges, revealed them closing fast.

"Attack from cover," he reminded his group as they powered upward to meet the assault.

Staying in the open would leave them outlined in the Marines' own radar and infrared. And that could trigger their most feared weapon: a flechette launcher that spewed out sixteen slowly spreading needle-point darts, with the initial aim radar-guided. Two, maybe three spikes a suit might be able to patch, and the oxy tank in back could probably deflect them, but any more and they would open too many holes for the suits' auto-seal to close off. Besides penetrating right through the flesh within.

Stop thinking about getting hit, Beck chided himself, and think about hitting something.

A mosquito-like whine inside his helmet told Beck one of the Marines had radar lock.

"Break!"

The group of Riggers darted off at different angles. An infrared flash flowered inside Beck's head, superimposed over the expanding green radar ball speeding toward him. It flashed by scarcely a meter from his leg.

In a moment all his group were behind cover. The manufacturing frame was close-packed with modules, pressurized passageways, electric motors, crane arms, and the superstructure to support it all. In absolute zero none of it registered on infrared, and with all exterior lighting within the cylinder doused, only radar or echo location would map it out before you smashed into something hard.

Beck's suit radar picked up the strutwork, but with such a confused mass he was thrown back to visual readouts. Too slow to be zipping in and out of the maze surrounding him, especially while getting shot at. So he relied on the rising and falling tones of echo-location, virtually *singing* his way through the beams.

He snuggled tightly behind a girder as another green-configured mass of spreading darts came in, then shot by.

Beck found himself terrified. And yet that fear did not affect him, except as a stimulant so sharp it spilled over into a countervailing exuberance. At the same time he wanted to huddle up behind something hard, and charge through open space handing out mayhem. Fortunately, the pulls of the extremes allowed him to settle somewhere in the middle.

Since most of the suit sensors were mounted on the helmet, you had to expose the helmet to get a reading. Clinging to the strut with his knees, Beck gave the mental command "freeze" and stuck out his head. He ducked back almost in the same moment. Nobody shot at him, but if some Marine's radar had been scanning, it might still be locking in on his position, awaiting a second chance.

Since he'd given the "freeze" command, the read-outs from the sensors in the moment he exposed himself presented themselves in a filmy representation on his faceplate. Infrared showed maybe six or seven half-exposed rust-colored clumps crawling down the strutwork sixty meters out. Marines, closing to engage. Radar and echo were too confused to read. The yellow lines of motion detection, still not a mature technology, indicated other objects, presumably Marines, flying past in the distance. Were they going to attack another position, or circle around behind?

"Padachevsky," he called on his vocal channel, since mental transmission under stress could get a wee bit garbled.. "Stay around thirty meters behind us. Keep alert for Marines attacking from the rear." The message was coded on a varying frequency; if the Marines picked it up, they could not decode it in time to do any good.

"Martin, Cass. We need rocket fire to blind their sensors. Proximity's good enough. The rest of you, full thrust on my command. We'll fly past, then loop around and take them from behind."

Risky, but he did not want to get pinned down in a sniper duel. In earlier planning sessions Beck had continually stressed aggressiveness. Repugnant as it might be to his feelings, a battle of attrition favored the Riggers on straight numbers. Also, the Marines' had a clear advantage in long-range fire.

Rockets streamed off from Martin and Cass behind him, bursting around the Marines' positions, though an actual hit was unlikely. Rocket and flechette fire answered back. Beck peered cautiously around the girder, after first drawing himself four meters further up from his last position. Bursts of infrared glowed across his front. The rockets should blind the Marines' sensors, though of course it blinded his as well.

"Now!"

Giving his thrusters a mental command Beck shot from the strut, zooming up and forward. One big advantage the Riggers had over the Marines was that while the Marines had voice command over their thrusters, freeing their hands, the Riggers with their implants could control their own thrusters with mental commands, which were considerably faster and much more instinctive regarding direction.

Beck flew straight into the infrared glow, extending his laser rifle on its shoulder swivel. What lay beyond only visual and echo could tell him. Visual was next to useless trying to pick out the Marines' black uniforms from the black background, and he was flying too fast and the Marines hugging cover too close for him to get enough of a reading to aim by.

Behind him Martin and Cass ceased firing. The glow turned to rust, began to shimmer. The Marines would be locking on him and the others any moment now.

He better pick them up first.

Eighty meters from take-off.

"Loop!"

It was as if his thrumming nerves, not the thrusters, were accelerating him into the roll, an inverted Immelmann where he dove down in a semi-circle, flipping at the bottom.

A mosquito whine.

Beck did another, tighter, upward loop. Green streaks flew past.

Spinning at the top he located a heat signature. At the same instant echo danced humming off a projection along a girder twenty meters away. Mentally Beck joined the two and thought, *"fire!"*

A yellow-orange line shot out ahead of him. As he swooped in behind, it stayed constant on its target.

Infrared spurted in gouts from his target lock.

Suit breach. The heat signature quivered like a column of smoke caught by a sudden gust of wind; the shaking of the Marine's suit as the pressurization whiffled out it.

A dead man. Or woman.

Green lines throbbed in from below and left. Panic, then the realization that they were moving too slow to be a clutch of flechettes.

Marine, or Rigger? The Riggers had left their transponders off because there was no way to shield them from the Marines' sensors.

Beck didn't dare fire. Instead he zoomed toward the nearest girder, hoping to work above the approaching figure until he could determine what it was.

A scream in his earphones.

Then Cassie's voice, on a different channel: "Suit breach! I have a suit breach."

"Whoever's closest, help Cassie," Beck ordered. "Carefully."

The girder was closing fast. Beck waited till the last moment, rotated to hit feet first, then braked hard with his thrusters.

Impact, harder than he intended. Had the suit not been powered his legs would have been broken. Still, the sudden deacceleration sparked a flash of yellow across his eyes. His head spun from the sudden surge of blood to his brain, then cleared. Mostly. Enough that he maintained thrust to keep from bouncing off the girder and giving some Marine an easy target. A clutch of green lines shot by, very close. One deflected off his helmet with the loudest clang he'd ever heard. Again he saw yellow flashes.

And heard another scream.

"Get Cass to an airlock!"

Why had he said that? What else did he think anyone was going to do? The question was if anyone was in position to do anything at all. Her suit would self-seal — up to a point. Beyond that point you'd be blind in ten to thirty seconds, and your lungs would explode in ninety, if you could hold your breath that long.

Meanwhile, the pressure venting from a major breach would make it almost impossible to control your own flight.

And the scream?

Someone dead. Probably Cass.

Primal anger surged through Beck. One of his people gone. *His* people. His Riggers.

Beck locked onto the girder with the sides of his boots and leaned out.

Amid the clutter of strutwork below him he saw nothing of his own people except dull, shifting blurs of infrared maneuvering behind girders, and one suit — a Rigger's suit — drifting slack, leaking heat. Two Marines likewise drifted. Two more Marines were twisting around their girders like snakes, shooting off flechettes in a frenzy while trying to dodge laser fire that came at them from several directions.

Two or three more of the enemy remained outside his perception. Where, dammit, *where?*

One way or the other he'd find out. For now he was the one best positioned to take out the Marines below.

Clumsily, more so than his thick gloves would explain, Beck worked loose one of the shrapnel bombs hooked to a bandolier crossing his chest. Two safeties; manual and mental. He thumbed off the one, thought the four-number code for the other.

Generating power from the waist and shoulder since his legs wrapped the girder, he hurled the bomb toward one of the Marines below. Tracking on infrared and motion, he issued a mental command and burst the bomb as it drew opposite the Marine. Infrared flashed bright enough to trigger his faceplate filter.

Knocked loose from his perch the Marine spun, twisting crazily upward, waving his arms and legs as he tried to get his orientation and his thrusters in alignment. Before he could manage the task, three lasers converged on him, leaving him dead and twitching as heated red air rushed out through the gaping rents in his suit.

Beck ignored the other Marine, who was still shooting. He peered around searching for the others he'd lost track of. Feeling them right behind him no matter which way he turned.

Echo pinged like a ballpeen hammer in his head. From left and above. Close, much too close.

Green lines showed a shape swooping down like a hawk on a mouse. Echo climbed in staccato notes. Beck was already jetting away at the jetpac's best imitation of Warp 10.

The very quickness of his release threw him to the right. At this speed it would be too hard to swing back under cover without going into a feedback loop of over-corrections.

He watched the red shape trail green lines as it swerved after him. He fired his laser but they were crossing each other too fast in a shallow X pattern and the yellow-orange line appeared to swerve behind the target.

The mosquito buzz crescendoed as the Marine's radar zeroed in. The buzz turned to a shrill ululating whine. Target lock.

Beck did a number of things all at once, through mental commands and gyrations of his body. He swerved right, hoping to gain a half-second before the radar locked on again. Then, holding his breath, he waved back in toward the Marine's last target lock.

A clutch of darts shot past, so close he couldn't believe they'd missed him, and wasn't sure they had.

Weaving like an eel, Beck drove upward. It was counter-intuitive, but the less distance between him and the Marine, the less time it gave the radar to secure a lock.

His sensors were going mad. For one of the very few times in his life he suffered information overload and could not interpret the data coming in. Going against an instinct born of fear, he maxed out his thrust.

Something smashed into him. The Marine had been diving while he climbed. They caromed off each other, cutting their thrusters at once because their bodies were starting to tumble and the thrusters could turn you into a human pinwheel, the g's knocking you unconscious within seconds.

They were flying fast, no more than three meters apart, and who knew what lay ahead because they had no time to look. Beck was too busy to register his own panic, but adrenalin was about to shoot out his ears.

The Marine brought his flechette gun into line. Beck braked hard and flipped to put his pacs and helmet between him and the muzzle. An all-embracing *clang* was transmitted through his oxy tank, which he prayed would hold.

But the Marine shot ahead.

Beck cut his thrusters back in and got radar lock on the black shape before him, with the yellow-orange flash of the thrusters on either side.

A human being. Fleeing. Another space-farer, like him.

Beck hesitated.

The Marine pulled hard to the left, all but a right angle. Nicely done.

Beck twisted after him. Visual showed the Marine's back, streaking in a tight curve in front of a mass of girders.

Beck fired.

Red wisps spun off the Marine's back as he kept trying to pull around in a circle too tight for Beck to get target lock.

Then the wisps exploded into a streak of flame as the laser cut through the oxy tank.

The flame pinwheeled as Beck shot past.

He felt nauseous.

Braking, then sheltering behind a girder, he watched as the Marine's suit fabric began to whiffle apart. Vapor shot through the rents, turning at once into ice crystals — blood, and whatever other body fluids were being released. The suit shivered violently from depressurization. Arms and legs spiraled like the arms of a galaxy as the still burning tank drove it out toward the stars.

THIS IS WAR!

It didn't help.

Chapter 31

THE MARINES BECK'S GROUP had engaged were all dead.

So were Galen and Martin. Cass, who'd reported a ruptured suit, was missing. And realistically, dead. The out-venting air from the breach would have lit her up in the Marines' infrared.

The survivors answered his questions in clipped tones. Even in the bulky suits you could detect a huddled quality among them. No one was injured. Savakis had a minor suit breach, but the self-sealing mechanism held.

Two of the Riggers had grabbed a flechette rifle in favor of their own lasers. Beck thought about it. The flechette rifles were a fearsome weapon. But without the helmet of the Marine who'd carried it, you could not get a radar lock and would essentially have to point fire. He passed.

He had never been so tired in his life. He could tell from the voices and postures of the others they felt the same. But they followed him silently toward where the fighting had moved closer to the hull.

The comm channels were revving into the red zone. Riggers were searching for their comrades, searching for Marines who'd shot at them one moment and vanished from view the next, crying out warnings to comrades that the enemy was headed their way.

Occasionally a scream sounded. Or even more chilling: "*Mayday, Mayday, I have a suit breach.*"

Some of the Riggers, especially the young ones, were hearing for the first time a sound most of the older ones knew all too well.

The sound that occurs when a strangled person drifts far enough into agonized semi-consciousness that the breathing reflex finally overwhelms the will. That one cut-off gasp, and the moist, rasping *POP!* of the lungs exploding.

In a suit you might go a long time past the ninety second limit of someone unprotected. You had a mouthpiece on standby to supply pressurized oxygen, barring out the vacuum. If your helmet itself wasn't breached, it could take a while for the absolute zero of space to crawl up through the rents in your suit, freeze your lips and face, and finally the muscles underneath, so that your mouth went slack around the mouthpiece and the vacuum at last seeped past.

Best not to think about it.

Yeah, right.

Deciphering the frantic calls over the comm channels, Beck led his group in toward the cup-shaped end of the *Hawking*, where the solar sails where anchored and controlled.

He and his five survivors jetted past fierce, small-scale creeping and sniping battles along the way, with both sides too closely engaged to break contact without getting shot in the back.

Some of Beck's fighters wanted to stop and pitch in. But he was now in contact with Kuende Adebayo, overseeing the battle from the Command Hub. And sounding atypically nervous. She informed him that the crisis was now at the hull itself. Several groups of Marines from the six ships had fought their way through and were moving ever closer to where they could lock explosives onto the anchor points for the solar sails.

"Haines reports being heavily engaged," she said. "The Marines are pushing their way through to Anchor Three."

Beck wasn't entirely sure what that meant; feeling heavily engaged and *being* heavily engaged could be two different things. But the fact that Haines was so alarmed meant he likely needed help no matter what the actual situation.

"I'm moving in on his position," he reported back, moving on without tender endearments on either side.

A few minutes later she called in to report that the Marines were in the act of attaching a heavy mine to the anchor point.

Beck cursed under his breath. He'd known having only four main anchor points was a weakness. If one of the points lost integrity, the other three could hold the sails on — for a while. But an instability would be created that would eventually lead to harmonic resonance, which would rip the sails to pieces.

By the time he even knew about the sails it had been too late to change the design, but it only reinforced his opinion that when it came to engineering, Kuende's band of rebels, though brave and surprisingly resourceful in some ways, couldn't build a coffee-maker.

As Beck moved in, Haines called. "They're working in to Anchor Three. We're slowing them down, but there are too many of them for us to stop. We need reinforcements now."

"Whether you get reinforcements or not," Beck told him, "you hold your positions or die at them. I'm just a few minutes away."

"Who the fuck do you think you are to tell me what to do?" Haines fired back.

"Haines," Kuende broke in. "Hold your position, or the battle is lost. And do what Beck tells you. With*out* bitching about it."

"Fine, then. I'm ready to hold fucking position, if it kills us all. But you think a whole lot more of that son of a bitch than I do."

"Goddammit, are you going to whine or fight?" Kuende yelled. She didn't usually allow her temper such free reign. "Beck is in charge. You will do what he — *shit!* Look, there's something else I need to take care of." And she switched channels.

Beck sped forward at max speed, weaving and twisting through the superstructure in a most hazardous manner. Several times his group was shot at, but no one was hit and he ordered them not to pause to return fire. He badly wished he hadn't lost Galen, Martin and Cass; experienced Riggers capable of thinking clearly under stress.

And his friends.

Damn, he wished this battle had never happened!

But it had.

Homing in on Haines' channel, he closed in on Anchor Point Three.

Chapter 32

Later, in that period when myths are born more around the needs of the moment than the facts on the ground, it would be said aboard the *Hawking* that Earth's first attempt to stop the habitat failed so badly, it never dared attempt another.

Which might be true. But it certainly didn't feel so one-sided to those doing the actual fighting. To them it remained the most terrifying experience of their lives, with the conclusion unknown until it was finally over. And the list of dead was simply appalling. Heroes to the future, but great gaping holes to those who'd known them in the past.

Several times on his way to hook up with Haines Barber, Beck heard that mosquito whine in his head and twisted violently into evasive action, aware of the green lines of a flechette cluster speeding his way and the girders he had to dodge, narrowly. Fortunately none of his people were hit.

He found Haines and his fighters spread out in a semi-circle around Anchor Three. They had sheltered amid the thick tangle of superstructure clustered around the end cap of the cylinder. A desultory sniping duel was going on with the Marines similarly hidden. In Beck's opinion, neither side showed much initiative.

Were the Marines in fact cowed by the unforeseen demands made on them by this environment they thought they'd been trained for?

Or were they waiting for reinforcements?

His radio told him fighting continued fierce and uncertain all over. The Marines had chosen to attack all four anchor points. And bogged down on all of them. But they'd gotten closest right here. And if they left a holding force on two of the others, they could likely force their way through to Anchor Three.

"How many people have you got?" Beck asked Haines, slithering down the back side of a girder to join him behind the shelter of a clamping point where five beams came together to be braced by a star-shaped flange.

"Nine besides me," Haines replied, peering cautiously out around the flange, not to get visual, which was worthless here, but his other feeds.

"And them?"

"Seven or eight? There were more, but they made a charge toward the anchor point and we depressurized three."

"Okay."

Haines should have made a counter-attack after repulsing the Marines' charge. Now they were locked in target practice. Neither side was going to win any time soon.

Unless the Marines got help.

From occasional flashes of motion or infrared, Beck put the distance between him and the enemy position at sixty to seventy-five meters. He couldn't tell for sure how many of them there were, but he presumed Haines could halfway count, at least.

Now, with Beck's people added, they had fifteen Riggers. Be foolhardy to wait for better odds.

"We're going in."

Haines helmet spun around toward him. Not that Haines had to turn his head to see him; his suit sensors covered 360 degrees. It was just a human reaction even Beck had not yet managed to discard.

"Going in? What the hell are you talking about? They're behind cover. They'll blow our asses off."

"Shut up and listen."

He knew he should be more collegial. But the *Hawking* stood a real chance of getting stuck here, all because Haines got jelly in the belly when he had the chance to drive the Marines off.

"You take eight in on a straight-line assault. Slow, making full use of cover. The idea isn't to overrun them, but keep them occupied, and blind their sensors. Move and shoot, move and shoot. Keep a heavy fire on them whether you have target lock or not. Meanwhile, I'll fly my five over, then loop around and come in behind them. We'll fire as we pass, then brake hard, find some cover, and catch whoever's left between two fires."

He just hoped Haines at least had the command presence and the sense of responsibility to keep his people moving forward. It was hard to make people leave a nice snug bit of shelter.

"Loop around?" Haines exclaimed. "Fire as you pass? Who the hell do you think you are, the Red Baron? While you're 'looping around,' whatever that means, they'll swat you like flies. Then the rest of us will be outnumbered."

"Not if your assault force does it job. Just keep advancing and keep firing, that's pretty simple, isn't it? Once we come in behind them it's all over."

Haines chuffed into his helmet. "Oh, it'll all be over, says General Patton. My question is, for which side?"

"Look. We don't have time for any more of your bullshit. The fact that they haven't made another rush for the anchor point tells me they're expecting help. If it comes, we won't be able to stop them."

"Oh, now you can read the future?"

Kill him here and now?

No. It would look bad in front of the others.

"Listen to me. I mean *listen*, instead of thinking up snide comments while I speak. You had a chance to repulse these people, and you blew it."

"You can't tell me—"

"Shut up. You've been mouthing off for years about overthrowing Earth rule. Just so long as you never had to actually do anything but talk. Now the *Hawking* is up shit creek, and all your talk doesn't make a paddle no matter how good it sounds to you. We're going in. It all comes down to this. We win, or Earth does."

"Man," Haines muttered. "All I can say is if Kuende put you in charge, you must have qualities that aren't apparent to the eye."

Okay, kill him.

"But okay," Haines said. "We'll do it your way."

That was the best he was going to get. Beck explained the plan to his own group of Riggers, who had done something much like it a little while before.

And lost three out of the nine of them.

"Now," he told Haines, who after the briefest of hesitations, two seconds short of where Beck would have killed him, began to crawl forward along the girders. His Riggers followed after, hugging girders and machinery. Immediately the fire on them, which had grown rather half-hearted, intensified.

"Shoot back!" Beck shouted. "It's your best defense."

So they did. Wildly. But that would still blur the Marines' sensors.

Up to a point. One of Haines' group took a clutch of flechettes directly in her faceplate. She didn't even have time for a shriek.

Beck feared the rest might go into hedgehog mode, but after a few expressions of shock they returned the fire as they went humping forward like caterpillars across the superstructure.

At heart, he thought, most were still Riggers, even if young and mouthy and poorly led.

Soon his infrared hazed over into a generalized cloud of dull red, sparked repeatedly by quick, intense glares.

"Let's go."

They pushed hard off the hull under full thrust. They had only echo to guide them among the girders as they climbed above the Marine position; radar was too confused.

He weaved this way and that, missing chunks of steel by centimeters. They took no fire. Nor delivered any, because despite his statement to Haines, no targets presented themselves from the haze.

Then having circled past the red clouds, Beck led them looping back in.

There was less distortion from this angle. Of course that worked both ways. Beck expected to hear the whine of radar lock at any moment, and see the green lines streaking toward him.

If the Marines had an officer or a seasoned non-com, he was either dead or else shitting his suit, because it was not until Beck's attack force started firing almost directly into their backs that the soldiers even knew they were there. Belatedly the survivors swiveled around, first trying to grope or jet their way toward cover, then trying to get target lock as the six Riggers flew forward, ducking over and under the beams as they came.

Beck eye-guided his laser onto a blob of red, then tried to hold the yellow-orange line on its center as it bounced on a tight, irregular trajectory, apparently trapped among the girders. Finally the center flowered into quickly-dissipating mists of bright red as both blood and air whistled out through rents in the suit.

Green lines swarmed him like angry bees, but he kept moving and firing, moving and firing, and somehow flew through the storm as the Marines grew too panicked to wait for radar lock, and just pointed at the light show crossing the interiors of their faceplates they hadn't the experience to sort out in the seconds, or less, they had.

Beck blew up another ball of infrared with his laser rifle.

"Halt!" he shouted. "Take cover!" His force was taking fire from Haines force still shooting at the surviving Marines.

We've done it, he thought exultantly. We've won.

He was about to convey the news that Anchor Point Three had been secured when something tore his lower leg off.

It can't be that bad, he made himself think as he banged hard into a girder. He checked the impulse to look down toward his leg the way he really, really wanted to. That much pain indicated there was something down there he'd rather not see. Red flashes signaled "suit breach" in his face mask.

Shit.

Okay. At last Beck looked at his leg. The suit over his calf was tattered. Reddened ice crystals sprayed through the holes.

Well, at least the leg was still attached. That might be good for something. The rent being in a lower limb, the suit had automatically tourniquetted his calf just below the knee. The rest of him would be okay. For a while. He called for an injection of pain killer through the stent in his arm that was part of the suit.

By then the fight was over. Which took Beck a few seconds to realize because everyone was shouting to each other. But the Riggers in the frontal attack were wriggling forward rapidly, making only a cursory effort to stay under cover, and no one was shooting at them.

"Haines, take the roll," he said. Barber called out the names of everyone in the battle group. Figueroa and Rothstein didn't answer. By this time Beck felt no grief. Only gratification that they'd lost only two out of fifteen suits.

What the hell was in that painkiller? A baby aspirin?

"Beck's been hit," someone said. He wasn't tracking as well as he'd like.

"Jesus, man, look at your leg!" exclaimed someone else.

"I'd just as soon not, actually. Okay people, listen up. Good job. You've shown the Marines are no match for us in space combat. But don't start telling war stories yet. There may still be more along. We're going to regroup on the Anchor point. No matter what comes at us, we *must* hold it."

He jetted down to the hull. And reversing by habit to take the impact feet first, banged into it clumsily. The suit was powered; it would do its best to accomplish what your nerve impulses told it to. His lower leg muscles, such as were left, appeared to be lacking a certain subtlety.

Dammit to hell! He was grateful to the medicos for saving him from drug addiction and all, but addiction was for later, and this pain was right fucking *NOW!* The vacuum was skinning his leg alive.

"Do you need help getting back inside?" asked someone. He knew the voice, sort of, but couldn't identify it.

"No, no, I'm fine. Don't worry about me, worry about that fucking anchor point. All hands, right? Get behind some cover and be ready to fight. Haines, you're in charge. I'm going back to the *Hawking*."

He felt guilty as hell, but he wasn't worth a whole hell of a lot like this, and in a few minutes more he'd be worth a lot less, with so much blood gone and his lower leg freeze-dried.

Did the fucking tourniquet really have to be *that* tight?

Beck knew, he just *knew*, there was something more he should be doing, but for the life of him he couldn't think just what.

And so concentrating on his own problems, he flew across the face of the end cap, headed for an airlock.

Chapter 33

BECK NEEDED AN AIRLOCK to get into the *Hawking* and see what anyone could do to save what remained of his leg. Not to mention his life.

But he didn't dare use any of the access points within the circumference of the manufacturing cylinder. Too much chance some lurking Marines would zap him in the back. Then gain access to the hull, where they might form a bridgehead for others.

So he jetted up close along the out-curving hull. Several times he passed near fighting. He wanted to stop and join in, but that wasn't smart. Fatigue was digging deeper and deeper into him.

Shock.

So he kept on flying, keeping his thrusters low for minimum heat signature. He knew he should be more stealthy, scan an area before crossing it, but by now he wasn't sure that if he stopped for a visual recon he'd ever remember to start again. You'd think when your life depended on it you could pay attention, but Beck was finding it wasn't so simple.

He'd called up another dose of painkiller. Useless. Well, he at least wasn't going to die a drug addict. Some of the pain was from the way the flechettes had made hamburger out of his leg. The rest was from space flash-freezing his skin. Despite the suit tourniquet, absolute zero was working its way up slowly but inexorably through muscles and bones. If he was out here much longer he'd lose the whole damn leg. But you couldn't let yourself be ruled by panic.

He could feel himself growing more light-headed. He turned down his audio inputs to stop from getting his mind pulled this way and that trying to follow the battle. Several times on his journey up the end cap he failed to negotiate a girder completely and his wounded leg would hit. *That* was fun. It all kept distracting him from the very important task of staying alive.

Which way was he going?

It came to him suddenly.

Was he lost? Moving in circles?

Beck stopped, holding a girder to check out his surroundings. Through a gap in the strutwork the moon's multi-faceted face, so much closer than seen from Earth, shone dull gold.

Beautiful, just beautiful. When had he stopped noticing that? And the stars. Such glory.

This was his world. His true world.

He was so terribly tired.

"Beck? Beck Egan? Are you still on channel?"

Haines Barber's voice. Beck looked around, saw an infrared signature at seventy-five meters and closing.

"What are you doing here?" he sent.

"Didn't you get Kuende's message?"

"What message? No, I didn't. I turned audio down. What did she say?"

"There's a med team standing by at Airlock Three-Fourteen. She wanted someone to make sure you got there."

"And you left your post for that?"

"All was quiet. The Marines are pulling back from the whole face."

"You should have sent someone else."

"Just what I told her. But when Kuende heard you were hurt and on your own, she started to get frantic. So I promised I'd find you and get you inside. I never heard her like that before. You really got to her."

As he closed, Beck picked him up on visual. Haines sailed up to the adjacent girder over, five meters away. He grabbed the flange with one hand, the other holding the flechette rifle he'd taken from a dead Marine.

"Can you make it on your own?" Haines asked.

"Of course. Tell Kuende I'll be in soon. Three-Fourteen?"

"That's right. I'll call and tell her you're coming in. She'll still probably want me to come with you."

"Negative. You've still got work to do."

"If that's how you want it." Haines pushed lightly off and started off the way he'd come.

Was Kuende really so concerned over him?

Why do you doubt it? Whatever she does or doesn't feel about you, you really do love her. It's all so clear, from here. That should count for something.

Shut up, Beck told himself. He was having trouble thinking straight. Whatever his mind was babbling about, the rest of him wasn't following.

Are you dying, by any chance?

Shit, how would I know?

Swinging around the girder, Beck set his thrusters for slow and set off to find his way to the airlock further up on the hull where the med team waited.

A steel pipe hit him in the lower right back, drove through, tore out his stomach, then burst through his suit in front. Through flashes of yellow and black he saw green motion and silver on visual as it sped away, leaving his suit flapping like laundry in a hurricane, spewing out a storm of red ice.

Shock enveloped him. But only for a moment.

Haines!

Grabbing for his laser rifle Beck tried to swivel around, but the rapid depressurization of his suit was blowing him around all herky-jerky and he couldn't get control over his thrusters and his hands had grown distant and clumsy.

His sensors were reeling, disoriented. He could not even fix on his own position relative to the girders all around.

Another shock of flechettes, this time in the left side. Beck slammed into the hull. Pain was exploding all through his body. Yet at the same time a great emptiness filled him, draining the strength from his limbs.

Instinctively he mouthed the rubber breathing tube his helmet thrust forward in response to the breach in order to save his lungs. His arms waved feebly. One held the laser rifle but there wasn't anything he could do about it because he'd lost all connection. Then it was jerked away. A boot smashed him down against the hull, held him there.

There cannot *be* this much pain, Beck thought. In the whole world, there is not this much pain. More than he could bear; he would have screamed with it but he was sucking for dear life on the breathing tube.

Dear life? I'm dying, aren't I? Really, really dying.

He looked up to see Haines holding onto a girder with one hand, forcing Beck hard against the hull.

"Just so you know," Haines told him, "this isn't for revenge. I do hate your guts. I do hate the way Kuende thinks you're anything more than the dumb little wrench-jock you've always been. But I wouldn't kill you for that. Well maybe, if I'd known much fun it would be." His voice dripped with gloating.

Recovering the use of his hands — why did they still feel so far away, like they were mounted on springs? — Beck tried to push Haines' foot off his chest.

Dumb idea.

Pain was tearing into him on all sides. Not only had his insides been torn up by the flechettes, the sudden depressurization was causing his internal organs to swell up and press against his ribs. Skin was being freeze-burned over his whole torso.

Such pain! Beck wriggled and thrashed, trying to run away from the agony.

"*This,*" said Haines, "is about the future. My future. I don't want you in it. So I'm just going to stand here for a couple more minutes and watch you die. Is your helmet pressure still keeping out the vacuum? That will stop pretty soon. Then the cold will start creeping up, and your face will turn numb, and you'll try and you'll try to suck on that mouthpiece, but ... I give you three, maybe four minutes. Want to place a bet?"

He laughed. Most fun he'd had in a long while.

Beck was under no illusion that he was going to survive this. He and his suit were both too badly mutilated.

But he had one last job to do.

Haines was not going to be part of the *Stephen Hawking's* future.

But Haines simply had too much leverage. Beck couldn't shift his foot a centimeter, even with the suit amplification.

It's work. Another job, no more.

He still had one of the shrapnel bombs. Below Haines' line of sight, as he ground his foot happily into Beck's chest.

"P-p-p-please," Beck blubbered, trying to distract his tormentor.

Haines laughed even louder.

And while he did, Beck reached down and detached the bomb.

Worked loose the safety.

At last Haines saw it. And panicked. Grabbing the flechette rifle in both hands, he swatted the bomb from Beck's grasp with its stock. Beck's limbs were just too cold and numb to counter.

But by using both hands, Haines had just lost his anchor point. He stared at the bomb floating away, wondering how far it would go before it exploded, and torn between the dangers of it above and Beck below.

Not much of a Rigger. Slow reflexes.

Beck twisted with everything left in him. In the same motion he grabbed the boot against his chest and rolled Haines sideways.

Haines tried to shake loose, but his efforts only bounced them both away from the hull. As the two men floated free, Beck twisted

Haines' ankle around. Then climbed up his back. Along the way he grabbed the vibra-saw Haines carried in a scabbard on his thigh.

That got Haines really excited, but he didn't know what to do about it except try to poke the muzzle of the flechette around behind his head to shoot Beck. But Beck wriggled down a little way, and Haines could do nothing but twist.

With just this one little last burst of vitality, Beck meant to do good works.

"You talk too much," he sent.

Then he rammed the vibra-saw up into Haines' crotch. Because even dying and in terrible pain, Beck remained a pragmatic man, and that was an attack for which Haines had no possible counter.

That scream, and the ones that followed, broke right through Beck's helmet filters. Haines kicked, and arched, and twisted, all at once, repeatedly. Still Beck pushed up, gashing the suit in front and behind.

When the screams broke off into a choke, then a shrill whimper, he stopped. He pushed the body away from him. Escaping pressurization sent the dying man turning somersaults as he drifted away, spewing ice crystals.

Beck threw the saw into the darkness.

There. That's a job done.

You will *not* give up.

You're kidding.

No, man. For Kuende. For Maeda. For the man you want them to remember.

I'm torn to shit! It fucking *hurts!*

One last job.

Yeah, yeah, okay!

He cut in his thrusters. Heading for an airlock, any airlock.

His progress too slow. Air was blowing out the gaping rents of his suit, swinging him first to one side then the other. If he boosted thrust he'd drive himself into the hull or a girder because he didn't have the control to stop himself.

Kuende, I'm still trying.

But he knew it wasn't going to happen.

I loved you.

Fuck it hurts!

Keep going. Can't be that far now. Who knows? You might make it. Surprise everybody. You most of all.

Then a new pain started. In his face, as the cold started seeping in past the neck seal. You couldn't tourniquet your head the way you did a leg.

Beck clamped down hard on the mouthpiece so that the vacuum, when it came, wouldn't creep past and explode his lungs.

Or tried to; everything was turning numb. Not painless; the water molecules in his skin and cells were starting to freeze and expand, and aside from his already dead leg there were few parts of his body *that* agony couldn't reach. Numb in the sense he could no longer control his muscles.

Beck finally knew the vacuum had defeated his neck seal when the blowtorch flared against his eyes.

He wanted to scream. But if he did he'd spit out the mouthpiece and his lips were too numb to clamp down on it again.

His guts were bursting inside him, fire flayed him from the eyes on down, the flechettes had torn big chunks out of him, and he was increasingly turning into this little ball of pain in a great big echoing empty chamber.

Then his chest too began to ache as the lungs started pushing out against it.

Don't breathe through your nose!

This is it, isn't it?

Yeah.

Within a minute maybe, ninety seconds probably, two minutes at the most, you are going to feel your lungs blow out.

Okay. You always suspected you'd die in space.

On impulse Beck swerved away from the hull. His sensor signals were fading, but he detected one gap in the strutwork that gave him a clear path into open space.

He went to full acceleration.

Out toward the glowing moon, the sparkling diamond stars, a dimension defined only by eternity.

And one final thought.

HOME.

ABOUT THE AUTHOR

Richard Quarry writes science fiction, fantasy, crime, and historical adventure. His short fiction can be found in *Fiction River* and *Blaze Ward Presents*. He lives in Seattle, where he enjoys hiking the hills and beaches of the Northwest with his wife Claire. For more of his books go to richardquarrywriter.com.

The Big Empty is the first of the seven-book sf series *The Evolved*. For a preview of Book 2, please turn the page.

And if you enjoyed this story, please consider leaving a review. I'd appreciate it.

Point of No Return

WAXY LEAVES BIG AS Mirai's outstretched hands arced from scaly trunks. The overhead spray that mimicked rain had ceased a few minutes before, leaving beads of water clinging to the leaves. Even partially shaded by the foliage overhead, the veined green surfaces sparked tiny prisms in the light of the cylinder's longitudinal panels.

Yellow, orange, and purple flowers sprouted in clusters among the leaves. The bees which had fled the spray buzzed back, drifting from flower to flower.

This was Mirai's favorite part of the Sector Three arboretum. Most of her friends found it too close and too humid. Nor did they care for the way the thick-bodied bees kept bumping into them, stingless or not.

Which was part of the attraction. At seventeen Mirai Allan placed a high value on blazing her own trails. She also liked being alone, which for all the habitat's immensity was hard to do aboard the *Stephen Hawking*. She even enjoyed the spray, though it dampened her stretchy top and pants, making them bunch up in all the wrong places. By staying to the center of the crushed-rock footpaths she escaped the worst of the artificial drizzle. With water so precious, the gardeners concentrated the sprinklers further back, toward the plants that most needed it.

Mirai exerted her will to avoid flinching when one of the black-and-yellow bees blundered into her. Though she still brushed them away from her face with a little more urgency than her calm and collected self-image might choose.

Really, you'd think the bees would be smarter than to fly right into you. Fat, stingless, and slow, it was fortunate for them that there were no predators aboard the *Hawking*. They'd just be flying dinners else.

Even the sickly-sweet smell of the flowers didn't deter Mirai, though her friends made gruesome jokes about what decaying horrors the ignorant farmers who cultivated this area might have hidden amid the thick-clustered ferns.

Mirai Allan was her own woman.

She especially liked the parts where the trail narrowed and leaves long as her forearm met close overhead. Like a living cave. Here you could pretend to enter some part of the forest you'd never seen before, which might hold who knew what mysteries? It was a little-girl sort of thing to do and harder to maintain as the years wore on, but Mirai still clung to that thrill of anticipation. Though vast, after seventeen years the *Stephen Hawking* didn't offer much in the way of startling new vistas. Or much new at all.

Nor did it today. After one last short, dark passage, the path left the jungle section and opened into more open forest. Mirai squinted slightly against the brightness of the overheads as the crushed rock of the jungle path faded into a slightly domed, mossy track.

To her left beehives dotted a horseshoe-shaped field. A boy about her own age sat amid them at a wooden bench, assembling a square frame from wooden slats.

Christian, obviously. All the gardeners were. Mirai thought she might have seen him around a time or two, lurking in the woods like the others, shifting quietly around doing whatever gardeners did. Soft-footed and graceful. Or else ominous, depending how on you looked at it.

You didn't see them sitting out in the open very often. Didn't often see them close to her own age, either. In the markets sometimes, but not here.

It came to Mirai that in all her life she'd never spoken more than half a dozen words at a time to a Christian. All while buying food or the occasional crafts piece.

Nor did she have much reason to do so now. In fact if the very thought of approaching someone of such alien beliefs hadn't started butterflies churning in her stomach, she'd have walked on by.

But foreboding was a challenge. And Mirai Allan didn't shy from challenges; she met them head on.

Head held high, she walked across the mossy grass. The bees swarmed more thickly here among the hives; the boy sat inside a virtual cloud of them. One bumped into her shoulder, another off her cheek. She forced herself not to react. She was ruled by her mind, not by undisciplined emotions.

The boy looked up from his work as she approached. Yes, her age or a little older. But not much. He wore his black hair cut short in the Christian manner; not according to any religious significance she'd ever heard of, but as one more symbol of their opposition to the Riggers, most of whom wore their hair long to drape over the "pigtail" connectors emerging from the base of their skull.

The look he gave was totally deadpan. Close to animalistic in its absolute lack of communication.

That look and that hair came close to turning her around. But Mirai stiffened her courage with her favorite nostrum of late: imagining herself telling the story in her dorm lounge.

As she came to his bench he pushed back his chair and stood. He was tall, wiry-looking, with corded muscles playing in his neck and forearms. At first Mirai feared that rising to his feet was meant to warn her off, and she stopped several feet away. Then she recalled how Christians clung to a host of archaic and sexist customs, such as the males standing when a woman approached.

What was the point of that? Except maybe to demonstrate they were most often bigger. Pretty much always, in Mirai's case.

His expression became more guarded. What did he think, she was going to beat him with a stick? What could possibly be threatening about her? She searched for an opening.

"Hello."

She tried to sound friendly. Even a touch effervescent, to show herself a woman of high spirits and boundless enthusiasm for life. But her effervescence seemed to have fizzled away.

He nodded noncommittally. Mirai was trying to suppress all the clichés about Christians and their narrow bandwidth, but he wasn't making it easy for her.

"What are you doing?" she asked.

He looked down at the bench with all the pieces of wood and a few archaic non-powered tools scattered across it. Some of the slats were joined together in what was clearly intended to be an open-sided box.

"Making a beehive. I mean," he corrected himself, "the frame for a hive."

"How interesting," she said, ignoring his slightly sullen tone. After all, he probably didn't get to talk to anyone outside his own community very often. Maybe he was afraid the conversation might turn more challenging, and he'd be left mumbling. No one wanted to look a fool. As a teenager, Mirai was acutely aware of that.

Only she was running out of conversational options herself. "That's pretty wood," she said.

He looked down at the slats.

"It's pine," he replied, in a slightly puzzled tone she didn't understand. Among the Riggers, wood was a scarce commodity. Every plant or tree that could be grown was needed to produce oxygen for the cylinder, whose atmosphere recycling system was being taxed close to its limits.

Or, many were beginning to mutter, a bit beyond.

You didn't cut down trees just to make them into trinkets.

But the Christians, who generally tended the woods and crops even outside their own Sector, had the use of any tree that died naturally. It was said that within their own Sector they even grew wood for no purpose but for building, because they rejected composites as much as possible, like they rejected everything else about civilization.

Wood for bees, well, maybe there were reasons for that. Pollinators were important. But to waste on that scarred and rickety workbench holding his archaic hand tools? The wood in that bench could be sold for ... well, a good many composite benches, anyway. And have credits left over. And the composite ones would be a lot stronger.

Stubborn people, she thought. Thick and slow-moving as the heavy black-and-yellow bees that weaved and buzzed between them. But she wasn't ready to give up just yet.

"So you're a bee-keeper?"

"Some of the time." He considered her, closed his eyes, and when he opened them again produced an heroic oration: "It's my favorite part of the job. I like bees. They're...." But here his stock of conversation ran dry.

"I like honey," she said, not exactly brimming over with witticisms herself.

"Do you?" His face brightened, like that was really important to him.

"Well yes."

Searching for some follow-up, she found nothing but, it's very nice. If this kept up they'd soon be speaking in grunts and snorts like Neanderthals.

He pursed his lips, deep in thought. His eyes as he appeared to weigh her were golden-brown and bright, with a gleam absent from his conversation. She thought his face plain and workmanlike, with a suggestion of sincerity about it she could not precisely identify. Strong chin, rather nice lips. He might have been good-looking with a touch more animation in his expression. But until the mention of honey came up he'd been holding himself bundled up.

"Wait here a minute, would you?" he said, having at last arrived at some conclusion. "That is, if you don't mind the bees. Or you could wait by the path. There aren't so many of them there. It's the hives that keep them coming and going."

"I like bees." Just not quite so many of them.

"Do you? That's great. Ah, I'll be right back."

He ran toward the far end of the opening, toward a white-painted wooden — of course — shed with a roof so moss-covered she couldn't tell what it was made of. Deep scars gouged the boards. The door sagged so much she couldn't imagine how it would ever close.

But she noted how he moved with an easy, natural motion, not like the kids she knew who ran for sport and were often quite good at it but always, she realized now, a bit tense because they always played to win something.

He ducked into the shed and in a moment was back. He handed her a glass jar with an old-fashioned screw-on lid. The Christians made such things. By hand. There certainly wasn't anything like that anywhere else aboard the *Hawking*.

Inside the jar was a richly colored golden brown jellyish substance.

"Here," he said. "Take this. It's honey. Just ... honey."

"Why thank you. How much—"

"No, no, no," he said, waving his hands. "It's just some I made for myself. But if you like honey, and bees, you really should have it."

He'd grown quite loquacious. Was honey part of some secret Christian cult? There was a somewhat alarming eagerness in his eyes, but nothing that Mirai recognized as a signal he intended to grab onto her or anything.

He simply seemed pleased to share something with her. Which was why she'd approached him in the first place.

She unscrewed the lid. It took all her strength, and she saw him lean forward on the verge of offering his help. But just because some men might be stronger didn't mean she was weak. So bearing down hard, though the ridges on the lid bit into her palm, she twisted the jar open. He hadn't brought a spoon or anything else to eat with. Probably didn't recognize anything beyond her fingers might be necessary.

Mirai hesitated, her instincts rebelling against eating anything that some dust-covered Christian dug out of a rotting shed.

But she would *not* be a slave to convention. With a feeling of abandon she dipped in her forefinger, scooped out a generous dollop, and as it started to drip down off her finger quickly ducked her head and stuck the finger in her mouth, bearing down with her lips to scrape off the honey as she pulled her hand away.

The sensation was startling. First from violated expectations; she'd expected something almost unpleasantly sweet. She didn't get that at all. There was an element of sweetness to it, certainly, but subdued. Rich, even earthy, a background rather than the whole experience. The texture had a barely perceptible graininess, and a flavor she identified as wheaten without really having much experience to go on, simply because it was so substantial as to be almost breadlike.

But the word that kept repeating was that same "earthy." Not a very natural concept aboard the *Hawking*, where the "dirt" was formed from ground-up asteroidal rock thickened and fertilized with chemicals. But an evocative one. A picture of a vanished blue planet, now no more than a legend. An idea of growth, of nourishment, of life where the horizon stretched outward and down, instead of climbing up and turning back in on itself.

Suddenly all these bees buzzing around took on a new meaning. They worked. They labored. They didn't feed their young on the over-sweet, drippy substance she'd previously known as honey. They fed them this. Food, real food. The bounty of the earth, even here in the vast desert between star systems.

Mirai couldn't understand why the moment struck her as so meaningful. She'd never before thought it strange that the majority of what she ate differed only in details of processing and organic content from the materials that made up the dwellings and furniture where she lived.

Now she felt she had been cut off from a central part of human experience. That all those jokes about "you are what you eat" after all bore a tragic component because the corollary was that she, along with everyone else she knew, was artificial. A construct as much as a living, breathing person with free will.

But that didn't make any sense.

Did it?

Mirai Allan was a most searching seventeen-year-old.

She came back to the here and now. To the taste of honey in her mouth, and the boy waiting eagerly for her judgment.

"That," she said, "is delicious. More than delicious. It's ... inspiring."

He smiled broadly. "You like it? The honey we sell your people" — belatedly he winced at that *your people* — "is sweetened and has all kinds of stuff added. I don't know exactly what and don't want to. They tell me that's what sells. This here, well, I don't know that I'd have thought to call it inspiring, but...."

Their eyes locked together. Experienced a moment of shock. Not in romantic discovery, or even lustful interest. Just recognition of a common experience so rare aboard the cylinder as to be unknown not only to their experience, but anything they'd ever heard from their forebearers.

The boy gulped. "But it is, isn't it? Inspiring, I mean. In its way."

Then all at once they were laughing, both of them, madly, with that glorious teenage conceit that together they had just discovered something that would forever remain known only to them.